A Music City Rom-Com

DON'T YOU WANT ME

JOANNA ILLINGWORTH

This is a work of fiction. All characters, organizations, and events portrayed in this novel are either products of the author's imagination or are used fictitiously.

Don't You Want Me. Copyright © 2024 by JoAnna Illingworth

All rights reserved.

No part of this book may be reproduced in any form or by any electronic or mechanical means, including information storage and retrieval systems, without written permission from the author, except for the use of brief quotations in a book review.

Jacket Design & Illustration: timtamdesigns

www.joannaillingworth.com

To everyone I've worked with in the music industry who said, "you should write a book about the music industry."
This one's for you.

CONTENT HEADS UP

For readers who like a content heads up, this book contains an off-page death of a sibling, off-page death of a parent, a toxic mother, and mentions of being abandoned as a child.

CONTENTS

One	1
Mad About Brad	
Two	8
Leapfrog At Your Own Peril	
Three	13
All Tree Climbing Is Prohibited	
Four	20
The Alcove	
Five	24
A Sparrow By Any Other Name	
For Immediate Release	29
Six	31
A Real Kick In The Pants	
Seven	38
This Is Way Worse Than Sexy Thor	
Eight	45
I'm Being Haunted By An Alcove	
Nine	53
Hot like Ice	
Ten	56
The Past Tense Of Rendezvous Is Rendezvous	
Eleven	61
Instagram Polls, Gastric Distress and Other Reasons I'm Spiraling	
For Immediate Release	69
Twelve	71
Psyched	
Thirteen	80
Horse Kacey Musgraves Has It Out For Me	
Fourteen	86
We Need To Talk	
Fifteen	93
Upon Reflection, The Chop Pants Were A Mistake	
Sixteen	103
No Love No Joy	
Seventeen	109
At Least We're Taking Butt Rock Off The Table	

Eighteen *Pack It Up*	116
Nineteen *Irreconcilable Differences*	122
Twenty *Nerves Akimbo*	128
Twenty-One *The Cheek Pain Is Worth It*	135
Twenty-Two *Uggos Need Not Apply*	141
Twenty-Three *Room For Two In The W*	147
Twenty-Four *K.O.'d By T.O.*	157
Twenty-Five *Should've Gone Commando*	163
Twenty-Six *Despite All My Rage*	168
Twenty-Seven *Wait Until The TikToker Hears About This*	174
Twenty-Eight *We Can't Have Things In Common. That Would Ruin The Vibe.*	182
Twenty-Nine *Rock, Paper, Scissors, Shit*	186
Thirty *We're Writing This One In Permanent Ink*	193
Thirty-One *Banjo By Six*	200
Thirty-Two *Better A Wilt Than A Wither*	207
Thirty-Three *What Good Is An Almost*	212
Thirty-Four *Alcove, Bunk, Whatever It Takes*	217
Thirty-Five *Bullseye*	222
Thirty-Six *Zero Out Of Ten*	226
Thirty-Seven *When Trust Goes Bust*	231
Thirty-Eight *Coincidental Catastrophe*	236

Thirty-Nine *Not Even Bryan Adams Can Fix This Mess*	241
Forty *Right Here. The Whole Time.*	252
Forty-One *Seen*	258
Forty-Two *That Time Emily Grits Her Teeth So Hard She Chips A Tooth*	262
Forty-Three *Could've Been*	269
Forty-Four *A Lovejoy By Any Other Name*	273
Forty-Five *The Truth*	277
For Immediate Release	285
Forty-Six *Contract High*	287
Forty-Seven *Appearing In Studio*	292
Forty-Eight *Marick, Everybody*	297
Acknowledgments	301
Also by JoAnna Illingworth	303

ONE
MAD ABOUT BRAD

MY DUFFLE BAG stuffed with t-shirts, bras, and socks slips off my shoulder onto the ceramic tile floor of Cass's entryway. I stare down at it, shoulders drooped.

"The final remnants of my relationship with Brad the Bass Player."

"I think you mean, 'Yay, I'm finally free of that loser,'" Cass says.

I considered leaving everything behind with a dramatic door slam but some of my vintage t-shirts are irreplaceable. Brad probably would have given them to Shelley, the sexy little minx who teaches his spin class. Or was it Sherry? Shelby? Doesn't matter. I'm moving in with my best friend and her geriatric great aunt while Shelley/Sherry/Shelby is moving into my boyfriend's downtown loft.

Ex-boyfriend, I mean.

Cass sets my guitar case down next to my duffle bag, everything I own stacked into little piles in the entryway.

"How sad is it my entire life fits into two suitcases, two duffle bags, one laundry basket and three boxes I stole from behind the liquor store."

"And your guitar," Cass says.

I push out my bottom lip and blow a stray strand of hair out of my eyes, the same strand I wrangled back into my topknot five minutes ago.

"I am never dating a musician again." I say it emphatically, like a decree. If I had a gavel, I'd bang it.

"Mind if I record you saying that so I can play it back in a month?" Cass says with a knowing grin.

"I'm serious this time."

"As serious as the last time or the last, last time?"

I count down on my fingers. "No singers, no guitar players, no bass players, no keyboard players, no drummers." I close my eyes and sigh. "*Especially* drummers."

Cass's dog, an ancient French bulldog named Chop, toddles into the entryway and sniffs the contents of my life. When he doesn't find anything worthy of his attention, he wanders back into the living room. Much like the male population of Nashville, he is bored with me.

"I dated a drummer once," Cass says. "She had the most incredible shoulders."

"Right? Drummers and swimmers." I pick up one of the boxes and follow Cass down the hall to my new room.

It's technically her great aunt's house, the exact opposite of the palatial Hollywood Hills house my sister bought but never truly lives in. She and my mother travel so much I mostly grew up there alone with the house staff and empty rooms full of designer furniture.

Granny G's house is warm and inviting, painted a bright garden green on the outside and all the other colors on the inside. The kitchen is wallpapered in tropical birds and there's zebra print wallpaper in the hallway bathroom. The living room is a mismatch of fabrics, shag rainbow rug under a plaid couch next to a floral overstuffed chair. The walls, painted in varying shades of the rainbow, are barely visible underneath layers and layers of framed photos and memorabilia and random art pieces Granny's collected over the years.

"Things you love should be on display," she's always said, and she loves a lot of things.

"On second thought," I say, passing a metal sculpture of a roaring tiger on the wall, "I might make an exception for a drummer. But definitely no lead singers. There's always three of us in the relationship—me, him, and his massive ego."

"What about a producer?"

I shudder. "They always want you to 'come out to their car' to listen to a 'sweet track' they just recorded."

"But you'd think they'd be good with their hands. All those little buttons and knobs they have to turn on the mixing board."

Cass opens the door to my new room. It's small but nice. And free. There's a queen bed with white fluffy bedding and Cass cleared out the closet for me. Granny G's sewing machine is set up in the corner and the walls are covered in dozens of framed photographs and colorful art on canvas. Over the bed hangs a giant oil painting of Granny G, nude, from when she lived in Paris in her twenties. I've seen it before, but seeing it now, over the bed I'll be sleeping in, is a lot.

My life must really be in shambles if I'd rather sleep under Granny G's nude than ever date a musician again.

"Maybe this break-up with Brad is a good thing," I say, dropping the box onto the closet floor. "In fact, maybe I'll just be celibate for the rest of my life. Way less drama that way."

Cass pulls her phone from her back pocket and points it at my face. "Say it into the microphone."

I lean forward and loudly declare, "This is Mari Gold reporting live from my last and final break-up. I am done with men. Forever."

"I think you'll need to use your real name to make it legally binding."

I push out a loud breath and flop down onto the bed. "Pass."

Since I moved to Nashville from L.A., I've been burning through guys at an alarming pace. I didn't come here with the intention to conquer the men of Music City, but the thrill of being somewhat anonymous has been intoxicating. Nashville is rich with hot, young musicians looking for a good time not a long time. Most of them could care less who I really am or who my family is. But the few who do care have made things… complicated. Men, at least the men I'm attracted to, continue to be painfully predictable.

The mattress dips as Cass falls next to me. "Are you ready to talk about it?"

"No." She waits, knowing I'll tell her anyway. "I overheard Brad on the phone to his friend." I look over at her. "He was talking about my sister."

"Oh no," Cass says. We've had this conversation before.

"We'd been dating six months," I say. "We were *living* together. Yes, it was more about the cost of rent than true love, but still. I thought I could trust him. I thought he'd be cool about my sister being a pop superstar. The second he found out he began plotting how to dump me and meet Polly. I'm two thousand miles away from L.A. and have, once again, been bypassed in favor of my sister. How does this keep happening?"

"You do know the fact that you're LOVEJOY's sister is the worst kept secret in Nashville."

"Maybe. But at least I don't lead with it."

Introducing myself as Penny Lovejoy is like saying my last name is Grohl or Cyrus or Parton. The second people learn I'm a Lovejoy they form an immediate assumption about me, about my songs, about my reasons for being an artist. That, or they want an automatic in with my famous sister.

That's why I left L.A., to get away from the Lovejoy circus and make my own way as an artist in Nashville. In L.A. I was only ever LOVEJOY's sister or John Lovejoy's daughter or Candy Lovejoy's nuisance. A few years after my father died, my mother got into management, namely turning my older sister, Polly, into LOVEJOY. (My mother's a stickler about the capitalization. It's essential to *the brand*.) When she remembers I exist, my mother waxes poetic about turning me into a pop superstar like my sister and, in her words, "make so much money we'll be swimming in it." I keep telling her I'd rather dig ditches than be anything like my sister.

Nashville's a fresh start away from my family, away from the assumptions that I'm anything like them when I couldn't be more different. I'm here to become something else, something closer to the truth of who I am. I just need to figure out who that is.

My mother, loudly disappointed that I "abandoned the family," cut me off in every way she could. I've been working three different jobs but it still doesn't cover an apartment on my own.

"Brad was an empty-headed know-it-all," Cass says. "Good riddance, honestly."

"Do you really think that or are you just being nice."

"Both."

The bedroom door creaks open and Granny G swirls into the room. She's in a toucan-themed caftan, bright red lipstick, dangly gold earrings peeking out from her silver curls.

"Hello, little flower. I'm so happy you've come to make a home in our garden."

I hop off the bed and lean down to hug her. She kisses me on the cheek, leaving a lip print. Chop comes in, his chunky butt wagging in approval.

"I can't thank you enough for letting me crash here until I can get my life together."

"Stay as long as you need," Cass says. "We're family."

"I love you, but I don't think my mother's ex-husband's aunt's great niece truly counts as family."

"In Tennessee it does," Granny G says with a wink. "Our home is your home, sweet Mari. We're so glad you're here."

"Thanks, Granny. You two are truly lifesavers."

Cass's phone buzzes in her back pocket. She checks it and cocks her head to the side like *here we go*.

"It's Jackson."

"I'll leave you girls to it," Granny says, backing out of the room with Chop and shutting the door.

Cass swipes open the call and we sit next to each other on the bed so we can both see him.

"My two favorite ladies," Jackson says with a giant grin. He's in a Hawaiian shirt, unbuttoned, his blonde hair slicked back like an investment banker. "I'm having a little get together and I need you here."

"How little," I ask because Jackson Lord's get togethers are always over-the-top events. He's the unofficial Nashville host. He knows everyone, is friends with every kind of friend group. His house is always crowded and fun, but I don't know if I have it in me tonight.

"Just a few friends plus my two favorite ladies who are on their way right now," he says. "Right? You're on your way?"

Cass and I exchange a knowing look.

"We can see all the people behind you," Cass says with a laugh. "It looks like more than a few friends."

"I've been moving out of Brad's all day," I say, hoping he'll catch the hint. "Put us down as a maybe."

"Screw Brad. He's a terrible bass player and, coincidentally, not invited." When Cass and I don't heartily agree he adds, "There's food."

"Food?" I say, suddenly remembering I never ate lunch and it's now past dinner.

"I'll see you in thirty," Jackson says and ends the call.

"What do you think," Cass says. "You wanna go?"

I pinch the bridge of my nose. "I figured tonight would be about taking a very long shower and getting into bed to watch hydraulic press videos until my eyes burn."

She hops off the bed and claps her hands together. "Or, option B, we go eat Jackson's free food. Then you can come home and watch all the hydraulic press videos you want."

The last place I want to be is at a party. But I *am* hungry. And Jackson's parties always have the best food.

"Fine. But I'm going just like this."

Damp tendrils of my dark wavy hair are falling out of my sweaty topknot. I'm braless in my oversized Spice Girls t-shirt with the arms cut out and my denim shorts are too short for public consumption, part of my strategy to show Brad what he's missing out on.

Cass unzips my duffle and roots around until she finds a pink lace bra and tosses it to me. "At least put this on."

"Don't tell me you, a gold star gay, are scared of a little boob flash."

She shrugs. "Fine by me. But if you're gonna fly free, at least flash the good one."

"How do you know I have a good one?"

Cass laughs and pulls me out into the hallway. "Everybody's got a good one."

TWO
LEAPFROG AT YOUR OWN PERIL

IN TRUE JACKSON LORD STYLE, his little get together is a full-out rager. We have to park halfway up the street since his circle drive is jammed with leased Teslas and BMWs, the cars of choice for Nashville's wanna-be elites.

"I thought this was supposed to be a casual thing," Cass jokes as we make our way to the backyard.

"It wouldn't be a casual Lord hang without a full bar and a DJ."

"Don't forget the sushi bar."

I gasp and clutch my chest. "I would never."

Jackson's Brentwood home is, in a word, colossal. It's technically his dad's property, but he spends most of his time on set in Vancouver so Jackson claims the house as his own. The massive backyard has an outdoor kitchen bigger than some of the apartments I've lived in. There are five cabanas surrounding the guitar-shaped pool, a hot tub in the shape of a guitar pick, a fire pit with seating for thirty, a putting green and three separate balconies coming off the back of the house.

It's just after eight but the backyard is already wall-to-wall people. The drinks are flowing, the music is pumping, everyone on their best see-and-be-seen behavior. I'm out of place in my shorts and t-shirt, most of the girls in sparkly party dresses and fresh waxes.

"Penny Lovejoy and Cass Zimmerman," a sing-song voice calls, "my two favorite people."

Jackson, fruity drink in hand, finds us through the crowd and pulls us into a three-person hug.

"It's Mari Gold," I say with a knowing smile. "We're in public."

"Stage names are for stages, not friends," he says. "Besides, I keep telling you. It's okay to use your real name to get your foot in the door. Let your talent win them over, yes, but you still have to get in the door. Lovejoy is how you get in the door."

On some level, I know he's probably right. Everyone has a Nashville story about how so-and-so met so-and-so at a party and ended up with a number one single. It's Nashville legend, meeting the right person at the right time and all your dreams falling into your lap like spilled soup. Jackson and Cass believe I'll get my opportunity if I just get over myself and let people know who I really am.

Fresh off the sting of Brad's betrayal, I'm not so sure.

"We're here for the food," Cass says.

"Right this way," Jackson says, pulling us through the crowd.

We don't make it ten feet before someone's stopping us.

"Hey, Jackson, who are your friends?" A dark-haired guy in black jeans and a fitted black t-shirt smiles at me but his eyes are too wide, like he swallowed a too-big bite and it's stuck in his throat.

"Mike, my man," Jackson says, shaking Mike's hand while slapping him on the back, "meet Mari Gold, amazing songwriter and singer, and Cass Zimmerman, hairstylist to the stars." Jackson turns to us, a car dealer smile on his face. "Ladies, this is Mike Wilson, an up-and-coming producer here in town."

"Nice to meet you, Mike," I say, feeling entirely awkward meeting a producer while wearing shorts the same length as my butt cheeks, my first Nearly Naked Network Moment.

"Mari Gold, right," Mike says coolly. The way he's looking at me makes the hairs on the back of my neck stand up. "Jackson played me some of your stuff. Spicy."

"Did you send him the right songs?" Cass asks Jackson, who shrugs like, *don't look at me.*

"That's an…interesting take," I say.

Mike puffs out his chest in that aloof way I've seen on a lot of these guys in L.A.—nervousness that comes off douchey. "You've got a certain flavor. I love songwriters with flavor. Of course, it's not really the kind of stuff I work on."

"No?" I give Jackson a look but he's scanning the party, ready to move on to the next influential.

"What I'm doing is really fresh. Very in the moment," Mike says. "Kinda like what LOVEJOY's doing."

We've been at this party a total of five minutes. Maybe ten. I thought it would take at least thirty before someone brought her up. It's almost a challenge, seeing how fast his demeanor will change, how quickly the conversation will shift, if I tell him who I am. The curse of being related to someone wildly famous—I'm the girl people meet once and immediately forget in favor of my sister. No one ever comes back for seconds with me.

A mosquito lands on my arm and I swat it away. It's hot, the muggy April night too steamy to be comfortable. All I want is a cold drink and salty food and this so-called producer is name-dropping LOVEJOY like it's a power move.

"You're her sister, right?" He says it with a gotcha glint in his eye. He shifts his weight, rolls his shoulders, so proud of himself.

Jackson and Cass simultaneously gape at me. They're no doubt waiting for me to punch this guy in the jaw or scream in his face or fully hulk out, clothes ripping as I tear the party apart in a LOVEJOY-infused rage.

I hold Mike's gaze, my mouth set in a firm non-smile. "Yep. Ever since I was born."

"Fascinating." He mentally calculates how quickly he can shake me down for info. "You ever do any writing with her?"

Cass lets out a loud snort and then mumbles *sorry*, her eyes roaming the party for an escape route. I smile so wide I can see the tops of my own cheeks. "Why do you ask?"

"Just curious. You know, you don't look anything like her."

People love to point this out, how my sister and I look nothing alike. Polly's waifish and petite and blonde and sparkly-shiny where I'm tall and solid, built more like a basketball player than a lip-gloss model, the opposite of shiny. Probably why everyone leapfrogs over me to get to Polly.

"Then how'd you know I was her sister?"

"I'm good buddies with Brad Fowler. He mentioned it when he and I worked on a project together a couple weeks ago."

Brad the Bass Player strikes again.

"How nice of him," I say, my hands balling into fists at my sides. "I'll be sure and send him a fruit basket to say thanks."

Mike, oblivious, says, "I'd love to hang with her sometime if she's ever in town. Some of the things I'm working on could really vibe with what she's doing."

"I bet," I say, deadpan, surreptitiously elbowing Cass an S.O.S. message.

"You could come too," Mike offers. "Would be cool to work on a collab."

I should be nice, should pretend to care about what he's saying, should play along with his LOVEJOY collab fantasy, but that way lies madness. I came to Nashville looking for meaning, to find my roots, something to become and believe in. Being upstaged by my sister wasn't part of the plan.

"Would you excuse us for a sec?" Cass says. "We're just gonna hunt down some beverages. I saw a lime green concoction on my way in that looked interesting."

I lift my downturned smile, hoping it looks sincere. "Great meeting you, Mike."

"Yeah, you too. Let's catch up later? I'm serious about the collab."

I give him a thumbs up and throw Jackson a look I hope

conveys how much I do not want to meet any more Nashville Clingers thankyousomuch.

Once we're far enough away to not be overheard, Cass presses her thumbs into her temples and gags. "Why did you admit Polly's your sister to that slimeball?"

"Ill-timed compulsion? Heat stroke? Unfortunate verbal diarrhea due to break-up distress?"

She nods. "Alcohol. We need alcohol."

There are two bars set up on the far side of the pool, both with long lines in front of them.

"I'll get a place in line," Cass says. "See if you can scrounge up something decent in the kitchen so we don't have to wait."

THREE
ALL TREE CLIMBING IS PROHIBITED

I HEAD over to the outdoor kitchen hoping no one else thought to raid Jackson's personal stash. When I open the fridge, it's empty except for a lone bottle of ketchup and what appears to be a pitcher of sweet tea. I decide cold and wet will do until I can get something stronger.

On the counter are stacks of white solo cups with *JL's Pool* printed in gold on the side. I pull one from the top and push it against the ice maker in the door of the fridge. Instead of cubed ice, a huge clump of crushed ice dumps into my cup. I sigh and toss the ice into the sink. I jam my thumb against the cubed ice button and try again. More crushed ice falls into my cup.

I growl in frustration and toss the offensive ice and the cup into the sink.

"Ice crisis?" A voice next to me, deep and flirty.

He sounds exactly like the kind of guy I could get into trouble with, which is exactly the kind of guy I'm not supposed to be getting into trouble with. I'm here for free food and drinks, nothing more. I'm turning over a new leaf. I'm a serious artist as of today. I'm focusing on me, on my music. I officially cannot be swayed by a deep voice and what is likely, based on nothing but a feeling, an incredible jawline.

I hold my hand up without looking at him. "No thanks."

He chuckles. "No thanks?"

I should have stayed home with my hydraulic press videos.

"Look, man," I glance over, and then up, and my breath catches in my throat. He's so much worse than my five-second judgment predicted. Tall and angular, sharp nose and chin that catch the light perfectly, shaggy brown hair that's wavy and disheveled in an intentional way. Full, pink lips. Bright, curious eyes. A day's worth of stubble.

He's not attractive he's...irresponsibly gorgeous.

"I'm not doing that," I say, more to myself than to him.

He smiles and leans against the fridge, his broad shoulders pulling in as he crosses his arms. "I feel like we're starting in the middle. Catch me up?"

I shake my head. "I realize this is a party and going up to a girl and striking up a conversation is the natural ebb and flow of things but, and there's no way you could have known this, I have removed myself from both the ebb and the flow. I'm choosing to focus on more important things at the moment."

He cocks an eyebrow like, *go on*.

"I've decided to live a life free of," I motion between us, "this."

He looks down at himself. "Wasn't aware I had put anything out there."

I roll my eyes because there's no way he doesn't know how his whole thing comes across. With that face? That body? He's probably never been turned down once in his life.

"I'm afraid I'm not in the zone, so to speak."

He runs a hand across his mouth, pushing down another smile. "So you think I came over here to, what, seduce you and carry you away into the night?"

"Well, no, because that would make you a vampire. Are you a vampire?"

He smiles, showing all his teeth. "Would that help my case?"

I've unintentionally made this into a game he's too happy to play.

"It'd be better than if you were a musician. Vampires I can resist. Musicians? Not so much."

"So me being a musician would be a bad thing."

I push myself up to sit on the counter and put some much-needed space between us. "It's a long story."

He reaches across me, his hard chest brushing against my elbow, and grabs a cup. He presses it against the ice lever in the door of the refrigerator and fills it with crushed ice all the way to the top. He scrapes a bite into his mouth with his teeth and says, "I've got time."

I can't stop looking at him. He's wearing fitted black pants and a nearly translucent white v-neck. I scroll through every memory I have to see if I've ever met anyone this attractive. I can't think of anything to say that isn't *let's get naked and do it on this counter.*

"Do you actually like crushed ice?"

He peers down into his cup like he's surprised to find ice there. "You don't?"

"No one does. When your drink gets too low it falls in jagged clumps and lands on your face and goes up your nose."

He peers up at me through a tangle of eyelashes so thick they weigh down his eyelids in that sexy/sleepy kind of way, so thick he blinks in slow-mo. A ceiling fan is whirring over our heads and his eyelashes flutter in the breeze, that's how long they are.

"You know, I only came over here to get a cup of ice because the line to the bar is so long, but now I'm invested. Tell me about these musicians of yours."

"I'd rather keep talking about ice. Safer topic. I prefer Sonic ice, by the way."

He nods. "Nugget cubes. Very manageable."

I instantly regret the giggle that bubbles up my throat.

"Is that why you've sworn off musicians?" he says. "Not enough ice in it for you?"

"Maybe too much," I say.

"Eliminating musicians from your dating pool must really narrow down the options. This is Music City after all."

He's cocky, but in that ultra-sexy-flirty way, like you want to slap him and kiss him in equal measure.

"I don't have anything against musicians. I am a musician. I just can't date them anymore."

He takes another bite of his ice and watches me with an amused look in his eyes.

"Top five worst dates with a musician."

"It's cute you think the horrors can be contained in a tidy top five. And they haven't all been bad experiences. Some of them have been so, so great. Well," I double check myself, "maybe not so, so great. Some have been a medium amount of great."

"But not great enough," he says knowingly.

A low hum vibrates through my body, like this guy has x-ray vision and is peering into my soul. Something in his eyes, the way his body moves as he's talking, is setting off alarm bells in my brain. Trouble is, I can't tell if the alarms are signaling something good or something bad. Maybe that's been my problem the entire time I've been in Nashville. I think run-for-your-life sounds like jump-right-in.

"Okay. If you think you can handle it. First was the guitar player who, after meeting for drinks, took me out to his truck to show me his gun collection. There was the bass player who made fun of my car when I picked him up. I should add, he asked me to pick him up because he didn't have a car and also asked me to give his mother a ride to Bingo with Jesus at the Methodist church. Then there was the drummer who could only meet me within a two-block radius from his apartment because that's as far as his ankle monitor would let him go. Another guitar player took me to one of those axe throwing bars and when I came back from the bathroom, asked if I'd gone number one or number two."

"No," he says, smiling behind his cup.

"Then there was the lead singer who, on our first date, kept one earbud in during dinner because he 'needed to catch up on his podcasts.'"

That one gets me a big laugh. "You can't be serious."

"I am one hundred percent serious."

"You said first date for podcast guy. Does that mean you went on a second date?"

I cover my face in shame. "Possibly."

"No wonder you've banned musicians."

"What about you?" I ask. "I imagine you've had better luck in the Nashville dating scene."

"I've never been on a date with someone who listened to podcasts the whole time, no."

"Too bad. That story kills when I meet people at parties."

He chuckles again, charmed.

Behind us, a too-loud LOVEJOY song cranks up and people tipsy enough to be uninhibited start dancing on either side of the pool. I sigh so loud he hears it over the music.

"Am I boring you?"

"It's this song."

He listens for a beat. "Not a fan of LOVEJOY?'

"You have no idea."

We watch the crowd, watch each other, long enough for the playlist to move on to a Sparrow song. Arguably more palatable but just as upsetting. Sparrow and LOVEJOY are the two artists I never want to hear and yet, everywhere I go, Sparrow and LOVEJOY follow me like bad debt.

I don't even know why I hate Sparrow, it's just always been the way. My mother hates them and has commanded I hate them as well. Something to do with my father, who was an original member of the band. Whatever went down between him and the Sparrow brothers, my mother refuses to talk about it.

"Dance with me," he says.

He doesn't ask, just says it, like us dancing together is a foregone conclusion.

"Why?"

"Because I wanna dance with you. And I think you might wanna dance with me."

I dramatically sigh and throw my head back. "I'm going to level with you."

"A good start."

"There's nothing I'd like more than to climb you like a tree at this very moment. But I promised myself I wouldn't do that anymore. I'm going to get serious about my art, my songs, work on making things happen for me. I'm focusing on myself, not hot guys who eat crushed ice. Lucky for you," I hook my thumb over my shoulder and point to the crowd, "there are about fifty girls in tight little party dresses over there who would absolutely love to dance with you."

He cranes his neck to look behind me at the crowd. "Do you think any of them would climb me like a tree?"

"Oh, for sure. Probably multiple at the same time."

"But not you."

He's subtly inched his way closer as we've been talking and now his hip is lightly touching my knee.

"I told you," I say, my resolve weakening with every swish of his eyelashes. "I've given up musicians. Forever."

"I never said I was a musician."

I give him an obvious once-over, letting myself linger on all the good parts. There are *so many* good parts. "I can smell it on you. You have lead singer ego."

He clutches his chest. "You wound me."

"It's not a bad thing. All the great lead singers have huge egos. It's how they get the crowd to fall in love with them every night. But then they think everyone off stage should fall in love with them too."

He sets his cup down and faces me, his hands on the counter

on either side of my thighs. His eyes are light hazel with flecks of gold and green. "I asked you to dance with me, not fall in love with me."

I lean toward him the tiniest bit. "The love part is implied."

He leans toward me the tiniest bit. "You've got me all figured out then."

"Like I said, I've dated a lot of musicians."

He grins like we've just invented our first inside joke. "I never said I was a musician."

We stay like that, our faces close, our eyes locked. Maybe I could do it, dance with him and that be it. Maybe I could touch his arms, fit my chin in the crook of his neck, let him squeeze my waist, and that be it. Maybe I could have this and nothing more.

"One dance," he presses. "After that, you can go back to your, what did you call it? Removing yourself from the ebb and flow?"

Trouble is, I can see how the whole thing will play out. We'll dance and then we'll kiss and then we'll find a quiet corner and then I'll give him my number and then he'll text and then we'll meet for coffee and somehow I'll end up at his place on his couch, in his bed, and then a month later I'll be moving back into Cass and Granny G's because things didn't work out. Again.

Or it could just be a dance.

I push on his shoulders so he'll back up. When I hop off the counter, we're standing so close I have to turn my face up to meet his. "One dance. That's all you get."

FOUR
THE ALCOVE

WE'RE ROUNDING the corner of the kitchen when two girls run past us, one holding a phone in the air and the other shouting *do not swipe don't you dare swipe*! As they're running, one of the girls trips and falls into us, pushing me and my dance partner into an alcove on the side of the kitchen wall. It's a small space, definitely not big enough for two adult people.

"Little tight," he says with a smile.

"Little? We're wedged in here so tight it will take a Costco-sized can of WD-40 to de-wedge us."

"WD-40?" he says, amused.

"Yeah, you know, the lubricant that—"

The look on his face shuts me up, but only for a second.

"I did not mean to bring up lubricant," I say, grinning.

Our bodies are crushed together, my boobs smashed into his chest, our knees knocking together, hips dangerously aligned. When we were pushed into the alcove, I threw my hands out and now have one on his bicep and the other on his shoulder, my thumb hooked into the v of his v-neck. I'm eye-level with his chin. When I look down, there's a long white scar across his collarbone. Covering the scar is a tattoo of a tiny piece of music.

"I knew it." I trace the tattoo with my thumb. "Musician."

It's three measures, a simple melody, and proof of my suspicion.

He huffs out a one-note laugh and I feel it against my body. "It's a melody my brother and I wrote when we were kids."

I shake my head. "That's so sweet I might actually pass out. Or maybe I'll pass out from the heat. It's like a thousand degrees in this alcove."

Neither one of us makes a move to leave.

"Why is there an alcove here?" he says. "What's it for?"

"A bookshelf? Maybe one of those huge vases?"

We watch each other, both of us plotting. I know where this is going, know I should stop it, but my brain is no longer in charge. I keep tracing his tattoo, running my thumb back and forth over the notes.

"Something I've been wondering about you," he says.

"You mean for the last twenty minutes we've known each other?"

His hands find my waist and his thumbs push into my skin. "You don't date musicians."

"As of today, yes."

"Are there any other banned activities? Say…kissing a musician? Kissing isn't dating last I checked."

He's right. Kissing isn't dating. And kissing him would be a great way to erase Brad the Bass Player from my memory. It'd be like a service this guy's providing, helping me move on with my life. Some might even call it a smart decision.

"Kissing might be okay," I say, "but only on a special occasion."

"What kind of occasion?"

My hands migrate to his neck. His nose brushes against mine.

"Like, Christmas. Or your birthday. Is today your birthday?"

He whispers against my lips. "I'm thinking of having it legally changed to today."

Then his mouth is on mine as his hands squeeze my waist.

The muggy night air and our mingling breath raises the temperature in the alcove one million degrees. My armpits are damp and he can probably feel my sweat mustache and I don't even care because holy *shit*.

It's not even the amount of tongue (a lot) or the way his hands are drifting higher on my ribcage (almost there). It's the way he's softly but purposefully licking my lips like he's catching the drippy parts of an ice cream cone. The way he's gently tugging my bottom lip between his teeth before moving to my top lip. The way his tongue curls around mine so seductively I moan right into his mouth.

I was expecting something frantic and illicit but this? He's so tender. Purposeful. Sensual. It's the payoff of a slow burn we haven't earned. If this is what it's like to kiss him, imagine the sex? It'll be like bungee jumping into an exploding firework.

We break apart, panting from the heat and *the heat*, and stare at each other like we just discovered kissing. His face reads complete surprise, his eyes hazy, pupils blown wide. His lips part, his breath coming in short puffs.

I swallow thickly and say, "It's so hot."

"You're hot," he says, and I would roll my eyes but we're kissing again, with purpose. His hands are on my ass and I'm scratching my fingernails up under his shirt, my brain firing so many questions and exclamations there's probably smoke pouring out of my ears. I'm both in the moment and above it, watching and screeching one long, loud WOW as his hands make another loop to my hips, my waist, my ribs, his thumbs sweeping across my pink lace bra. If we keep this up my body hair is going to catch fire.

I don't have a category for this level of instant connection. We're inventing it right now, discovering a new level of chemical attraction.

He tentatively dips a finger an inch into the waistband of my shorts. I pull away from the kiss with a loud smack. It's five million degrees crammed into this tiny space with someone who kisses like he's shipping out tomorrow. The alcove is too small, too exposed. We need a new location.

"About that dance I owe you," I say.

A hint of confusion passes over his face.

"We could go down to Jackson's lair. Basement, I mean. He calls it his lair, I don't know why. Anyway, I know the door code." His finger inches further into my shorts as I'm babbling. "And it's air conditioned."

He leans impossibly closer and puts a hand on the wall behind my head. The entirety of his long, lean body pushes up against mine. He lowers his mouth to mine in a searing kiss that leaves me breathless. When he pulls away, the open want on his face nearly makes me scream out loud.

His breath on my face is a box fan set to scorching. "I don't even know your name."

"Come to Jackson's lair with me and maybe I'll tell you."

We unstick ourselves from the alcove and slide onto the walkway. He holds his hand out and I take it, already feeling cooler and the tiniest bit clear headed. I lead him down the yard to Jackson's lair. We're almost there when we run right into Cass.

"Hey," I say, obviously breathless. I pull my hand out of his so fast it makes his arm swing at his side.

"Granny G fell," Cass says, her face etched in worry. "She's at Vanderbilt. We have to go."

My priorities shift in an instant. I turn to him and he's already nodding his head.

"Go," he says.

I head up the hill with Cass and then turn back.

"Sorry. This was..." I don't know how to finish that sentence.

"It was," he says with a devastating smile.

FIVE
A SPARROW BY ANY OTHER NAME

VERY PROUD TO SAY I'M four weeks clean of hot musicians. Cass has been marking off every day on Granny G's Ryan Gosling calendar hanging in the kitchen. Granny says it's to encourage me but I know Cass is counting down to my inevitable slip-up. Not to brag, but I haven't even flirted with anyone in a black crew neck just to be safe.

Instead of kissing lead singers, I've been writing my ass off and performing every chance I get. My best paying gig was a fiftieth birthday party for a wealthy Franklin woman. None of the partygoers paid much attention to my songs but since they paid me fifteen hundred bucks, I couldn't be bothered to care. I've mostly played open mic night at Steamers, the coffee shop where I work, which doesn't pay me at all unless I'm also making drinks.

I've written fifteen new songs, a bulk of them about the musicians I've dated. Songs don't count against my rule. I can write about musicians, just not sleep with them.

Okay, full disclosure, when I say I've written songs about musicians, most of them are about that guy from Jackson's party. It's borderline ridiculous since I don't even know his name, but I've never had such an intense, immediate connection with someone. If Granny G hadn't fallen that night, who knows what would have happened. I'm so relieved Granny's okay but I do wonder, if she hadn't had her accident, if I would have learned his name. If we would have taken things further. If I would have broken my rule the same day I made it.

"Order for Don," I call, setting a black coffee on the bar.

I'm working a double today, drowning in mobile orders.

A tall-ish, middled-aged man with shaggy brown hair and enough stubble to almost count as a beard walks up to get his drink.

He picks it up and pauses. "Hey, didn't I see you play at an open mic night here a few days ago?"

My heart swells. "You probably did."

"Yeah, I remember the hair."

A week ago I chopped my hair into a shoulder-length bob and dyed it the most luscious shade of lavender, like spun cotton candy. Cass, hair genius, did it for me. She wondered if it made me look too much like a pop star, like my sister, but I don't care. I feel amazing.

"You were really great." He takes a cautious sip of his coffee, his eyes on me. "Do you play out a lot?"

"Every chance I get."

"Write your own stuff?"

I smile. "Every chance I get."

He nods, answering a silent question. "Would you be interested in an opening slot on an upcoming tour? Fifty cities. Expenses plus a salary."

I gawk at him. "Quick question. Are you about to turn a pumpkin into a coach driven by some mice?"

He laughs short and quick. "My band is having a local competition to determine the opening act for our tour this summer. It's word of mouth around town, so pretty limited. I think you'd be perfect for it."

My brain buzzes louder than the espresso machine. His band? Fifty cities? A salary? This is it. This is the thing I've been working for, the thing one out of a million hopefuls ever gets the chance to do. And I'd be doing it on my own. No Lovejoy assumption, no sister expectation. No set-up from my mother. This guy, *who has a band*, saw me play and wants me on his tour.

"Name the time and place and I'll be there."

"You got a pen?"

I search around behind the counter and find two pens. I hand him both, just in case. He writes a name and email address on a napkin and hands it to me.

"Reach out to Jasmine. She'll get you all the details. Tell her Don invited you."

"I will literally be sending her an email the second you step out of this coffee shop."

He smiles as I clutch the napkin to my chest. "Tell me your name?"

Oh, right. My name. I reach across the counter to shake his hand. "I'm Mari. Mari Gold."

"Glad I ran into you, Mari Gold."

He turns to leave and I call out to him. "Wait. I hope this isn't rude to ask but, what's the name of your band?"

He waits a beat and I think I've screwed up, like if I was any sort of serious musician I would have recognized him.

He grins and slides out the door as he says, "Sparrow."

My stomach falls out of my ass.

Maybe I heard him wrong. Maybe he said another band that sounded like Sparrow, like Marrow. Farrow maybe. Arrow?

"Did the dude from Sparrow just ask you to audition for his tour?" my manager Sage asks.

"Shit, shit, shit, *shit*. Are you sure he said Sparrow?"

She eyeballs me like I've finally lost the last of my marbles. "Uh, yeah. You're gonna do it, right? Sparrow is like, huge."

Yes, huge. Their first big hit, "In A Dark Wood," was written by none other than John Lovejoy, my father. I grew up hearing stories about Sparrow, being told they had a falling out with my father, being told the Lovejoy family would never and could never associate with the likes of Don and Deacon Sparrow as long as any of us shall live.

A specific memory springs to mind. My mother swinging her half-drunk glass of pinot grigio in the air and proclaiming it would be a cold day in hell before a Lovejoy ever performed with the Sparrow brothers. She's had it out for Sparrow since they were just Don and Deacon Sparrow and my father, the three of them writing songs and playing gigs around Nashville, dreaming about making it big. My father ended up leaving the band right at the beginning of their fame and I've never known why. Whenever I bring it up, my mother abruptly changes the subject.

When I came to Nashville, I hoped an opportunity like this tour would come my way, but I never imagined it would be with the one artist I'm technically banned from associating with on any level. I've avoided them so much, I didn't even recognize Actual Don Sparrow when he came into my coffee shop. Technically speaking, this is the best and worst thing that's ever happened to me.

Opening for Sparrow could be my shot. Most people never get a shot and I've just been handed a massive one by the lead guitar player of a major band. How can I let it pass me by because of an old family dispute I'm not even involved in? Besides, if I end up on the tour, maybe I can find out what happened between them and my father. I'll be disinherited by my mother, but it's not like she's a pillar of support right now.

I call Cass and she picks up on the second ring.

"Serious question. Should I plunge into my family's dark past by auditioning to tour with the one band in all of music that's forbidden to me?"

"Hello to you," she says, "and absolutely you should."

I love that she's able to make this decision without any context.

"You think?"

"I need more details, clearly, but if what you're saying is you got an opportunity to audition for a tour with Sparrow, like, *the* Sparrow, the answer is yes no matter what."

Hearing her say the words solidifies what I knew before I even called her.

First, if I do this, my mother will actually kill me. Like, hire a hitman and erase me from the planet kill me.

Second, I am all the way in.

FOR IMMEDIATE RELEASE

SPARROW TO LIVESTREAM AUDITIONS FOR GRAND TOTAL TOUR OPENING ACT

Five Nashville Acts To Compete In Livestream Event With Winner Determined By Fan Votes

Livestream airs Thursday, May 15th at 9pm ET / 8pm CT with voting to immediately follow

Nashville, TN (May 14th, 2025) Breaking with tradition, multi-platinum folk rockers Sparrow are bringing out an unknown, up-and-coming artist as the opening act for this summer's Grand Total Tour. After narrowing the search to five Nashville indie artists, Sparrow is holding auditions via livestream with the winner determined by fan votes.

"This summer tour is for the fans," says Sparrow frontman, Deacon Sparrow. "They've been such a great support to us over the years so what better way to celebrate than bringing out someone the fans hand-picked. Plus, we love the idea of giving a young artist the chance to learn the ropes the way we did, out on the road."

All five acts will compete in the livestream airing Thursday, May 15th at 9pm ET / 8pm CT on Sparrow's YouTube channel. Voting will open immediately after and will be open for 24 hours.

About Sparrow: Top-selling American folk rock band Sparrow are five-time PHONO® Award-nominated, two-time PHONO® Award-winning, Streamers Billionaires Club recipients with five *Charts* Music Awards. Their debut album, *Sparrow*, is RIAA-certified Double-Platinum with follow-up *Closer* RIAA-certified Platinum. The band's single "In A Dark Wood" remains one of the most-streamed folk rock songs of all time with over one billion streams. Sparrow are Deacon Sparrow (lead vocals, guitar), Don Sparrow, (lead guitar, vocals), Randy Moore (bass, vocals) and Joe Collins (drums, vocals).

Press contact:
Emily Wu
emily@sparrowband.com

SIX
A REAL KICK IN THE PANTS

FIRSTSOUND NASHVILLE IS a sprawling rehearsal complex east of downtown. When I pull into the parking lot, the squat, colorless building looks more like an abandoned strip mall than the rehearsal space for some of music's biggest acts. Rows of loading bays line the outside stacked with semi-trucks either dropping off or picking up gear headed to tours in places like Birmingham, Cincinnati, Chicago, Philadelphia.

Jasmine, Sparrow's tour manager, called three days ago to tell me the band loved my audition video, to show up here tonight, that the band wanted me to perform an original for a fan-voted livestream. I have spent the last two days choosing my song, my outfit, perfecting my performance. I feel very ready and also extremely not ready. Either way, I'm here.

Before I left, Cass pulled the front half of my hair up into a messy knot so the lavender color pops against my dark brown roots. I added heavy eyeliner, five coats of mascara and a rich, plum lipstick.

"There's an electricity in the air about this audition," I told Cass while she did my hair. "Can you feel it?"

Cass, never one to exaggerate, said, "I feel it."

I'm in my black floral dress with tiny buttons all the way

down the front and a plunging neckline that shows enough cleavage to matter. I unbuttoned the skirt up to my mid-thigh after I pulled on my lucky black Doc Martens. The final touch was a cropped leather jacket I found at Music City Thrift for eight dollars.

"You're gonna win this thing," Cass said once I had the whole look together.

"We don't even know who the competition is," I said.

"Doesn't matter. With your voice, that song, and this look? It's inevitable."

As far as I can tell, I don't look like a Lovejoy. It helps I've always looked like me and no one else, not my mother or my father or Polly. I came out of the womb fighting against being a Lovejoy.

I pull my guitar case out of the backseat of my beat-up Civic. Inside is my father's six-string PRS acoustic, the guitar he wrote his biggest hit on, his favorite one to play. I have my favorite photo of him taped to the back. He's with my mother. She's smiling so wide her eyes are pinched closed and his face is buried in her neck. He's holding a mint green Les Paul and wearing a cowboy shirt covered in tiny orange flowers. I don't know why it's my favorite photo—you can't even see his face—but something about it has always drawn me in.

I head across the lot to a set of concrete stairs with a rust covered railing and pull open the frosted glass door. Inside, the narrow hallway is crowded with black road cases and hand trucks stacked high with plastic tubs and sagging brown boxes. The walls are covered in framed tour posters—Zach Bryan, The Avett Brothers, Jelly Roll, Brandi Carlile, Noah Kahan, KISS. Down the hall there's a poster from Sparrow's last tour and I take a moment to study it. Deacon and Don Sparrow are front and center holding their guitars in the air like they just took a bow. In another time and place, I imagine my father standing next to them. My heart flutters at the thought, at me being here instead of him, carrying his guitar to audition for the band he started.

Jasmine said the auditions are being held in Room F. I pass two men in navy Dickies and faded black t-shirts and find a grey metal door marked Room K. Doubling back down the hall, I find Room H. Room G. No F.

"You look lost," a voice says, walking up behind me. When I turn around, the first word that comes to mind is stunning. The woman in front of me is perfection—a blunt black bob angled sharply at her chin, dark eyeliner winged out to a fine point, her mouth a severe slash of red lipstick, black structured blazer layered just so over an impossibly tight pencil skirt, shiny black spiked heels with a pointed toe. I walked in feeling confident in my boho indie rocker look but standing next to her worry I'm coming off like an un-showered flower child.

"What gave it away?" I ask, holding my guitar case up. "Do you happen to know where Room F is?"

"You're Mari Gold, aren't you? I'm Emily Wu, Publicist."

She's immediately intimidating and I do my best to match her confident energy. I heard once that making it in the music industry is twenty-five percent talent, twenty-five percent confidence and fifty percent dumb luck. The talent's in my blood. If I can manifest the confidence, I'm hoping the dumb luck will follow.

"Right this way," Emily says, crooking a black pointy fingernail over her shoulder as she swishes past me.

She leads us down a hallway over-crowded with more gear and framed tour posters. When we get to Room F, she pulls open the heavy, grey metal door. It's cool and dark inside, a suspended strip of can lights aimed at a wide stage set up on the right half of the room complete with a drum kit, monitors, mics, the whole works. There's a couple dozen people filling up the other half of the room, their identities obscured by the dark.

"Cheddar," Emily calls and someone turns and walks over to us. He's wearing a black hoodie which, in the dark room, highlights his pale white skin. His cropped brown hair is the same color as his friendly eyes.

"Hi," he says, extending his hand. "Chet Hurr, but everyone calls me Cheddar."

"Cheddar runs digital marketing for Sparrow," Emily says. "This is one of our contestants, Mari Gold."

"Mari Gold." He sing-songs my name and bends forward at the waist like he's going to sniff me. "Such a great Lizzy McAlpine cover for your submission video. We all loved it. And might I say, impressive set-up doing that YouTube video to get folks to vote for you."

After we found out I was chosen to audition, Cass filmed a new video with special guest Mari Gold. Her YouTube channel, Sapphic Sammies, where she makes different sandwiches based on famous lesbians, started as an inside joke with her now ex, but it's blown up in the last year or so. When I worried about putting myself out there so publicly, Cass rolled her eyes.

"You do realize if you go on this tour you will be playing in front of thousands of people every night."

"What if no one buys my stage name? What if they all know I'm really Penny Lovejoy?"

"You'll already be on the tour. Who cares after that?"

After posting the video we had to delete about ten comments asking if I was Polly Lovejoy's sister, which initially made me panic, but it all seemed to blow over after an hour or two.

"You saw that, huh?" I say, nervous he knows my real identity.

"Everyone saw it. Total stroke of genius. Who runs your socials?"

"I do? I mean, the video was my best...my manager's idea. She runs the Sapphic Sammies channel and thought it would be a great way to promote the contest."

Okay, so, I just panic-named Cass as my manager to the head of Sparrow's digital marketing. No way that will come back to bite me.

"Is she here? I'd love to pick her brain."

"No, she's…with another client tonight." Hair client, that is.

"If this contest doesn't work out maybe you two can come work on my team."

I can't tell if he's joking or not.

Cheddar's phone buzzes and he excuses himself, pulling Emily away with him. I scan the space for Sparrow, hoping Don is here and I can say hello, when a short woman wearing all black with a round Afro comes over to me.

"Mari Gold?" I nod. "I'm Jasmine Milner." She has a small diamond stud in her nose that sparkles in the stage lights.

"Jasmine!" I want to hug her but opt for professionalism. "So good to meet you. Thanks for all the great info you sent."

"Info is my specialty. The other contestants are gathering over here." She motions for me to follow her. "I'll be announcing the line-up in just a few minutes. Oh, and there are snacks and drinks at the table in the back, if you need. You can hang out, mingle, get some water, whatever makes you comfortable. For the livestream, only the artist performing will be on camera so you won't have to actively watch if you don't want to."

Ha. As if I won't be studiously scrutinizing every move they make. While Cass is doing her client Zoe's hair tonight, they're watching the livestream on her laptop and will be texting me with updates.

"Thanks, Jasmine," I say, my outer-confidence shining, my inner-terror trembling like a high strung chihuahua. "I'm really excited to be here. Is Sparrow coming for the audition?"

Jasmine smiles and pats my arm. "Big fan, huh?"

If she only knew.

"The whole band won't be here, but Deacon and Don will be. They're usually the ones to handle these types of front-facing things. Should arrive any minute, at least if they know what's good for them. I don't think those dudes have been on time once in the last twenty-five years."

"Oh?" I ask, trying to mask my immediate interest. "Have you worked for them that long?"

She laughs and winks conspiratorially. "I'm not as young as I look, honey."

Jasmine hurries off to talk to someone manning one of the three cameras set up at different angles around the stage. My heart races as I casually walk back to the snack table to grab some water. Jasmine probably knew my father, maybe knows my mother. But if she knows I'm a Lovejoy, she didn't let on in the slightest.

I'm texting Cass to let her know I may or may not have named her as my manager when Jasmine claps her hands and calls the room to attention.

"Hi, everyone, so glad to see all of you here. While we kept this audition word-of-mouth, we still received quite a few submissions. Y'all are the ones who really stood out for us. Deacon and Don Sparrow should be here any minute so I'm just gonna call everyone's name to make sure we're all here and then we'll go over some of the details for the audition." She looks down at her phone and then back up at us. "The Hopkins Family Band?"

A face-matching group all holding various stringed instruments raise their hands. The youngest one, who looks to be around twelve, raises his fiddle.

"royalties?" Jasmine calls.

A girl with bright pink hair along with three emo-looking guys all nod and wave to everyone.

"Shades of Grey?"

Four guys all wearing solid grey raise their hands. One of them is holding a grey bass and another, a grey acoustic. I've never even seen a grey acoustic, which means it's probably hand-painted. While I admire their commitment to a theme, their grey overload is making my chances at winning look better and better. I can definitely beat a twelve-year-old, a Paramore wannabe and a band leaning too heavily on a color scheme.

"Mari Gold?"

I say *here* too loudly and immediately feel dumb. The pink-haired girl smiles at me.

"Kick Raines?"

I look around and don't see anyone else other than a handful of people milling around the snack table.

"Kick Raines," she says again.

"Over here," comes a gravelly voice from the dark corridor by the door. We all turn to look as a tall, dark-haired guy saunters in, guitar case in hand. Two guys follow behind him, one carrying a bass guitar case.

My breath catches in my throat when his face comes into view in the dim lighting.

Because Kick Raines is him.

The him.

From Jackson's party.

From the alcove.

The one with the big hands and the soft lips and the eyelashes that defy logic.

He's here.

He's a contestant.

SEVEN
THIS IS WAY WORSE THAN SEXY THOR

I CANNOT PROCESS the mirage walking toward me looking like forbidden sex in painted on jeans. When our eyes meet, his narrow as he tries to place me. I watch his face as his brain makes the connection, hesitating a fraction of a second.

"Wow," he says right as I say, "what are you doing here?"

"Okay, great," Jasmine says, launching into her speech about the competition, a speech I now cannot hear because Best Kiss of My Life is standing right in front of me grinning like I was the best kiss of *his* life.

He looks as stunned as I feel, which is very, very stunned. My brain is emitting one loud unending screech, like I've slammed on squealing brakes but the car's still plummeting over a cliff. How is he here? How, exactly, am I supposed to compete against his whole…everything?

This has to be some sort of unspoken competition violation, like a bride forbidding hot bridesmaids so she doesn't get upstaged. *Contestants must be of average attractiveness so as not to distract from the headlining act.*

That's when it hits me.

Oh God, my song.

I wrote a song about the alcove, about him, about that night.

It's objectively better than any song I've ever written, which is why I chose it for the audition, but I never imagined I'd be singing it *in front of him*. He'll for sure know I'm singing a song about his hands on my hips and his tongue in my mouth and exactly how much I liked it and I will have to die dead on a livestream in front of thousands of people.

"What are you doing here?" I ask again.

Our guitar cases clank against each other. I set mine upright between us like a barrier. He mimics my action, giving us even more separation.

"I'm here for the Sparrow audition." He looks around with a fake sort of shock. "Is this the wrong room? Jasmine did say Room F, right?"

"But you never said…that night when…you never said you were a musician."

"Never said I wasn't."

He has a self-assured twinkle in his eye and it's all roaring back now. His look-at-me charisma, the way he read lead singer the second I laid eyes on him. He was and is the kind of guy who winks and gives you finger guns and you don't even care because he's *that attractive*. I'm moments away from the biggest opportunity of my career and suddenly I'm up against someone so hot it burns your retinas.

"I was hoping I'd run into you, you know, around town," he says. "Never imagined it'd be here, us competing against each other."

"How did you even get here?"

"Same way you did I imagine."

It's too much, seeing him and being near him when he's consumed so much of my thoughts over the last few weeks. It's like seeing a celebrity in the wild. You think you'll know what they look like but in person they're always so much more. He is more. Too much. I'm drowning in shock.

"Are you any good?" It's a ridiculous thing for me to ask since it absolutely doesn't matter. He'll get votes just for looking into the camera with that face. I bet he could sing the ABCs while banging spoons together on his knee and people would clamor to vote for him before the song was over.

"On stage or in the sack?" he asks. "The answer to both is... wait, are you still off musicians?"

He follows that zinger up with a toothy grin and oh my God I am going to commit a felony. Best Kiss Ever or no, I do not intend to lose my long-awaited spotlight. I'm here to win, not be bested by Captain Lady Boner in solid black Chucks.

"Kick Raines," he says, hand out.

I take it and look him pointedly in the eye. "Kick, that's...an interesting name."

"Maybe I'm an interesting guy."

"Is that why you're so comfortable seducing strangers at parties?"

I pull my hand away and fluff my hair with my fingers.

"I'll admit," he says, his voice all husky and knee-bending, "it's not often I come across a half-naked girl in an outdoor kitchen talking about crushed ice and making suggestive," he pauses, pursing his lips, his eyes doing the damn sparkle, "suggestions."

"Your memory is a bit more salacious than the reality of the moment. I was fully clothed."

He scratches at his neck, his fingers grazing over his clavicle tattoo. "You're different."

"Different than what?"

"That night." A small, secret smile pushes against his mouth. "The alcove."

The word alcove falls off his lips like an invitation. Hot liquid want pinballs between my thighs.

Bing! Bing! Bing!

But I made my rule for a reason. Now is not the time to break it.

"Look, that whole thing was...great, but...I wasn't supposed to ever see you again."

He wiggles his fingers out to the side like he's a Toro at Rancho Carne High School. "Surprise."

I roll my eyes but I'm also smiling so wide I instinctively raise my hand to cover it. I hear my name and turn my head away from Kick, attempting to listen to what Jasmine's saying since we've already missed the bulk of it.

Our bodies are half facing each other, half facing the stage. Kick sets his guitar case on the ground. He crosses his arms and widens his stance, making himself the tiniest bit shorter. His hair is a riot of dishevelment that's completely begging for someone to run their hands through it.

The way I ran my hands through it.

The way I want to again.

He leans in close and puts his lips right next to my ear. "Love the hair." I look straight ahead like I didn't hear him, but I can see his smirk out of the corner of my eye, like he's already won the unnamed competition between us. "I didn't take you for a pop princess." When I narrow my eyes at him, he shrugs and says, "I figured you were more *folklore* less *Lover*."

I give him a slow, measured head-to-toe once over. "I absolutely did take you for a rock god wannabe with artfully rumpled hair."

He feigns surprise. "You think my hair is art?"

We're flirting. We shouldn't be flirting.

My body is still very attracted to his body, humming at his proximity, pushing me to drift closer to him while my brain fights to move farther away.

My body needs to get it together.

Because this guy is a musician and my immediate competition, both of which mean he's a hard no.

Don't say hard.

Oh God.

"You still haven't told me your name," he says.

I catch his eye, looking for his angle. "I'm Mari Gold."

He pauses long enough to make me nervous. "It's great to officially meet you Mari."

"We'll be collecting votes for twenty-four hours," Jasmine says, "so about this time tomorrow, one of you will be joining Sparrow for their Grand Total Tour this summer. Sound good?"

A few contestants clap and I snap to attention. The audition has already started. I need to get my head in the game. Now that Kick Raines has entered the competition I'm going to have to work even harder to win.

Jasmine checks her phone. "We'll get started in about ten minutes as long as the guys get here on time. Shades of Grey, you're up first. You can go ahead and get set on stage."

"Jasmine, I'd like to get a few photos before we start," Emily says, "for the press release?"

"Emily. She's the one who invited me here," Kick murmurs into my ear, which seems like an excuse to get close to me. "Who invited you?"

"Don Sparrow." It comes out exactly as sassy as I intend for it to, but he grins at me.

We leave our guitars and climb the three stairs up to the stage. Jasmine and Emily get to work assembling us all into two long rows. Emily puts Kick next to me, both of us right in the center with Kick's two bandmates behind us.

"Isn't this adorable, Goldie? Our first photo together," Kick says, nudging me with his elbow.

"Don't worry. Once I'm on the tour, I'm sure there will be lots of photos of me you can download and admire. You can show your friends the one that got away."

"I don't see you running."

His breath is on my ear and my cheeks burn with the heat of it. How is he so cavalier about this? You'd think he knew I was going to be here and planned this whole thing.

"Kick? Mari?" Emily says, calling us out like little kids talking during class. Pink-haired girl catches my eye and gives me a wide-eyed thumbs up, like *good for you get it girl*.

Emily snaps a few photos with her phone. I try to look cool and unaffected but probably look terrified. I came here thinking all I needed to do was give a kick ass performance and now I'm completely thrown off by Kick Raines' elbow brushing my arm.

We all file back off the stage. Shades of Grey stays on to plug in their guitars. The lead singer runs through a vocal warm-up full of hmms and oohhs and bum bum bums, sliding up and down the scale.

I whip my phone out of my unlaced boot and walk away from the other contestants, making sure Kick doesn't follow me, and call Cass.

"Why are you calling?" she barks on speaker. "What happened?"

"Remember the guy? The one from Jackson's party a few weeks ago?"

"Mari, there are bigger things to focus on at this exact moment than some stranger danger make-out. I know you said it was epic but the livestream starts in less than five minutes. You need to focus!"

"He's here."

Long pause. I can totally see her face in my mind and its equal parts comical and stressed, mouth open in shock and brows drawn together in horror, eyes half-scared, half-pissed.

"What do you mean he's there?"

"The guy whose tongue surface I memorized is a contestant. He's competing against me to win the opening slot. His name is Kick Raines and *he is here.*"

She lets out a low whistle. "Plot. Twist."

"And he walked in looking all smug, like, haha guess what I'm here. He even made a snide comment about my hair. Called me a pop princess!"

"Asshole. Your hair looks incredible." She pauses. "And yours will too, Zoe."

"Do you remember the time Jackson invited us to that Johnny

Cash tribute show downtown at the War Memorial Auditorium? Colton Rhinehart performed?"

"Didn't he do 'Hurt?'" Cass wonders.

"I was there that night," Zoe says.

"Anyway, remember after Colton's performance I was going on and on about how he's a sexy Thor and I wanted to ride him all the way to Asgard?"

"We turned around and he was standing right behind us," Cass says and Zoe laughs.

"Watching Kick Raines walk into this rehearsal space was worse than Sexy Thor." I'm trying to keep my voice as low as possible. "What am I going to do?"

"What do you mean what are you going to do?" Cass's voice gets all high and pitchy, the yin to my low whining yang. "You get your perfectly styled ass on that stage and blow everyone else out of the water. I don't care if that dude's name is Kick or Stomp or Smack. The fact is, you, Mari Gold, are a shining star and no one else is going to get in the way of that. This audition is for you."

She's right. This audition is for me. I'm here to prove something, if not to Sparrow, at least to myself. I can't let anyone, not even Kick Raines, get in the way of that.

I hang up with Cass and look over at Kick and his overly confident grin, his sparkling eyes framed by those hideously long eyelashes, and I make a decision.

I am going to kill this audition.

EIGHT
I'M BEING HAUNTED BY AN ALCOVE

DEACON AND DON SPARROW show up about a minute before the livestream is supposed to start. The mood in the room shifts the second they walk through the door, every head turning toward them, spines straightening, eyes widening, low whispers laced with excitement filling the room. I've been in the same room with people far more famous than the Sparrow brothers but even I'm dazzled.

Deacon's arm is slung around a young blonde woman wearing a super short slip dress with fishnet stockings and stacked combat boots. I'd guess she was his daughter but the way his hand is grazing her ass says otherwise.

Don looks exactly as nondescript as he did in the coffee shop, like any other forty-something man in Nashville. I instinctively move to go say hello to him but Jasmine hurries both him and Deacon onto the stage to intro the competition.

"Don't worry," Kick says, sidling up next to me, "I'm sure they'll hang around for autographs afterwards."

I flash him a squinty-eyed, close-lipped smile, the face equivalent of flipping the bird. "It's cute the way you think you're so cute."

He starts to say something back, but the livestream is starting. Deacon Sparrow is immediately magnetic behind the mic. It's obvious why he's the front man, all personality and charisma even just walking up onto the stage. Don stands to the side, quietly supportive. Based on my internet research, Don's the real brains behind the band and writes all the songs, or does since my father left the band, but Deacon is the undeniable showman.

"Hey there everybody, I'm Deacon Sparrow," he says into the mic, spotlight shining on his face. He's weathered and handsome, lines around his eyes and a five-day beard, his brown hair streaked with enough grey to be sexy before tipping into old. His t-shirt and jeans hang on him just so, obviously picked out by a stylist to look effortless, thrown together, maintaining his cool guy appeal. Don's the step-down version of Deacon. He's just as handsome, but dimmer, like he puts in fifteen percent less effort in being famous. I wonder how my father would have looked next to them if he were still here. If he'd be on stage with them, intro'ing the competition.

"We want to thank y'all for tuning in to our big livestream event tonight for our Grand Total Tour this summer. Tickets are selling fast by the way so get 'em while you can. It's a little last minute, but we thought we'd do something a bit different for this tour. As most of you know, we got our big break on a tour with The Beaumont Brothers when we first started out, so we thought, hey, this summer we're gonna do the same for another up-and-coming."

Deacon looks over at Don, who nods in agreement.

"We kept the contest word-of-mouth around town here in Nashville but still got over five hundred video submissions. We know Nashville is Music City but wow! So many great artists submitted songs making it really hard to choose our top five, but we did and they're all here tonight. I know you're going to love them as much as we did! Now, don't forget, as soon as the livestream is over, voting begins. We need your help to pick who you wanna see with us out on the road this summer."

Deacon cups his hand over his eyes and looks out past the cameras and the lights. "Jasmine, who's first tonight?"

"Shades of Grey," she calls back before turning around and giving Cheddar a look like *I told him that already!*

Shades of Grey is waiting on stage, standing behind Deacon and Don, ready to go. They wave when Deacon turns around and finally notices them.

"Oh, cool, alright. Check 'em out and give 'em a vote if you like what you hear," Deacon says. "Shades of Grey, everybody."

Deacon and Don leave the stage and Shades of Grey's lead singer takes the mic.

"I bet they're embarrassed," Kick says, back in my ear, whisper-shouting over the loud rhythm of the kick drum, "all showing up in the same color."

I elbow him away from me and keep my focus on the band while also keeping an eye on Deacon and Don's movements around the room. They've got their heads together with Jasmine, not even paying attention to Shades of Grey. Deacon's arm-candy hovers next to him as she swipes through her phone.

Kick shuffles closer. "I like your look, though. Very nineties cool girl. You look incredible."

He's smiling with his eyes. That damn sparkle that's slowly wedging itself between my temples like a popsicle brain freeze.

"Shut-up, please. I want to hear this."

He runs his thumb and finger across his lips and mimes zipping them shut. I'd be charmed if I wasn't trying so hard to mentally take him out at the knees so he won't be able to perform.

Shades of Grey, while ridiculous looking, are amazing. Fully pop, their singer is boisterous, like Tigger hopped up on Pixy Stix. The band is tight, perfectly in sync with each other. And they all look like they're having the time of their lives, which, I imagine will be very vote-getting. Most bands let the lead singer do all the wooing, content to play their part getting the notes right, hitting the beats. This band is all in, including the drummer who's smiling and singing the lyrics even though he's not mic'd.

At a glance, none of the other contestants seem to be intimidated by Shades of Grey's performance. I'm doing my best to maintain my confident veneer while avoiding eye contact with Kick and stuffing down the waves of nerves rolling through me. I'm worried Don or Deacon or even Jasmine will hear something of my father in my voice, worried what Kick will do when he hears my song about him. I'd switch to a new song but I'm already rehearsed to perfection. If I switch now, I could flub the lyrics, forget the bridge, crash and burn in front of Sparrow. As much as I'm sure to be wildly embarrassed, I have to keep the song I planned to perform. It will be worth it when I get on the tour.

Thirty seconds into The Hopkins Family Band's song, I relax a tiny bit. They're talented, sure, but not the kind of act to open a Sparrow tour. royalties are good, but not as good as Shades of Grey. They're a bit too eclectic, like a rock band with a grudge. And the lead singer's chewing gum while she's singing.

Cass, via Zoe since Cass's hands are occupied doing Zoe's hair, has been texting me throughout the audition, rating each act on a scale of one to five for stage appeal, vocal appeal, and song choice. So far, no one's fared over a three-point-five.

Every time a new text comes in, Kick hovers over my shoulder to see what we're talking about.

"Nosey much?"

"I just can't imagine what would be so important it would tear your very serious concentration away from the competition."

"If you must know, my best friend and I are discussing the pros and cons of our fellow competitors."

His eyebrows jump and he tries to read my screen before I shove it under my arm. "Got a list in there about me?"

"I don't want to break your heart, but not everything is about you."

Until you hear my song about you, I think.

I hate how relaxed he seems, how unrattled. The other artists are antsy, eyes roaming the room, blowing out big breaths, shaking out their arms and walking in circles. Kick's leaning against the air all liquid and loose, like he does this kind of thing every day, like he can't wait to be done and go get midnight pancakes.

royalties finish their song and Kick lightly bumps my shoulder with his fist.

"I'm up next. Can't wait to see what you write about me on your little list."

"I'm pretty sure it will start with dumb and end with ass,"

He laughs like I've started another inside joke between us.

He and his two bandmates step up onto the stage, forgoing the makeshift stairs on the side since the stage is only a couple feet off the ground. I can't help but admire the way his body moves as he steps up, bends over to pick up his guitar cable, adjusts his strap over his shoulder. I notice his bass player and drummer match each other—same thick dark hair, same wide-set eyes, same bulging biceps, same brown skin. Twins.

I make an effort to wipe all emotion from my face so none of my churning thoughts will be visible. It's a challenge because I have what my mother says is a see-through face. I wear my emotions right on the tip of my nose, good or bad.

Kick's black Les Paul is visibly weathered. I hope it's because he bought it second-hand and not because he's played it for years. He plugs it into the amp and strums it a couple times before he smiles into the mic like he wants to make out with it. I know how the mic feels. A tingling sensation stings my cheeks and I smash my teeth together.

"I'm Kick Raines." His voice low and flirty and rough. He looks away from the camera and finds me, looks me right in the eye as he says, "This is 'I Kissed Her In An Alcove.'"

My entire body goes rigid, like I've died and rigor mortis has already set in. This absolute *dude* of a *guy* wrote a *song* about the *alcove*?

He lands a hard strum on his guitar and the song kicks into high gear. I'm still trying to determine what genre they're doing —Pop? Rock? Alt-folk-rock-tinged-with-pop?—when Kick starts to sing. From note one, to no one's surprise, Kick Raines drips charm and sex appeal and boy next door and aloof rock star—a fangirl smorgasbord of hotness. My mouth drops open against my will and I hope I'm obscured enough by the bright stage lights that he doesn't see me. Because Kick's voice.

Kick's.

Voice.

It's liquid smoke. A crackling fire. The kind of voice you want whispering dirty things into your ear as he unbuttons your jeans.

On stage he's all energy and joy, a frenetic knee-jerk of wildness that's mesmerizing to watch. He's stomping the stage with his black sneaker and making eye-contact with every single person in the rehearsal space, especially the camera. He's attractive and attracting, all of us unconsciously shifting closer to the stage, mesmerized by his charisma.

I squint into the darkness across the room and see Deacon and Don are watching him. Slip Dress is whispering in Deacon's ear and motioning to Kick like, *look at him.*

Honey, we are all looking at him.

My cheeks burn, but not in the good way. Kick's more than my competition, he's everyone's competition. I want to hurl him WWE-style off the stage, slam him over the head with a metal folding chair. Want to hang him by a wedgie from the top of the Batman building. Want his voice to crack or a guitar string to break, something, anything to give me even the slightest chance at winning.

Somehow I hear the lyrics through the smoky sex haze the room is now engulfed in and wow I am in so much trouble.

It was just a party

Time to kick back
Had no idea I'd meet her
My heart too black
But she told me she was interesting
By the way she didn't care
Told me I should want her
Think she liked the way I stared

He smiles into the camera as his arm pumps up and down on his guitar.

Then I kissed her in an alcove
We took it fast we took it so slow
To party people we put on a show
When I kissed her in an alcove

My phone buzzes in my hand.

Cass: THIS is the guy from Jackson's party?

I grimace and look back at Kick. He's reached the lead-up to the bridge and he's spinning, his guitar chord wrapping around his legs like a serpent. Then he reverses, spinning in the opposite direction to unwind himself and it's obvious he's rehearsed this move. I wish I could say it's not working for him but it. so. is.

I can't process the lyrics, too stunned by the theatrics of his entire performance, his face, the way he leans into the microphone like he wants to put a baby in it. He keeps glancing my way and I worry people will know I'm the girl in the alcove. When I look around the room, everyone here is the girl in the alcove, too busy drinking him in to care what he's saying. He is so going to win this thing.

As his song comes to a close, my knees start to quake. I don't know if I can beat him. If I was voting, I'd vote for him. I don't know how any person with eyes and ears and repressed sexual desire wouldn't.

I look down at my buzzing phone.

Cass: This is still Zoe. Cass says do not spiral, she can feel you spiraling.

Cass: She says sure, he wrote a song about you but yours is better

Cass: IT IS BETTER (she said this in all caps)

Cass: She says you've got this. He's good but you're great.

Cass: She just yelled for you to get on that stage and BLOW THEM ALL AWAY

On Kick's last note, the entire room loses it, cheering and clapping like they just witnessed a star being born. Cheddar's got his pinkies in his mouth, whistling. Even Jasmine's grinning and clapping. I politely clap long enough to look like I mean it before crouching down to pull my guitar from its case.

It's time for Mari Gold to show the world what she's made of.

NINE
HOT LIKE ICE

KICK and I pass each other as I make my way up the stage stairs.

"Was it good for you?" he asks, knocking his shoulder into mine.

Does he want me to comment on his performance? The fact that he sang about the alcove? Even if I had something clever to say, which I don't, I'm about to do the exact same thing. I'm basically swan diving into my biggest humiliation while also hoping it's my moment in the sun. The duality of the moment has me wound so tight I'm on the verge of passing out and rolling off the edge of the stage.

I smile up at Kick and bat my eyes, nothing but sweetness.

"Watch and learn, Ice Boy."

The room settles, waiting for me to begin. I plug my father's guitar into the amp and adjust the strap across my shoulder. I can't see Deacon and Don through the stage lights, but I hope they're watching.

"Hi, I'm Mari Gold." My voice rings out confident and clear over the sound system. "This is 'Hot Like Ice.' Thank you for voting."

I can feel the room shift as I play my first chords. Everyone else was loud and energetic, playing like they were hanging off the back of a speeding train. My toned-down, acoustic approach is giving me space to draw them in, and I do, one note at a time.

Springtime night, but heat so high
Distraction on my mind
Cicadas singing, moon dark sky
Not knowing what I'd find
He came wandering, looking like a wish
Made conversation so nice
Heat was rising, moving us close
Between us we could melt ice

Then we kissed inside the alcove
His kisses sweet as honey
Who he was I really don't know
But I loved the way he wanted me
Inside that alcove
Inside that alcove
Inside that alcove

I hit the chorus like I'm falling in love in this moment, on stage, in front of the cameras. When the first *inside that alcove* hits, the high note soars as I draw out the word through the measure. I think it sounds amazing. I know it feels amazing.

I don't look at Kick. I keep my focus on my lyrics, my guitar, the camera. Because this moment is for me. For the memories I never got with my father. For every moment like this we never got to do together.

I howl the bridge, my voice filling the room.

In the alcove, secrets don't matter
In the alcove, we don't need to know
Anything but each other
'Cause anything goes

As my song ends, there's a too-long pause and I worry no one liked it. But then the applause starts, loud and enthusiastic. I smile wide to the camera and take a half-bow.

Beat that Mr. *Kissed Her In An Alcove* foot-stomper, microphone-seducer.

"Great song," Don Sparrow says as I step off the stage. "Really glad you made it here."

"Thanks to you," I say with a big smile.

He shakes his head. "You earned it."

I freeze in place. It's impossible for him to know what those three words mean to me, but they mean the entire world.

"I'm just glad we ran into each other and that you'd seen me play. It's an honor to be able to audition for you."

He shakes his head, refusing the compliment. He looks around before he says, "We need new blood on the tour to help us sell tickets. So, we need you as much as you might think you need us."

"I can't imagine a world where I would be a ticket draw for you guys. You're legends."

"Suck up to the voters, not me," he jokes.

Since I have his attention, I dig a little. "Your song 'In A Dark Wood' changed the game. It won Record of the Year, didn't it?"

"You know your history," he says with a friendly smile. He doesn't mention my father, who wrote the song, and I'm not sure how to bring it up without sounding like a fangirl.

I shrug, casual. "I dabble."

"Don," Deacon calls from the doorway.

"You're being summoned," I say.

"Your audition was really good, Mari. I'm sure you'll get lots of votes." He pats my shoulder reassuringly. "I hope to see you out there. Good luck."

I thank him as he leaves to meet up with Deacon and, for the first time in a long time, it feels like my life might finally be on the right track.

TEN
THE PAST TENSE OF RENDEZVOUS IS RENDEZVOUS

I'M PUTTING my guitar back in my case when Emily pulls me aside, her red lips pulled into a devilish smile.

"You two know each other, don't you?"

"Who?"

I know who. I don't want her to know who.

"You and Kick." She crosses her arms and taps her fingers like a plotting villain. "Your songs were about each other."

I'm working to come up with the right thing to say when Kick walks by and she yanks him into our small circle.

"You two," she motions between us, "you hooked up at a party."

"No," I say right as Kick says, "not exactly."

Emily shakes her head, her eyes bright. "This is utterly fantastic. You wrote songs about each other without knowing the other would be here? I couldn't make this up if I wanted to."

"We're still eligible, right?" I ask, because if Kick Raines and his alcove song boot me out of the competition, I will singe his dreamy eyelashes off one by one.

"More than ever, I'd say. But just so I have it straight, you met at a party, clearly got intimate or whatever," she winks, "and had no idea you'd both be at the audition?"

Neither one of us admits it, which pretty much confirms her suspicions.

"And you didn't know about each other's songs?" she asks.

I shake my head as Kick says, "Your song was really good. Like, really good."

"Yours was amazing," I say. No point in denying it now.

Emily steeples her hands, her pointy nails poking into her chin. "I don't suppose you'd give me a quote about your party hook-up for a press release?"

Kick raises his eyebrows at me like, *you wanna?*

"Absolutely not," I half-yell. "This isn't about…that. I'm here for the music. Nothing else."

Kick chuckles. "You sure about that?"

In this moment, I'm sure of little else. If I wanted to be a gimmick I'd let my mother spin me into LOVEJOY the Sequel. Polly's the one who would use a situation like this as leverage, not me. I left L.A. to do something authentic, something real. I want people to know me because of my music, not because I kissed Kick Raines in an alcove.

Emily points at us as she walks away, taking steps backwards so she's still watching us. "Just fantastic."

Kick doesn't move, stays right next to me like he's waiting for me to say something.

"I can't believe you wrote that song." I say, not looking at him. "You made me sound like some no-name girl you made out with at a party."

He barks out a laugh and shoves his hands down the front pockets of his jeans. "You do realize that's what you were, right?

He's got a smirk on his face I either want to kiss or smack with my guitar.

"But I wasn't too far off, was I?" he says. "Looks like we're both harboring a lot of…emotions from that night." He motions with his head up at the stage. "You just sang your heart out about how my kisses were sweet as honey."

Everything in me is screaming *flee* but I can't move, can't look away. I think it's leftover shock from seeing him here in the first place.

"You weren't supposed to hear that song," I mumble.

He dramatically cups his hand around his ear. "What was that?"

"I never thought you'd ever hear that song, okay?"

"But look at us now, together again, hopped up on alcove memories." He eyeballs the dark rehearsal space. "This studio has some dark corners we could make good use of, if you're interested."

I am interested. My middle name is interested. I might quit music and go back to college to major in interested. But I came here to get on the tour, not do the tongue tango with an overgrown puppy.

Kick and I are locked in a heated staring contest when Emily trots back over pulling Cheddar by his arm.

"Tell him," she says, eyes dancing. "Tell Cheddar about your little rendezvous."

"It wasn't a rendezvous," I say right as Kick says, "We met at a party a few weeks ago."

I throw him a look and add, "We didn't know, I mean, I didn't know he'd be here. And he didn't know I'd be here."

Cheddar's eyes cut over to Emily, a sly grin on his face. "This just got so much more interesting. Fans are going to go wild over this."

"But the competition is over tomorrow," I say. "There's nothing to go wild over."

He shakes his head. "Check your socials. I bet you're already getting traction about this. Way to go, seriously. I wish I'd thought of it."

I kick my foot up to pull my phone out of my boot, which causes Kick to raise an eyebrow. I have dozens of notifications, maybe more. I'm still scrolling when Cheddar says, "See?"

"That's not…we didn't…this wasn't a strategy."

"Unlike the alcove," Kick jokes. "And the lair."

"There was a lair?" Cheddar asks.

I should kick them both. Hard. In the shins. With my Docs.

"I can't wait to see how this plays out," Emily says, urgently tapping something into her phone.

In less than twenty-four hours, the competition will be over. I'm more concerned about getting votes than letting whatever this is *play out*. All I want is to be taken seriously as an artist. It's unfair I've somehow landed in a situation worse than being a Lovejoy.

Cheddar and Emily exchange a knowing look before turning to smile at me and Kick like serial killers trying to convince us they're not serial killers. My phone buzzes with a new text.

Cass: Socials are exploding. You're already a hashtag. (This is still Zoe by the way, in case you wanted to say anything too personal.)

Me: I'm a hashtag?

Cass: Well, you and Kick together. #Marick

"We're a hashtag," I say to Kick. He beams like we just won the sixth-grade science fair.

"Like I said." Emily waves a hand through the air. "This whole thing between you two is perfection."

I go to argue but she and Cheddar move on, heads together, plotting.

"Kick Raines, I swear to God. If this somehow disqualifies us from the competition—"

"Emily said it wouldn't."

"But if it does…you will pay."

I glance up at him and he's watching me, lips parted, a mischievous look in his eyes. "How, exactly, would you make me pay, Goldie?"

"Stop flirting with me. We're competitors now."

"Don't tell me. You don't date competitors either?"

"No, I just don't date you."

A dangerous smile spreads across his face. "But you do kiss me."

"Did. I did kiss you."

"You could kiss me again. We could leave here right now and you could kiss me…anywhere you want."

I lean in, raise up on my tiptoes, get close enough to brush his lips with mine.

"Tempting," I say. But instead of giving in, I pull back, pick up my guitar, and walk away.

"So that's it?" Kick calls after me. "After everything that's happened between us you won't even ask for my number?"

I spin around to face him. "Why would I need your number?"

His hands go to his hips. "To rub it in when you beat me, of course."

I know he doesn't mean it, know he's just trying to be flirty or obnoxious or both, but the idea of it lights me up inside. Because *I am* going to win and will definitely want to rub it in when I do.

"Can't get over me, can you?" I say.

"Wrong again." His eyes burn into me. "Over you is exactly where I want to be."

We're ten feet apart but it's not enough. His voice, thick with want, touches me everywhere. It's all I can do not to throw my guitar on the ground and jump into his arms.

But I need this tour more than I need to answer the desire pounding in my core.

By some miracle, I shove down my inner-voice telling me to give in and force myself to turn around and walk away.

Kick's eyes follow me all the way to the door.

ELEVEN
INSTAGRAM POLLS, GASTRIC DISTRESS AND OTHER REASONS I'M SPIRALING

THE ENTIRE INTERNET thinks I had sex with Kick Raines.

It didn't take long for people to put together our songs were about each other since we both sang about alcoves. Like idiots. It sent voting into overdrive (which is good) but the social commentary has been...colorful. Voting ends in ten minutes and for the last hour I've been neck and neck with Kick Raines, the last guy on earth I should be tangled up with (again). Thanks to our songs we're a hashtag crammed with all manner of sexual assumptions about what we did, how we did it, how many times we did it.

"Everyone's acting like they'd rather subscribe to our Only-Fans than listen to our music," I say, pacing the living room floor.

If Cass wore glasses, she'd be looking at me over the top of them like she wasn't born yesterday. "Wasn't it you who said, and I quote, 'Look at him.'"

"Just because he's wildly attractive doesn't mean..." I lose my train of thought thinking about it.

"I hope you were safe," Granny says from the overstuffed floral monstrosity that is her favorite chair. She's watching the Gameshow Network, calling out answers to questions one hundred Americans answered and eavesdropping on our conversation. Chop is on the footstool in front of her, dozing.

"All we did was kiss," I say, loud enough for her to hear me over the overly excitable gameshow host. I sit down on the couch next to Cass. "And maybe some over-the-clothes action. And a little bit under the clothes."

Cass exhales through her nose like she's equally proud of me and also maybe doesn't all the way believe me. *"I make it a rule not to ship real people,"* she reads from her phone, *"but Marick is my life now. If these two don't get together I will no longer believe love exists. Unless Kick wants to date me and then I will force Mari Gold to board a ship to outer space because BOY IS FINE."*

"Lovely," I say.

She keeps reading. *If anyone's interested in Marick fic I've got some posted to AO3 under MarickHeartsandAlcoves*

"There's fanfiction? Already?" I'm half tempted to read it.

"Refrigerator," Granny yells at the gameshow host.

"They weren't even on screen together and still their chemistry made smoke come out of my laptop."

Cass takes a breath and I butt in.

"Easy for them to say. They don't know the real Kick. They don't know that he's so…so…he's…"

"Yes, you've been saying," Cass says, rolling her eyes.

"Chicken casserole," Granny hollers, clapping when a contestant echoes her.

"At least I'm not getting tons of 'aren't you LOVEJOY's sister' comments."

I balance my laptop onto my knees. Every time I refresh the voting page, Kick pulls ahead by a dozen or so votes. Then more votes for me on the next refresh. None of the other contestants are even close.

"This is torture." I toss the laptop aside and launch myself off the couch just to sit down in the swivel recliner and spin around and around and around. "What will they do if it's a tie?"

"Don't make yourself sick, little flower," Granny says, eyes glued to the TV. "Bruce Springsteen."

"I didn't think people would be so invested," I say, "even though Cheddar all but crystal ball'd it. I sort of thought the fan vote was just for publicity and Sparrow would pick the winner. It is their tour after all. You think they'd want a say in who plays in front of them every night."

"Yeah, but then you and Kick sang those alcove songs," Cass says. "People are invested now. Hugely. In the music, sure, but mostly in the two of you."

"That's exactly what I don't want," I moan. "How did I move to Nashville to build something authentic only to end up in a PR stunt? If that's all it took I should have stayed in Los Angeles. My mother would have made me a household name by now."

I move back to the couch, open a new tab and type Mari Gold into Google. Way more results pop up than I'm prepared to face. A lot more. One of the top results is an article on *Music Now*.

INDIE ACTS VIE FOR COVETED OPENING SPOT ON SPARROW SUMMER ARENA TOUR

Looking to involve their fanbase in their summer dates, Sparrow announced a fan vote to determine the opening act for their Grand Total Tour. Five Nashville up-and-comers competed via livestream to win the coveted spot and spend the summer hitting the road with the platinum-selling rockers.

Surprising livestream viewers, two of the contestants, rocker Kick Raines and singer-songwriter Mari Gold, performed songs that appeared to be about each other from a romantic encounter they shared at a recent Nashville gathering. When asked about the origin of their songs, Raines was tight-lipped in his response.

"Mari and I met at a party in Brentwood," he said, "but we only talked for a few minutes. We don't really know each other. It was a surprise to see her at the audition and learn she's a really talented artist."

Despite Raines' claim he and Gold don't know each other, social media platforms have lit up with speculation about the two contestants.

Voting is open until May 16th at 8/9pm ET on the band's YouTube channel. Tickets for the Grand Total tour are on sale now.

*Mari Gold could not be reached for comment.

"He gave *Music Now* a quote," I huff. "It says I couldn't be reached for comment, but they gave him a quote."

Cass's face scrunches into an I-told-you-so. "I did say you should check your DMs."

"I did! There's like a million of them! And not a few asking me about Kick's…anatomy. One person asked me if he's hung more like a banana or a hot dog."

"Halloween," Granny says before turning to me. "Even a cocktail weenie can be good if he knows what he's doing."

"Granny," Cass shrieks, "gross."

"The point is," I say, trying to erase dancing cocktail weenies from my mind, "he's trying to act like—"

"He's talking about you," Cass says.

"What? Where?"

She turns her phone around and it's open to Kick's Instagram stories. There are several of him talking about the contest, asking for votes. The camera, even on a poorly lit Instagram story, absolutely adores him. He's got a poll up, asking people to guess who's going to win, me or him. Cass votes for me and we see the votes are evenly split down the middle. I take it as a good sign since people are on his Instagram voting for me.

"You should be doing stuff like this," Cass says. "I know you don't want to engage the trolls but if he wins, it's because he's interacting with people, giving quotes to *Music Now*."

This is all moving too fast, too big, too much. I thought I had everything under control and now it's all spiraling against my will.

"Ski boots," Granny says with a loud handclap. Chop startles awake and barks.

"Refresh the votes," Cass says.

I pull my computer back onto my lap and hit the space bar. I'm back in first place. Barely.

"Seriously, what if it's a tie? Or worse, what if that smug bastard—"

"That you definitely don't want to bone."

"—that I *definitely do not* want to bone, beats me by ten votes?"

"He's not going to beat you," Cass says with an undeserved assuredness. "There's no way."

"You're gay. You cannot comprehend the full scope of his sexual energy."

"Excuse you. I may love the ladies but even I can understand his animal magnetism."

"Animal magnetism?" I ask, straight-faced.

"Look, I know this isn't the way you wanted it to go down, but at least it's happening? Your music is getting out there, your name is getting out there. Over forty thousand people have voted for you, which means forty thousand people think you're rad. That's a win."

Damn. She's always right.

I go back to dramatically spinning in the swivel recliner with my eyes closed, my heart swishing around in my chest with each turn of the chair.

Despite Cass's wise words, I hate that it's come down to a hashtag popularity contest. I thought entering this competition would be a legitimate judge of talent instead of a reality show in the making. Either way, I cannot be beat by Kick Raines. I'd rather be beat by that all grey band, which, would be super embarrassing. But being beat by Kick would be worse. So much worse.

The Alexa timer dings and Cass hits refresh. I jump up from the chair, wobbly from the spinning. We lean in like getting our faces closer to the laptop screen will change the results. Chop barks, wanting in on whatever we're doing.

"Did you win?" Granny asks.

Final Votes:

Kick Raines — 46,453

Mari Gold — 46,453

"That's not possible. It's not…that's impossible."

Cass's phone dings with an alert that Sparrow is going live on Instagram. She hits the notification, opening up the live.

Deacon Sparrow's familiar face is on the screen with his brother Don sitting silently beside him.

"Hey everybody, big news about our little opening act competition we've had going. We decided to let you pick a young Nashville artist to debut on our summer tour and wow, y'all really showed up for this contest in a big way. And that was very cool of you. All five of the artists who auditioned blew us away. We're glad we're not the ones having to make this tough decision, am I right, Don?"

Don smiles.

Deacon scans his screen. "I'll just wait for some more folks to get on here before we announce who you'll be seeing with us on tour this summer."

"I'm going to be sick," I say.

Cass grabs my hand and holds on. We're huddled around her phone, me anticipating the worst and her believing the best, the applause track from Granny's gameshow filling up the silence.

"We want to thank all of you again for voting," Deacon says, stalling. "Our digital media team told us y'all nearly broke the server."

"Does Don ever talk?" Cass says.

I shush her, my eyes never leaving the phone screen.

"We didn't really know what to expect with this contest and

truthfully, we got way more votes than we anticipated. As it turns out, there's a tie. Can you believe it?"

Cass squeezes my hand harder.

"All five acts were great and you guys should totally check them all out and give them some love, but, after counting all the votes, it looks like you really loved Kick Raines and Mari Gold and honestly, so did we. Those two really brought something special."

"And different," Don says.

"He speaks!" Cass shouts.

"That's right. Two very different artists, but different in very interesting ways."

My phone rings. It's Jasmine so I answer it.

"Hi, Mari, this is Jasmine Milner from Sparrow. I'm not sure if you've heard—"

"A tie?"

"Yes, exactly. Congratulations," she says.

"So, we've decided to take them both," Deacon says.

Cass smacks my arm and I nearly fall off the couch. There's too much happening at once. Hearts are flying up the screen on Sparrow's Instagram Live and Jasmine is saying something in my ear about schedules and bus assignments and Cass is bouncing up and down on the couch causing Chop to bark and turn in circles while Granny shouts "camper" at the TV. I'm in the middle of a joy tornado but internally I'm a jumble of sparked nerves. It's happening. It's really happening. I'm going on tour with Sparrow. I'll be singing my songs in front of thousands of people every night. I'm going to find out what happened between the band and my father.

And I'll be doing it all with Kick Raines.

FOR IMMEDIATE RELEASE

SPARROW ANNOUNCE OPENING ACTS FOR GRAND TOTAL TOUR

Five Acts Chosen From Online Video Submissions Competed In Livestream Event With Winners Determined By Fan Votes

Nashville, TN (May 16th, 2025) The much-hyped fan vote to determine the opening act for Sparrow's Grand Total Tour resulted in a surprising tie between energetic rocker Kick Raines and indie crooner Mari Gold. Ultimately receiving an astonishing identical number of votes, Sparrow opted to take both winning acts out for the summer tour.

"We couldn't believe the votes came in as a tie," says lead singer Deacon Sparrow. "These two young artists are both incredible in different and interesting ways and people clearly love them both. So, when it came down to it, we thought it would be great for the fans to see them both out on the tour. I can't wait to see the energy Kick and Mari bring to the show."

The Grand Total Tour will hit 50 cities this summer, launching in Indianapolis on June 5th. Tickets on sale now.

About Sparrow: Top-selling American folk rock band Sparrow are five-time PHONO® Award-nominated, two-time PHONO® Award-winning, Streamers Billionaires Club recipients with five *Charts* Music Awards. Their debut album, *Sparrow*, is RIAA-certified Double-Platinum with follow-up *Closer* RIAA-certified Platinum. The band's single "In A Dark Wood" remains one of the most-streamed folk rock songs of all time with over one billion streams. Sparrow are Deacon Sparrow (lead vocals, guitar), Don

Sparrow, (lead guitar, vocals), Randy Moore (bass, vocals) and Joe Collins (drums, vocals).

Press contact:
Emily Wu
emily@sparrowband.com

TWELVE
PSYCHED

WHEN JASMINE SAID I could bring a plus one to the tour launch party, Cass immediately began plotting her public role as my pretend manager. The party's being held at a hotel bar in midtown. It's the swankier part of downtown Nashville where locals go to get away from tourist-clogged honky tonks on Broadway but still feel like they're So Nashville, an important distinction. I'm not totally sure of the dress code so I keep it neutral—army green silk joggers with a black off-the-shoulder crop top and black slides. I layer a bunch of gold necklaces and gold bangles in case the party has an unspoken dress-it-up vibe.

Cass comes dressed to impress. The front of her bleached hair is sprayed into a stiff sideways point so that it looks like white waves rolling off the side of her head. She's wearing stacked white sneakers and wide-legged white denim pants with a black tuxedo stripe down the leg, a tight white t-shirt tied in a knot against her ribs and a cropped, hot pink leather bomber jacket, the lapels covered in pro-LGBTQ buttons. Fact: No artist in the history of music has ever had a better pretend manager than my pretend manager.

Since the announcement both Kick and I will be on the tour, I've been doing my best to keep up with the onslaught of comments and DMs and posts. Most of them demand to know if our songs are really about each other. I've largely ignored the question, but Kick whipped the rumors into a full-blown feeding frenzy when he left a comment on one of my posts saying he couldn't wait to be on tour with me. The kissy-face emoji he added really tipped it over the edge.

When I haven't been fielding comments about Kick and me-and-Kick and #Marick, I've been on pins and needles expecting to hear from my mother. I know any minute she'll try and worm herself in, take over, take a cut. It's been over a week since the announcement and she hasn't called. Neither has Polly. If Emily's as great a publicist as she says she is, my mother is definitely on her email list for press releases so she's either sent Emily to spam, hasn't checked her email, or has the word Sparrow blocked from all of her devices. I'm hoping it's the latter.

When Cass and I arrive to the low-lit bar, my hands ball into fists at my side. My goal was to glide into the party like someone who's done this a million times, someone cool, someone not at all nervous about opening a tour for Sparrow. Instead, I'm on the verge of running to the bathroom to hide in a stall.

"You belong here," Cass says, reading my mind.

I'm about to argue when someone by the bar calls out my name. We walk over to find Deacon Sparrow welcoming us with an outstretched hand, his other hand on the waist of a new girl. This one's taller than the last one, even taller than Deacon, with waist-length dark waves, heavily lined eyes and a gold septum piercing. She slides her arm around Deacon's shoulders and lifts a salt-rimmed drink to her lips, chewing on the stirrer.

"Hey there, I'm Deacon," he says, shaking my hand. "Loved your audition. Excited to have you out with us this summer."

My brain fires off question after question Mari Gold would never ask.

What happened between you and John Lovejoy?
Did you know he had another daughter?

Did you see any of him in me when you heard me sing?

"Thank you so much," I say. "It's so great to meet you, Deacon. I'm thrilled to be there." I grab Cass's arm. "This is my manager, Cass Zimmerman from…C. Z. Entertainment."

"Pleasure," he says with a polished grin. I notice he doesn't introduce his date. "You two like margaritas? You can't really do karaoke without a margarita or two in you."

"Karaoke?" I ask.

"Tour tradition. Everyone has a margarita, virgin if that's your pleasure, and everyone sings karaoke, for luck."

"I can absolutely do and have done karaoke stone cold sober," Cass says, "but a margarita with all the alcohol would be amazing, thank you."

"I'm in," I say, but I don't plan on drinking it. Margaritas make me do things like make out with hot strangers in alcoves. Although when I met Kick I hadn't had a thing to drink.

Deacon motions to the bartender, who brings over two margarita glasses filled with a bright neon slush.

"Special recipe," Deacon says with a wink as he hands them over. "Mari, you look so familiar to me. Have we met before?"

Sweat beads practically leap onto my upper lip.

"Don't think so," I say with a smile, praying my cover doesn't get blown before I even step foot on stage.

"She has one of those faces," Cass says. "Looks like an up-and-coming superstar if you ask me."

Deacon's about to say more when something catches his eye. Cass and I turn and see Kick Raines, bringer of destruction in painted on black jeans, walking through the door. He has an actual swagger, natural, like if someone told him not to walk that way, he'd have to put in effort not to be so…swaggery. He should be studied for science.

Kick makes a beeline straight for me, a half-grin on his face. "Hey there, Goldie."

We stare at each other too long, but I can't look away. He draws me in so easily with those eyes, that mouth.

"Kick, right?" Cass says, breaking the spell. "I'm Mari's manager, Cass Zimmerman."

"So nice to meet you," he says shaking her hand. "Wait, aren't you the Hot Dog Sandwich Girl?"

"*That's* where I know you from," Deacon's date says.

Cass immediately fumes next to me. Two weeks ago, she posted a new video for Sapphic Sammies. She made a sandwich for Sarah Paulson based on her Nurse Ratched role—a turkey hot dog covered in pickle relish and sauerkraut with hot sauce on top. She thought it was cheeky and funny, but the comments on the video got heated with people debating whether or not a hot dog is a sandwich. The debate moved to TikTok and went absolutely everywhere. There are TikTok accounts named things like AHotDogIsNotASandwich where people hotly debate Cass's video and whether or not she's evil for insinuating a hot dog is a sandwich. While she loves how many views she's racked up, she hates being called Hot Dog Sandwich Girl, especially by strangers.

"That's me," Cass says with a thin smile, "in the flesh."

"I made that hot dog. It was legit." Kick rubs his thumb across his bottom lip. I decide to write a song about that specific action as soon as I am able because good lord. Thumbs like that and lips like that require a memorial in song.

He turns to me. "Manager, huh? I didn't realize you were such a serious artist." His smile is playful when he says it, but I wonder if he's putting on a front. He acts so breezy causal all the time, like none of this affects him, but there's no way this tour doesn't mean as much to him as it does to me. The deal was to be The Opener, not one of the ones opening. He has to at least be mildly irritated to share the spotlight with me.

"Kick and Mari, so glad you could both join us tonight," Don Sparrow says, joining the party.

We all exchange introductions, Don telling us how impressed he was with our auditions. I'm cooking up a question, something to open the door to what I really want to know, when Cheddar comes over and demands their attention.

I feel Kick's eyes on me and throw him a look. "Where's your band? Or plus one or girlfriend or…whatever."

It just hit me in this moment that he could have a girlfriend. It's been over a month since that night at Jackson's party. I'm sure someone like him doesn't stay single for long.

His left eye half winks, an almost wink, like he rethought it half-way through. "Band couldn't make it tonight. But don't worry, they'll be on the tour with us." My stomach does a summersault at the mention of *us*. "Hey, since you don't have a band, did you need to borrow me and the boys to fill out your set? I'm sure they'd be down to help out since it's just you and your acoustic. Might be fun."

"That's actually a great idea." Emily's vaporized out of nowhere, a tumbler of amber liquid sloshing in her hand. "Maybe you two could even do a song together, yeah?"

Suddenly everyone's paying attention, including Don, Deacon and Cheddar, all eyes on me and Kick. I don't even want to be on the same tour as Kick Raines, let alone *on stage together*. I need to shut this down before it gains traction. I look at Cass and telepathically tell her to be my pretend manager and jump in. She sees it and, blessedly, speaks fluent telepathy.

"But their styles are so different," Cass says. "I think it would really fill out the night to have them doing their own thing, separately, give more variety to the show overall."

Emily takes a drink and says, "Maybe."

Deacon throws a disinterested hand up. "I'll leave that to you and Cheddar. This whole thing was your idea anyway. You guys are in charge of that part of the show. Oh, look, there's Nic."

He and Don leave to go say hi to this Nic person, Deacon pulling his date with him, which leaves Emily semi-glowering at me and Kick.

She aims a long, pointy, pink shellacked nail, first to me, then to Kick. "This thing brewing between you two, we need to capitalize on it. The fans love you together, voted you both onto this tour. Maybe we should give them what they asked for."

Kick nods in rhythm to the music playing from the loudspeakers, but I can't tell if he's agreeing with Emily or humoring her. There's no way he'd want to do a song with me. His style is too hectic, too party boy loud, too sexy chaotic. My music is emotional, deep, moving. My songs need to be absorbed with eyes closed, heart open. Kick's songs are body shakers, tambourine breakers. We cannot perform together.

"Think about it," Emily says before flittering off to talk to more important people.

"Maybe we'd be good together," Kick says. "We already know we're good at…other things."

"Are you ever serious?'

"I'm serious about spending more time with you."

He smiles and leans over the bar to motion to the bartender. I take the opportunity to pull Cass with me and head over to a table full of appetizers. I need snacks if I'm going to be dealing with Sparkle Eyes all night.

"Umm, what was that?" Cass says, picking up a taquito and biting it in half.

"You mean Emily nearly crashing and burning my entire existence? Can you imagine? Me and Kick Raines doing a song together? No way. Not ever."

"I'm talking about you and Mr. Smooth Talker Sexy Eyes. With the flirting and the sexual tension. I thought he was supposed to be your musical nemesis."

I turn my head as slowly as I can, letting her know she could not be more wrong.

"He's an ass."

"An ass you wanna do bad things to. I've never seen your flirt face live and in action. It was truly something to behold. And his flirt face can be seen from outer space."

I spoon some queso onto my plate. "He's just trying to rattle me."

"Yeah, rattle you all night long."

"Hey, Mari." Cheddar says from behind us. We turn around and he's smiling. "You and your friend like karaoke?"

"Would do it as a career if I could," Cass says. "Cass Zimmerman. Mari's manager,"

"I'm Chet Hurr," he says, nodding. "You can call me Cheddar."

"Cheddar. I dig it."

"If you haven't already, get your name in the queue because trust me, singing a Whitney Houston song backed up by an animatronic band is the only way to live."

That's when I notice, which, how did I not notice until now? At the back of the bar is a stage set-up with four life-size animatronics. Like, Chuck E. Cheese level, massive, furry, creepy, dead-eyed animatronics. There's a polar bear wearing camo pants playing drums, a pig in a leather jacket playing keys, a cow in a cowboy hat playing bass guitar and a horse in a long black wig with a sequined bomber jacket playing guitar. They're the back-up band of nightmares. I can't decide if, when activated, they'll rock out or try to murder me.

"Oh. My. God." Cass is enamored, her love of all things kitsch kicking into high gear. She shoves her plate at me and already has her phone out taking photos to show Granny G.

Cheddar leaves to round up more singers and I feel Kick shuffle up behind me.

"I bet you're a Celine girl." His voice is low and husky, an invisible fingertip tracing down my spine.

I don't turn, letting him talk to the back of my neck while I balance Cass's plate and add guacamole and blue tortilla chips to my plate.

"Celine Dion is a goddess, but no, I'm not a Celine girl." I turn to face him, "I guess you don't have me as nailed as you think."

"Oh, I'm gonna nail you, Goldie."

My mouth drops open. I know he only said it to get a reaction from me, but my thighs are quivering all the same.

"Let me guess," I say, "you do a mean Journey cover? You and your brother got a karaoke machine for Christmas and tortured your family with spirited renditions of 'Don't Stop Believing' around the Christmas tree?"

He shifts, goes far away for a moment, his mind focused on something only he can see. His eyes well up and for a second it looks like he's about to full-on cry into the salsa. I'm trying to think of something to say while wondering what exactly I said wrong when he shakes his head and pops back into the present, back to his loose, confident self.

"Journey rules," he says, wrapping his lips around his thumb to suck off some stray salsa. "Not my go-to, though."

I realize too late I'm staring at his mouth and quickly turn away, nearly slathering Emily Wu and her dry-clean-only black silk blouse in guacamole.

"Oh," I startle, righting my plates. "Sorry. That could have been a situation."

"You two can't stay away from each other, can you," she says, looking between me and Kick.

"We just happened to be getting food at the same time," I say. Emily needs to get over her dream of making us a thing like, now.

She bats her eyelashes. "I'd love to get a quote from you both for the tour launch press release. Tell me how you're feeling about opening for Sparrow."

She holds her phone up, her voice memo app open to record us. I look at Kick and he's looking at me like, go ahead. I'm still startled from nearly slathering Emily in guacamole and curious about Kick's emotional reaction to my comment about his brother. I reach deep down for the sincerest thing I can say, sure I'll say something I'll regret but hoping for something inspirational. I need to get this right, need to convey how much this means to me, how it's not about Kick or a rivalry or a contest. That I'm here to show the world the artist I know I can be.

"I'm psyched."

That's what I say. *I'm psyched,* a phrase I've never, ever uttered until this exact moment.

Emily doesn't bat an eye. She turns her phone to Kick who smiles a million-dollar smile and says, "As an artist, it's so vital to learn from those who've gone before you. To me, this tour is such a huge opportunity to learn from a band who's already paved the way for so many. I mean, they're legends! I couldn't be more honored."

I close my eyes and will the floor to turn into quicksand, swallow me whole, and melt me into the Earth's core.

When I open my eyes, he's inches from my face, grinning. He chomps on a tortilla chip and saunters away knowing he's just thrown a gauntlet the size of Horse Kacey Mugraves' teased bouffant. I feel certain every partygoer felt the ground rumble beneath its weight.

I inwardly harumph and go sit at a table in the middle of the floor, not too close to the stage but still in the mix. Cass finds me and plops down in the chair next to mine. I'm stewing, not ready to tell her about my press quote embarrassment, when she points to a tall, burly man with a thick blonde beard that reaches to the middle of his chest and small eyes that disappear into his bushy eyebrows.

"That's the band's manager, Nic Johns," she whispers.

I remember seeing him at the auditions but didn't know he was the band's manager. "How do you know this?"

"We manager types tend to stick together."

"Uh-huh. What else do you manager types do?"

She smiles, showing all her teeth. "Perform, baby."

THIRTEEN
HORSE KACEY MUSGRAVES HAS IT OUT FOR ME

I LOOK UP and Nic's climbing onto the small stage in front of the frozen animatronics.

"Bet he does Lynyrd Skynyrd," I say.

"Or Hootie and the Blowfish."

"Or, like, Jars of Clay."

We're giggling when the opening beats of "7 rings" from Ariana Grande starts playing and Nic, who is a beast of a man, throws an imaginary ponytail over his shoulder and blows kisses to the crowd as the animatronics awkwardly jerk to life. The crowd is immediately into it at a surprising level.

"So it's *that* kind of party," Cass says, eyes dancing.

She runs up to the karaoke DJ and puts her name in while Nic prances across the stage like he's wearing stacked, spiked heels. The animatronic band lurches and exaggeratedly blinks behind him, a full half-beat behind. The entire bar comes to life, scream-singing the lyrics with him, wolf-whistling and shouting like it's a competition and Nic's already won. It's an exuberant, uninhibited display. Even the bartenders are dancing.

Jasmine gets up next, which I find surprising. She doesn't seem the drunk karaoke type, but the second she launches into Aretha Franklin's "Bridge Over Troubled Water," I realize my mistake. Jasmine can flat out sing. Everyone eggs her on like it's Sunday morning church and she's singing the Holy Ghost into the room.

"Who is *that*," Cass yells into my ear. I follow her finger pointing to a statuesque Black woman standing off to the side. She has a braided updo that accentuates her heart-shaped face and is wearing lime green short shorts that highlight her extremely long legs. I look over at Cass and she's practically drooling.

"I must meet her," Cass says right as the DJ calls her name like a game show host.

"Cass Zimmerman, come on dowwwwnnnnn."

She nearly tips over our wobbly table as she eagerly hurries to the stage. The opening strains to Pat Benatar's "Hit Me With Your Best Shot" come on and Cass, who's always so alive and ready for whatever the world has to offer, plunges in, blatantly flirting with her new crush.

Kick plops down at the table next to mine. He tips his chair back and nudges me.

"She's pretty incredible."

"You have no idea." I look at him watching Cass. "She's gay, you know."

"What," he says, affronted, "I can't admire someone in their element without making it sexual?"

"I have a feeling you make pretty much everything sexual."

He leans in close, his palm-branch eyelashes inches from mine. "Is that one of the bullet points on your little list about me?"

I tear my gaze from his and take a sip of my margarita. I will not be bewitched by his sleepy-eyed grin, no I will not. Besides, Kick's still my competition as far as I'm concerned. And you don't fraternize with the enemy, that's rule number one. Actually, rule number one is never join a cult, but the fraternizing thing is up there.

When Cass hits the chorus she gets the entire room up and

dancing—Nic, Deacon, Deacon's date, Jasmine, Don, Cheddar, even Emily. They all love her. As they should.

Up next is Sparrow's keyboard player, then a guitar tech. I guess Deacon was right. At the tour launch party, everyone does karaoke.

We're too many songs and margaritas in when Cheddar runs onto the stage and grabs the mic, pointing right at me and Kick. "Who here thinks the new kids should sing a duet?"

Applause breaks out and all eyes turn to me and Kick, all of them saying yes, get on the stage right now. A loud, deep voice behind me shouts, "Do it."

"Oh, no," I say, "I don't—"

"Come on, Goldie." Kick stands up from the table next to me and holds out his hand. "Unless you're scared?"

I get up from the table and bat his hand away. "I'm not scared of anything."

"My kind of woman."

I march ahead of him and look for Emily on the way up, feeling certain she has a satisfied smirk on her pinched face. She's sitting near the front, gloating. I bet she put Cheddar up to this, trying to prove her point that Kick and I should sing together. She's about to realize her mistake.

Up close, the animatronics are even more dead-eyed, their eyeballs like big round, polished Magic 8 balls possessed with an unidentifiable evil. I turn my back to them and put on my best performance smile. I take the mic in front of Horse Kacey Musgraves, ready to one-up whatever cheesy performance Kick tries to do.

"I picked a song for you," Cheddar says, motioning to the karaoke DJ. "Do you guys know 'Don't You Want Me' from The Human League?"

I lean away from the mic. "You know this song?"

Kick keeps his eyes on me and says "hit it," into the mic, flashing that confident smile he never seems to lose.

The track starts, a synth-heavy eighties beat. Kick pulls his mic off the stand and looks out at the crowd, shaking his hips like he's trying to earn singles in the waistband of his jeans. I attempt to match his energy, dancing in front of my mic stand. Emily's scheming aside, I'm going to win this duet and show Sparrow I'm the rightful artist to be opening their tour.

Kick turns to me, eyes flashing, and sings the first line like it's just the two of us. Like we rehearsed this before the party. He's not even looking at the lyrics on the screen.

I'm swaying to the music but can't look away from him. He gets closer and closer, singing right to me. It's for show, I know this, but heat climbs up my neck and into my jaw, singeing my cheeks. I turn to the crowd and get them to clap in time to the synth beats but he's still in my space, singing to me like we're completely alone, like we aren't on display in front of the entire Sparrow crew and management team, in front of all the members of Sparrow.

The chorus hits and we wail into the mics about how much we want each other. It's too wrong and so right. Tiny heat explosions sizzle down my neck and my chest. Our voices sound like they were designed to sing together, like we're two parts of one whole. I want to hate this, want it to be a train wreck, but we're incredible.

The crowd goes wild, whistling and hollering like we planned to reveal our secret chemistry at this exact moment. All their reaction does is amp up our performance.

When it's my turn to sing the verse, I dance in a circle around Kick, forcing him to follow me with his eyes. I'm performance flirty, stage sultry, playing it up as wildly as I dare, making the audience believe I want him as much as he wants me.

I pout my mouth into a kiss when I sing the word *you* causing Kick to stare at my lips. Which makes me stare at his lips.

This song was a bad idea.

We go full out on the last chorus, singing right to each other, our noses nearly touching, flirting so hard my molars ache.

By the time the song ends, our arms are wound around each other's and our mics are in each other's face, our heavy breaths on each other's lips. The crowd loses it and gives us an enthusiastic standing ovation. Kick untangles us and takes my hand in his, sending an electric current shooting up my arm as we take a dramatic bow.

I hop off the stage as quickly as I can, the applause still roaring. When I get back to our table, Cass is wearing the biggest smirk I've ever seen. And she's added a third chair to our table, now occupied by the leggy girl in the lime green shorts.

"Mari Lorraine Gold. What are you doing?"

"Since when is my middle name Lorraine?"

"You two practically procreated in front of Horse Kacey Musgraves."

"Cheddar picked the song," I argue. "What was I supposed to do?"

She eyes me, unconvinced. "In that case, you won't mind if I post a video. Because Mo took video. This is Mo, by the way. She's on the merch team."

"Nice to meet you," I say.

"You two were really something," Mo says with a twinkle in her green-shadowed eyes.

I shrug and take a huge bite of a black bean egg roll. "Post it or don't post it, I don't care. It's not like it meant anything."

"Post what?" Kick says, pulling up a chair.

"Cass filmed our song," I say.

He whips his head toward her. "I'm gonna need that video."

"Are y'all gonna do songs like that on the tour?" Mo asks. "Cause I'd pay to see that again."

"I can't tell if you're serious or making fun of us," I say.

"I'm completely serious," she says. "I bet other people would pay to see it, too."

Kick and I exchange a look, his side more curious and mine more horrified.

"That is not happening, Kick Raines," I say, turning back to my food. "Do not get any ideas."

He steals an egg roll from my plate. "I'm full of ideas, Goldie."

FOURTEEN
WE NEED TO TALK

WE'RE LEAVING for tour in two days and I am extremely not ready. There's so much to rehearse and pack and plan and stress over. I need to choose my stage clothes and my bus clothes and my daytime clothes. I need to pack all of the shoes but not too many shoes. I'm only allowed one large suitcase and an overnight bag and no configuration of packing cubes will contain what I absolutely must bring.

Instead of dealing with my unzippable suitcase, I'm working my last shift at Steamers. I don't really have time to be here, but I promised Sage I'd help out as long as I could since I'm leaving so suddenly.

"Hiatus," I said when Sage and I talked about it. "I'll be back after the tour."

"You'll be a superstar after the tour but thank you for faking humility. Door's always open when you need it, but I know you won't need it."

Of all the jobs I'm quitting to go on tour—dog walking, food delivery, house sitting—I'll miss working with Sage at Steamers the most.

I'm restocking milk when Cass comes in for a decaf latte before her next client.

"You look panicked," she says when I walk out front with a gallon of milk in each hand.

I set them down and touch my face, eyes wide. "But I've been using a new moisturizer."

"You've rehearsed your set," she says, ignoring my snark. "We've gone over your wardrobe essentials. You have all the info from Jasmine. You're ready. You can do this."

"You're sure you can't come with me?"

Cass smiles wistfully. "Wouldn't that be a dream? But there's no space for me on the bus. Plus, I have clients with urgent hair needs."

"Hair needs can wait. I'm about to be on tour with my family's mortal enemy playing my untested songs to massive crowds every night."

"And living on a bus. With Kick Raines."

I leave that comment hanging and go to make her drink. I'm putting the lid on when a text comes in from an unknown number.

Unknown: I think we should talk. Before the tour

I show it to Cass and she whistles. "He wants you."

"He wants something, but it isn't me."

Me: Who is this?

Unknown: Your alcove lover. Hopefully that narrows it down?

I save his number as Do Not Kiss and shove my phone back in my pocket.

Do Not Kiss: Have you seen the video of our karaoke song? People really love us together, Goldie

Do Not Kiss: We should probably talk about that before we're sleeping together every night

Do Not Kiss: On the bus, I mean

Do Not Kiss: I don't want you getting any sexy ideas

Do Not Kiss: Unless I DO want that

Do Not Kiss: Which is another thing we should talk about before the tour

Turns out it only takes six texts to wear me down.

Me: Please stop text bombing me like a bored housewife

Do Not Kiss: How could I be bored when I'm texting my favorite duet partner?

Me: So singing karaoke duets is a favorite pastime of yours?

Do Not Kiss: Only when they're with you

"You do realize you're beaming at your phone, right?"' Cass says.

"I'm not beaming. I'm close-lipped partial-smiling. It's a very neutral expression."

"Who's on your phone that's got you smiling like that?" Sage says, joining us at the counter.

"Karaoke guy," Cass offers.

"Oh yeah, I saw that video. He's hot," Sage says.

"Would you two shut-up? I'm professionally texting a person I will be on tour with about said professional tour. That's it."

Cass and Sage fist bump each other.

Me: I'm working at Steamers in midtown. We close at nine. Come by.

I show Cass the messages.

"Smells like the start of a beautiful love affair."

I roll my eyes and shoo her away. "Go do hair."

An hour later Kick walks into the coffee shop in grey sweatshorts, a white crew neck and a backwards baseball cap. He's sweaty, like he's just getting back from a friendly pick-up game of basketball. He saunters over to the counter, a half-smile on this face.

Absolutely not, I tell myself. I will not succumb to the eyelashes or the forearms. I will not bend to the will of the grin. I will not be ruined by the way his hair curls out just so from behind his ears.

"How'd you get my number?" I ask, my way of saying hello.

"I Google'd Hottest Girl In Nashville and your number popped up." When I don't give in, he says, "Everyone's numbers were in the tour pdf Jasmine sent."

"Oh. Right."

My pulse pounds in my neck. I wish I could figure out what it is about him that sends me off balance. Every time I'm around him my brain malfunctions and I feel like I'm going to trip over the air and fall into his arms like a lovesick romcom character.

"Can I get you a drink before this big talk of yours?" I say. "It's on me."

"In that case, can I get an extra-large ice water?"

"We don't have crushed, only cubed."

His eyes dance, thinking about that night. The alcove. "I'll manage."

I grab a large cup and fill it with ice as I wave at Sage. "I'm taking my fifteen."

She nods and gives me a wink.

I motion for Kick to follow me to the patio outside. It rained earlier in the afternoon so the night air is pleasantly cool. We take the table furthest away from the windows.

"I can't believe you sent me a *we need to talk* text," I say as we sit down across from each other. "Who does that?"

"I thought it was important for us to sort some things out before the tour starts. Plus, I wanted to see you again."

"You're about to see a lot of me. Too much, probably."

"Care to test that theory?"

He keeps poking even though we're both hesitant to name it —the heat between us. The want. The way we can't stop looking at each other like if we don't devour one another right this second we'll die of starvation.

But it's just hormones. Pheromones. That urgent thing you get with some people. It's not anything worth risking a life-changing tour opportunity.

"I wanted to talk about you and me. How it's pretty obvious there's something between us." He lets that simmer for a beat. "After singing together at the launch party, I think it's pretty obvious to everyone else too."

He's not wrong. Cass's video of me and Kick practically making out on the karaoke stage has gone semi-viral, stoking the flames of relationship suspicions even hotter. Anyone who wasn't already convinced we were doing the dirty on a regular basis is now a believer. And yes, I can admit it felt incredible singing with him. Everything with him feels incredible. He's incredible. But for this tour to work, we can't be that, do that. We just can't.

"Here's the thing," I say, doing my best to keep my voice even, "this opening slot, this tour, it's really important to me."

He nods. "It's important to me too."

"Yeah, but there's...I have...I can't let anything, even something good, get in the way."

His smile fades. He looks more serious than I've ever seen him. "What if it's something really good?"

"Is it ever? Has a momentary fling ever been better than the fulfillment of a dream? I don't know about you, but this tour is something I've been working for, hoping for, for a long time. Guys come and go. An opportunity like this is once in a lifetime. I can't screw it up just because you're gorgeous and I like kissing you."

"I like kissing you too."

"Not the point."

"But it is the point. I've never...it's never been like that with anyone else. I can't stop thinking about that night. About you."

My cheeks burn. I haven't stopped thinking about him either and this conversation isn't helping matters. It would be so much easier to avoid it altogether. "We leave for tour in two days."

His eyes roam my face. He twists his cup in his hands. "So what do we do?"

He's made it clear what he wants, but he's letting me choose. It's not a hard decision. I have to pick the tour. Even when he's looking at me like I'm the fulfillment of his one and only wish, the tour has to come first. I search my mind for something concrete to say, something solid. Something that will put an end to the question once and for all.

"We have to keep things professional, like actors on a movie set."

"You mean like all the actors who end up together?"

I roll my eyes. "We keep it about the music, about the show and the songs. That's why we're doing this, isn't it? You didn't audition for the tour because of me. You did it for you, for your songs."

His expression turns hopeful. "What about artists who are serious about the music but are also friends? We can do that, right?" I can't tell what he's truly feeling. His tone is always so flirty, so carefree.

"What kind of friends?" I ask.

He lifts one shoulder in a shrug. "Not the kind who kiss in alcoves. Just the kind who sing about it."

I can't help but smile. "I can live with that."

I check the time on my phone.

"I need to get back." I stand up to leave.

"Wait. One question." He stands up and moves right in front of me, close enough I have to turn my face up to his. "If this tour wasn't happening. If we'd met earlier…"

He wants me to say it would be so easy. Fun. Insanely hot. Wild in the best way. He wants me to give in, to acknowledge the current buzzing between us.

"We can't live in what ifs, Kick."

"Think about it," he says, voice low. "We still have two days. We could spend some quality time together. Get it out of our system before the tour starts."

It's like he knows the exact thing to say to break down my defenses. Because yes, we could do some serious damage to each other in two days. Emphasis on damage.

"Keep it in your pants, Raines. We're friends, remember?"

He lifts his eyebrows. "You're the one thinking about what's in my pants."

FIFTEEN
UPON REFLECTION, THE CHOP PANTS WERE A MISTAKE

BUS CALL IS AT MIDNIGHT. Jasmine's detailed email informed us that meant the bus would pull out of the lot at exactly twelve o'clock with or without us. I'm dangerously close to testing that theory, so I hope it's an empty threat.

"You're really playing it fast and loose with this timeline," Cass says as she swings her car into the gravel lot. "It's two minutes to midnight."

"You can't rush an everything shower," I argue.

"Text me when you get on the bus," she says as I hop out of the car and wrangle my suitcase out of the backseat. "Text me in the morning. Just, text me all the time. Day or night."

"So you can keep tabs on Mo?"

She shimmies her shoulders. "We have a phone date in half an hour. But also because I love you and want to be there vicariously when the world discovers your greatness."

"Have I told you today I would be nowhere and no one without you?"

Cass beams. "Go be amazing."

I don't look back as I wheel my suitcase across the gravel lot, my overnight bag weighing down my shoulder. The storage bay doors underneath the bus are closed except for one and I shove my suitcase into the only space left. The door combination is scribbled onto my hand in black marker. It's also written in the email Jasmine sent but I knew looking it up while trying to board the bus would send my already twisted nerves into a tailspin. When I punch in the four digit-code, the lock opens with a loud click.

I pull the wide silver latch, heave open the heavy door and climb up the tall stairs. It takes some maneuvering to swing the door back closed, my too-stuffed overnight bag in the way. As I step into the front lounge, it falls off my shoulder at the exact same moment I hear Kick's sandpaper voice, a voice that could only be described as pure trouble.

"Nice jammies, Goldie."

I'm dressed for bed. Because it's midnight. And I didn't want to do the change-clothes-dance in the tiny bus bathroom.

Kick's sitting on the left-side lounge sofa, legs wide, arms propped up behind him. He's wearing long, loose basketball shorts and a worn, black Bryan Adams t-shirt. I'm still not used to the hot rush that races through my body at the sight of him.

There's only about two feet of space in the aisle between the two parallel couches—not enough room for my body, my overnight bag and my growing humiliation.

"Hey, Mari," Mo says with a wave and a grin.

I smile back at her. Kick's wonder twins and Mo are sitting on the opposite couch watching a vampire movie on a TV mounted to the narrow wall that separates the front lounge from the driver's seat. Emily and Cheddar are in a small booth next to the couch, both furiously tapping on their laptops, trying to look like they're not straining to hear every word.

My legs are knocking into the wonder twins but they don't seem to notice. Kick's eyes haven't left me for a second.

"Who's the cute little doggie all over your pants?" he asks, bumping my leg with his knee.

"Not that it's any of your business," I say with a huff, "but it's my dog, Chop."

Technically Cass's dog but I've adopted him in my heart.

Kick leans forward, elbows resting on his knees, and rubs his hands together. Because of the tight space, his fingertips brush against my pajama pants and I startle, nearly falling into Mo and the twins, whose names I still don't know.

Kick's mouth turns down into a sardonic smile. "You ready for our first night together?"

I glance lightning fast at Emily who's pretending she didn't hear it, but the tiniest grin is growing in the corner of her mouth.

When Kick and I agreed to be friends, I should have included an amendment about overt flirting. Based on what I know about him, he'd never be able to comply.

"I'll be sleeping in my own bunk. Alone."

Kick holds his hands up in mock defense. "It would probably be unprofessional to shack up night one, but thanks for the invite."

"Are you intentionally this irritating or did you take a class?"

"You love me," he says and my eyes dart to Emily. She looks pleased.

Jasmine comes through from the bunk area and clucks her tongue when she sees me. "About time you showed up, Miss Gold."

We do a sideways dance so she can squeeze past me, counting as she goes. Once she counts herself as number twelve she shouts, "We're a bus!" signaling to the driver that everyone's on board and it's time to get moving. The driver throws the bus into gear and makes a wide turn out of the lot. The motion throws me off balance and straight into Kick's lap, my hands on the couch on either side of his head. His hands are on my waist, the heat seeping through my hoodie and straight into my nervous system. He laughs silently, a puff of breath on my cheek.

"I could ask Jasmine to move me to a different bus, if my being here bothers you so much." His voice is low, only for me. "Wouldn't want to subject you to any undue," he squeezes my waist, "tension."

"Stop flirting with me," I whisper in his ear, "we're friends, remember?"

He cocks an eyebrow at me. "Friends can't flirt?"

"They're right here," Cheddar says, pointing his phone at me and Kick.

Nic is on the screen and chuckles when he sees me sitting in Kick's lap.

"Glad to see you two getting along."

"I'm just gonna," I swallow and look away from Kick, pushing myself up and off his lap and onto the couch next to him. Jasmine scoots in beside me, reading over a print-out of tomorrow's schedule.

"Here's the deal, you two," Nic says while Cheddar holds up the phone, "there's only one opener slot."

The bus hits a pothole and Jasmine and I nearly bounce off the couch. I grab Kick's arm to steady myself before quickly pulling it away.

"The good news is," Nic says, "you proved at the tour launch party you're dynamite together. Emily floated the idea to the band that you perform as a duo and we all love it. So, you share the slot."

Am I hallucinating? Is this a stress dream I'm having before the actual bus rolls out for the tour? Did my boiling hot everything shower raise my body temperature too high and I'm passed out on the floor of my steamy bathroom? Because I know Nic did not just say I'm sharing my dream slot with Sir Panty Dropper.

Kick's lips are pulled tight like he knew this was coming. The Vampire Twins haven't noticed anything's going on but Mo's watching me, her head shaking back and forth the tiniest bit. She warned me about this. I should have listened.

"I'm sorry, what?" I say, baffled.

"I don't care what you do," Nic says, "whose songs you play or whatever, but we want you to do 'Don't You Want Me.' Cheddar says some video leaked and the fans are wild for it and we're wild for whatever the fans are wild for. Good?"

My head flops back and I gape at the ceiling, wide-eyed, not believing my life. "No, not good. This wasn't the plan." I look over at Emily who's busily typing on her computer like she and Cheddar didn't just blow up the entire tour.

"We were told we'd both have opening slots," I say. "We're solo artists."

Nic nods. "And you both will be, together."

"Will this alter set time? Soundcheck time?" Jasmine asks.

Kick's saying nothing. Doing nothing. He's slouched on the couch, happy to be a man without a plan.

I look back and forth between Emily, Cheddar and Nic. "We're totally different artists. We've never played each other's songs, never worked together before. Can't we talk about this? The first show is tomorrow night!"

Nic shrugs. "Plans change. That's the biz. Work it out between you and be ready for soundcheck tomorrow at three. Oh, and you have twenty minutes to fill. Monty has the in-ears from your fitting and will get you geared up at soundcheck."

Jasmine immediately starts making notes on her print-out.

"You seriously don't even care what songs we do?" I bark. That gets the Vampire Twins' attention.

"We're doing new songs?" Twin Number One says. "Cool."

I can't believe everyone's being so flippant about rearranging the entire plan the night before the first show. I already have my own ten-minute set rehearsed and ready. It's tight. It's perfect. I can't re-do a whole new set and have it ready to play for thousands of people *tomorrow night*.

"We can't do this," I say, looking at Kick. "Right? Tell them we can't do this."

Kick shrugs.

"Look," Nic says, scratching through his beard, "this whole opener stunt was just a way to get ticket sales up for the tour, which Emily and Cheddar have done a bang-up job on. Do the song we want, do any other songs you want, and keep the online chatter going and ticket sales booming. Got it?"

With that, he ends the call like he didn't just pull the pin on a grenade and toss it into the middle of the tour. How did I go from opening the tour, to co-opening, to now sharing the stage with someone who was supposed to stay neatly in the made-out-with-once-at-a-party box?

"What was that about?" Twin Number Two says, keeping his eyes on the screen as a vampire rips someone's throat out with his fangs.

"We're playing with Mari, like, all together," Other Twin says.

"Right on," Number Two says.

"Emily?" I say, just shy of a screech.

She pauses her furious typing and sighs, gives Cheddar a knowing look before saying, "Here's the hard truth. Sparrow's last two singles...weren't hits. Streams are down. And when we announced the tour, ticket sales were dragging. We did the duet with Sabrina Shannon—"

"Huge numbers," Cheddar adds.

"—which got huge numbers, yes. But it wasn't enough to get ticket sales up for the tour. We came up with the opener stunt and hey, it worked!"

It would be great if everyone could stop calling my dream come true a stunt.

"Since the competition and you two making everyone fall in love with you, we've sold out the first five shows," Cheddar says, "and the other shows are closing in. So, good job on getting people talking. Our social engagement has never been better." He waves his hands in the air like we should all clap.

"Don't be so precious about it," Emily says, swiping a lock of dark hair out of her eyes. "This is a major tour and you're both lucky to be on it. It's time to be professional and do the job you were hired to do."

The way she says *hired* makes it sound like our talent had

little to no bearing on why we're here, like the fan votes were just a smoke screen.

Cheddar's back on his laptop. The twins go back to watching their movie. Mo leaves the front lounge, probably to call Cass. Jasmine gets up and pulls a water bottle from the fridge. "Night y'all," she says before going back to the bunks. Everyone's moved on. Everyone but me and Kick.

We look at each other for a long moment, a million thoughts passing between us.

"You can't be okay with this," I say.

"It doesn't sound like we have a choice."

"You're seriously not bothered we have to combine our sets? We don't even know each other's songs."

"We'll figure it out."

He's no help at all.

"I'm gonna go find my bunk," I announce. "I need a minute alone to figure out what the hell I've gotten myself into."

"Word," Twin Number Two says.

"Sorry, Mari," Emily says, not meeting my eyes, "the only bunk available is the bottom right one."

My stomach sinks even further, which, given the last few minutes, might mean I'm the new world record holder in stomach sinking. I traveled on a tour bus a few times at the start of Polly's career. The middle section of the bus holds twelve bunks stacked three high, six on each side. The only acceptable place to sleep is a middle bunk. Sleeping in a bottom bunk is basically laying on top of the massive, rolling tires which rumble your internal organs to a gelatinous goo. The top bunks require gymnast-level climbing to get into and once you're in, there's a constant risk of rolling out and falling to your death. If you do manage to stay in, the top bunk sways like a hammock in a hurricane. Seasick prone travelers shouldn't sleep in a top bunk, which includes me.

But woe be unto you if you end up in a front bottom bunk, particularly the one next to the bathroom. Anyone coming or going will have to walk next to your head, with only a curtain to separate you, and any and all bathroom smells will waft directly into your face. Despite Bus Rule Number One, No Number Two on the Bus, the bathroom never ceases to smell…bathroom-y. If I'm truly left with the bottom right front bunk, it's basically RIP sleep and RIP me.

I scowl at Kick and his eyebrows lift. "Unless you wanna share with me? I've got a middle bunk in the back. Be happy to squeeze."

I ignore him and climb off the couch, pulling my bag behind me. When I slide the door to the bunk section open, I walk through without looking back. It's quiet in here, or, quieter. The constant, loud rumble of the engine is already seeping into my brain like an insurance jingle, always there, always humming.

I flop down onto my knees to take stock of my newly assigned bunk. The curtain is pulled back and there's a pillow, a plush grey comforter and fresh sheets. The bunk includes a teeny tiny shelf at both the head and the foot of the bed. I do my best to shove my bag into the shelf at the foot but it doesn't fit. I'll have to sleep with my legs scrunched up to make room. Once I roll inside and pull the curtain shut, I fish my phone out of my hoodie front pocket and text Cass.

Me: I know you're about to have your phone date with Mo but you will not believe what just happened on this bus.

By the time she texts back I'm a year deep into Kick's Instagram, looking for what I don't know. It's all food and sunsets and selfies with a zillion likes.

Cass: Nicole Kidman's there? She's doing BGVs for the tour?
Cass: Sara Paulson?
Cass: BEYONCE?
Me: Yes. All three of them, obviously. We're about to do a champagne toast in the back lounge to celebrate our womanhood. Nicole's asked me to call her Nikki. Come join us!
Cass: Ask Sarah if she holds any resentment towards me about the whole hot dog sandwich debacle.

Me: This is fun.

Me: You not letting me tell you what just happened to me.

Me: Let's keep doing it forever.

Cass: Fine. Tell me what happened on the bus and I'll react appropriately

Me: They want us to perform as a duo.

Me: No. Wait. They ordered us to perform as duo.

Me: Me and Kick. A duo.

Me: What am I going to do??

Cass: I realize I haven't been your manager that long, but as your manager I'll say, I think you're going to have to perform with Kick.

Me: And of course during this whole terrible conversation I was wearing my Chop pants!!!

Cass: Excuse you, those Chop pants were a gift which you love because Chop is the greatest dog who ever lived.

Me: I don't want to be a duo. That was not the point of this whole thing. The point was to be me, not me-and-Kick

Me: And when the bus started moving I fell into his lap like some kind of gross meet-cute, which, can't exactly be a meet-cute since he's already had his tongue in my mouth.

Cass: So putting your tongue back into his mouth would definitely be a bad idea then?

Me: I know you think you're funny, hilarious even, but there will be no smooching. It doesn't matter how insanely hot he is and how insanely hot the original smooching was, this is a smooch-free zone.

Cass: I believe you.

Cass: Except that I don't.

The door slides open and I hear Kick's voice. There's a tense edge to it I've never heard before. He's on the phone.

"I didn't do this to hurt you," he says.

My mind immediately conjures up a new girlfriend he's left for the summer, a girlfriend who's none too happy about being left behind while Kick tours the country with the alcove girl. I swallow down the pang of jealousy that stings my jaw like a sour Jolly Rancher.

"No," he says, "that's not what this is. How could you say that to me?"

My girlfriend fantasy shifts. This sounds like something much deeper, his words tinged with a specific kind of sadness, like an old wound that won't heal. When I risk peeking into the walkway to hear more, he's already slid into his back middle bunk and pulled the curtain closed.

SIXTEEN
NO LOVE NO JOY

I WAKE up with a gnawing growl in my stomach and a missed call from my mother. She calls whenever she remembers she has two daughters instead of one, which means she calls about every other month. I still haven't told her about the tour and am hoping she hasn't learned about it on her own. Her often repeated speech about how I'll only make it in music with her as my manager is tiring. And I'd like to delay the shit storm that will spin my way when she discovers I'm out with Sparrow. With all the press releases Emily sends out, I'm shocked the shit storm hasn't already arrived.

Stepping into the front lounge, I smell the bagel tray before I see it. I devour half of an everything bagel with veggie cream cheese by the time I hop down the tall bus steps, my overnight bag slung over my shoulder.

Sleeping in the bottom bunk was a disaster. There was a stretch from three am to four am when I thought my teeth would vibrate right out of my head. And then there was the pothole that sent me flying and I bonked my head on the bunk above me. No idea how I'm supposed to become a duo in the next few hours as I'm currently running on no sleep, nervous to listen to my mother's voicemail, curious about Kick's mystery phone call, and stressed about coming up with a twenty-minute set from scratch. I head in search of the dressing rooms, desperate to brush my teeth, and hit play on my mother's voicemail.

"Penny, it's your mother. So sorry to have missed you! Hopefully I'm not calling too early. I have no idea what time it is in Nashville. Polly and I are in Dubai playing a private birthday party for, well, let's just say the birthday boy is very *royal* if you know what I mean. You wouldn't believe the decadence! I thought being invited on the yacht with John and Chrissy was amazing but being here...wow. You know, if you played your cards right, you could be here with us enjoying all the extravagant benefits of hard work. Let me know when you're ready to take the plunge!"

Typical voicemail from my mother, selling me on her lifestyle like it's a timeshare and she needs me to invest. I hit delete and am about to text Kick for a time to meet when I get two texts in a row.

Do Not Kiss: Went for a run. Let's meet on the bus in an hour to work out our set.

Jasmine: Could you come to the Production Office ASAP please?

We're in Indianapolis playing an outdoor amphitheater. The backstage area is a series of small concrete buildings around a giant white tent that serves as catering. There are bright arrows made out of neon colored tape on the pavement pointing to where we need to be: backstage, dressing rooms, catering, production office. I follow the production office arrow and find Jasmine in a small, windowless room with a couple desks and chairs. She's busy on her laptop when I walk in.

"Oh, hey," she says, waving me in. "Thanks for coming over so quickly. I just had a question about your paperwork. You didn't list a social or any banking information. We need both to get you paid."

I knew this would come up eventually and hoped, probably

stupidly, that I could find a way around it. I flop down into a metal folding chair in front of the desk.

"Could I just get a paper check?"

Jasmine smiles like I've made a joke. "I didn't think people your age even knew what paper checks were." She swings her laptop around to face me. "Just fill in the missing info and we'll be all set."

It's day one of the tour. I haven't even performed one show. I was hoping to make it a little further before having to fess up.

I stand up and close the door.

"Before I do that, do you have a minute? I need to talk to you about something."

"Sure, what's up?"

I sit back down on the edge of the folding chair and roll my hands into the bottom of my hoodie.

"Strange question but, do you happen to know Candice Moskowitz? Used to be Candice Lovejoy?"

Jasmine's face zips through a gamut of emotions including a tiny hint of fear. "Sure, I know Candy. Not many people in the industry don't know Candy." She laughs at that, like knowing my mother is an inevitability. "I haven't seen her in a long time. Her first husband, John Lovejoy, he was in the band with Deacon and Don back in the day. He played guitar and was quite an incredible songwriter."

She stops, waiting to hear my question, but I wish she'd keep going, wish she'd spill long-held secrets without my even asking.

"Yeah, I...I need to tell you about Candy. And I'd like to ask you to keep it between us."

Jasmine sits back in her chair and clasps her hands under her heavy breasts. "Are you in some kind of trouble with her?"

If she only knew.

"Candy...she's..." This is more difficult than I thought it would be. The truth is sticking in my throat like a dry sandwich. "She's my mother."

Jasmine's eyebrows draw together in question.

"I'm Penny Lovejoy. Candy and John Lovejoy are my parents."

She blows out a long breath and purses her lips. She opens her mouth to speak but closes it, lifts her hand to her temple, shakes her head. I figured she'd be shocked but she's having a full-on moment. I don't add any more details, waiting to see what she'll say.

"I'm guessing you don't want anyone to know that."

"You guess correctly."

"So you came on this tour to…?"

"When Don told me about the contest, he didn't know who I was. He doesn't know. And the whole thing felt like a great opportunity to get on a tour because of me, because of my talent, not because I'm a Lovejoy. It was important to me that I got here without using my family connection."

Her expression tells me she's listening, but she's also working something out inside her mind, her focus obviously split between what I'm saying and whatever her response is going to be. If she knows what went down between my father and the Sparrow brothers, she's not going to offer it easily.

"Does Candy know you're here?"

"No. I know she'll probably find out, but I'd like to keep her in the dark as long as I can. If she finds out, when she finds out," I decide to leave the family history lesson out of it in hopes I can get Jasmine to tell me herself, "she'll insist on acting as my manager even though I've repeatedly told her that's not what I want. I'm sure you know she manages my sister, Polly."

"Yes, she's made quite a name for herself. And Polly. I'm guessing Candy wants you to follow in your sister's footsteps."

"It's all very…complicated."

Jasmine barks out a laugh and claps her hands. "Ain't that the half of it." She studies me while I squirm in my seat. "I can't believe I didn't recognize you."

"Helps I don't look like Polly or my mother. Probably the only reason I was able to pull this off."

"But you got the family talent, didn't you?"

A blush creeps up my neck. "I hope so. And look, I'll put my real info on the paperwork, but can you make sure no one else knows? I'd really love to get through as much of this tour as I can without anyone finding out I'm a Lovejoy."

"And when people do find out?"

I shrug. "I'll cross that bridge when I have to."

Jasmine leans forward and rests her elbows on the desk. Her chair creaks at her shifting weight. "So, when Candy calls me about this mess, because you and I both know she will, what exactly would you like for me to tell her?"

An impossible question, but if I'm going to put my cards on the table, I might as well play the whole deck.

"I know something went down between my father and the Sparrow brothers before I was born. My mother's never told me any details, but growing up I was always taught that Sparrow was the enemy." Jasmine laughs at that. "It's another one of the reasons I didn't use my real name for the tour. I don't want my mother to cause any trouble but, you know how she is."

She nods like, yeah, of course. "Candy never was one to mince words."

I stand up to pace, unable to sit still any longer. "I guess what I'm asking is, if she calls, when she calls, if you'd just tell her everything's going great. I'm great. I don't need her to do anything, don't need her as my manager, that I've worked everything out on my own and you have everything you need. We're good."

Jasmine waits a long time before she says, "I'll see what I can do."

I sit back down, my eyes on the floor.

"Something else on your mind?" she asks.

"I don't, uhh, I don't guess you'd tell me, would you? What happened between my father and the Sparrow brothers?"

Jasmine laughs so loud and so hard I now know she's had a cavity filled in her back right molar.

"Listen, honey, that is not my story to tell." She shakes her finger in the air. "No ma'am it is not."

"But you do know?"

She's still laughing when she says, "Knowing and *knowing* are two different things."

Message received. I stand up to leave but turn back around at the door. "Thanks for the help with Candy. And if you ever decide you want to spill your secrets, you know where to find me."

I'm half-way out the door when she calls out to me.

"Mari?" I look back, my hand on the doorknob. "As long as it isn't hurting anybody, your secret's safe with me.

SEVENTEEN
AT LEAST WE'RE TAKING BUTT ROCK OFF THE TABLE

AFTER A QUICK SHOWER, I change into black cut-offs and my vintage Peter Gabriel t-shirt and head back to the bus to figure out what the hell we're going to do tonight. The expansion has been pulled out in the front lounge so there's more room to move around. Kick's sitting on the couch strumming on an acoustic and humming with his eyes closed. The muscles in his arm twist and shift as he strums. His long legs are stretched out in front of him, taking up all the extra space. He obviously showered as well. Damp waves of hair cling to the back of his neck.

"Are the vampire twins coming?" I ask, flopping down onto the opposite couch where my guitar case is propped.

Kick opens his eyes with a question.

I decide not to elaborate. "Thanks for getting my guitar."

"What's up? You look more irritated than usual."

"Dealing with some family drama."

He makes a face I can't interpret. "Family drama finds a way."

"And I can't shake how Nic talked to us on the call last night." My eyes sweep up to his. "The way he talked about us performing together was like…we're just set dressing they're moving around to wherever they think looks best."

Kick strums something slow and melodic. "Did you expect something different?"

"You didn't?"

He shrugs. "I think we've been thrust onto the big stage earlier than most people and they're going to remind us of that every chance they get."

The sincerity in his voice answers a question that's been simmering in the back of my brain. He's scared too. Unsure. It feels good knowing I'm not the only one.

"It's not that I'm not grateful to be here but, this entire process is starting to feel like I'm being stripped of my entire personality."

Kick laughs, a low rumble in his chest. "Pretty sure your personality could drop kick anyone who tried."

I swing my foot out and tap his leg. "Quit flirting. We've got work to do."

"But flirting with you is so much more fun."

The vampire twins saunter onto the bus, oblivious. "Who's ready to rock," one of them says. Kick motions to a bass case sitting in the small booth. One twin grabs it and scoots in next to me.

"I'm Mari," I offer. "Would probably be good for us to officially meet since we're now playing together."

"Cool, yeah. I'm Miguel. And that's Mateo."

"Yo," Mateo says. "And for what it's worth, I think playing together sounds rad."

At least they're not bothered by the shift in plans.

I unpack my guitar and settle into the couch, no idea how to start this rehearsal or what direction we should go in or what we should do. I worried over it the entire time I was in the shower, what songs I could pitch, what songs we could possibly do together, how I could incorporate myself into what Kick does, how to use the band on my songs. I didn't come up with a single answer. The probability that we bomb tonight is scary high.

"So, we have to learn 'Don't You Want Me.'"

"Ran into Nic while you were in the shower," Kick says. "He said they have a track, that we won't be playing for that one."

"Great. So now not only are we a duo, we're also singing to a track like literal karaoke queens. Super."

If I wanted to sing to a track, I'd be on tour with my sister.

"The video of you two doing that song was fire," Mateo says. "Still can't believe we missed that party. I do a killer Elton John."

The image of the two of us dancing and flirting in front of the entire band and crew jogs through my mind. I haven't been able to bring myself to watch the video. I don't want to see how good we probably look together.

"Maybe in front of drunk party-goers and wobbly animatronics but this is a huge tour. Are you aware of how many people are coming tonight? We're going to make asses of ourselves."

"You can do whatever you want," Mateo says, flexing his biceps, "but I will not be looking like an ass tonight or ever."

"I think maybe we should take turns," I say. "Like, I do one of my songs and you can do one of yours. How long are your songs, on average, because we have to keep it to twenty minutes and 'Don't You Want Me' is three minutes and fifty-six seconds and—"

"You counted?" Miguel asks.

Kick hesitates. "Or we could play with each other."

"That's what she said," Mateo says, snickering.

I sigh and close my eyes. I cannot believe I'm being forced to share the spotlight with overgrown boys who giggle at paper-thin innuendo.

Kick keeps going. "Are all your songs like the one you did at the audition? Kinda sleepy? I'm sure we could back you up on rhythm or something. I could add some BGVs."

My spine stiffens. Is he honestly suggesting my songs are *sleepy*? And that he can add some *rhythm and BGVs*? I feel sick, and not in a hyperbolic way. I am actually going to vomit in a trash can.

"And what would you have me do on your songs? A TikTok dance?"

"That'd be sick," Mateo says, smacking out a rhythm on the table.

A loud scream echoes through my brain. I want to make this work, but at this rate, we'll be doing exactly one song tonight, a *karaoke song* for God's sake.

"Our styles are different, sure," Kick says, "but I think we should figure out how to play together instead of taking turns. Or we could just learn some of your songs and back you up for tonight, figure out the rest later."

"That sounds nice in theory, but I don't even know how to sing with you. What's your style, anyway? Country? Pop Metal? Butt Rock with a side of Grunge?"

He shakes his head. "It's a vibe."

"No," I argue, "it's a genre explosion."

Miguel claps his hands. "Dude, that's what we should call our band. *Genre Explosion.*"

Mateo raises his hand over my head and Miguel leans over to high-five him.

"And where am I in that?" I say, glaring at Kick. "Do you even get what I do?"

"I don't know, sing your pain? Like, pain pop?"

"And what would that make you? Empty-headed noise rock?"

Kick sets his guitar aside and leans forward. "Not all of us need to share our heartbreak with the world."

"I seriously doubt you've ever been through a real heartbreak." It flies out of my mouth before I have a chance to stop myself. Because I know it's not true. The phone call I overheard last night is evidence enough.

"Why? Because I don't howl it into the microphone?"

"No, because of your face and the way you walk and just, ugh, your whole thing."

"You've been thinking about my thing?"

"That's what she said," Miguel says.

I swing my entire body over to glare at him. "Really?"

He smiles at me. "Maybe we should do some more covers, something current, like a LOVEJOY song or—"

"No way in hell we're doing a LOVEJOY song!" It shoots out of me too fast, too loud. They all stare at me like I just grew horns from my forehead.

"You really don't like her, do you," Kick says.

"We should do the alcove songs," Mateo says. "Both of them."

Kick and I lock eyes, scared, like Mateo just pried open Pandora's box with a crowbar.

When neither of us respond, Mateo shrugs. "I'm just saying, those songs got you all those votes, are the whole reason we're here on this kickass mega-tour being actual rock stars. Makes sense to play them."

Words tumble from my mouth out of order. "But not that's, those are, we're not...I don't know if that's such a good idea."

Kick rubs his lips together, thinking. In all his little quips and feather-ruffling he's rarely shown me anything solid, mostly hiding himself away behind his thigh-shaking grins. It's like he came on this tour just to irritate me and now that we're here and truly have to figure out what we're going to do, he's not sure how to flirt his way out of it.

"Kick?"

"Mateo's right," he finally says. "We should do the alcove songs. Together."

"Have you not been checking your socials? If we do the alcove songs we'll be sacrificing ourselves on the altar of AO3. I already feel like performing together will stir up unnecessary inspiration for the Marick conspiracy theorists whose sole goal in life is to prove that we...you know."

"What's Marick?" Mateo asks.

"It's their hashtag," Miguel says with an eyeroll. "Personally, I would have picked Gaines."

Kick picks up his guitar and plays a few chords from my song, my alcove song, like he's already thought about doing it on the tour.

"I think we can't worry about the conspiracies or whatever," he says, his eyes on his guitar. "What we need to do is give tonight's crowd the best damn show they've ever seen. Something they won't forget. And both of our songs about that night are," his eyes flick to mine full of heat and want and I have to cross my legs against the building pressure between them, "memorable."

The bus door opens with a loud whoosh.

"Knock, knock," Emily says, swinging the door shut and popping up the stairs. "You guys working on your set?"

"Yep," I say without looking at her, still disgruntled at her meddling.

"I told them we should do the alcove songs," Mateo says, his chest puffed out like he's saved the day.

Emily semi-glares back and forth between me and Kick. "That should have been a given."

Here we go. "But doing those songs will play right into the fan fantasies about me and Kick as...more than co-performers."

"Yes," she says, nodding her head so hard her hair nearly flips up into her eyes, "that's exactly what it will do which is why you have to do it. This isn't kumbaya hour, this is a major tour with thousands of people paying a lot of money to see the songs they want to see. Do you think Sparrow loves playing 'In A Dark Wood' every night? Hell no. But it's the song fans want to hear. And your fans, which by the way, are growing by the minute, want to hear the alcove songs."

All eyes turn to me, everyone sold on the plan, waiting for me to get on board. But I'm the one who'll be singing about kissing Kick. To Kick. With Kick. I'm the one forced to pretend it's just a song. I should ask Emily if she has Stevie Nicks's phone number. I could use the advice of a woman who's shared the stage with a former lover. Not that Kick's my former lover. Not that he ever will be my lover.

I need to stop thinking about the word lover.

"Anyway," Emily adds, "I just came by to tell you we'll be live-streaming your set tonight. Cheddar thinks it will be huge. If tonight goes well, we can start charging. It could be like selling an entire second show."

Her eyes light up with dollar signs and I half-wonder if she has a personal stake in this tour beyond publicist.

"Rock and roll," Miguel says and reaches across to high five Mateo again. Some of my hair gets caught in the smack.

I've spent the last couple weeks working up the nerve to play in front of more than twenty thousand people tonight, but a livestream? I look at Kick and there's genuine fear in his eyes. He hides it away before smiling at Emily, but not a real smile, not one of the smiles he gives me.

"That's great," Kick says. "Looks like everything's coming together."

More likely, everything's falling apart.

EIGHTEEN
PACK IT UP

SOUNDCHECK IS A DISASTER. Kick's in-ears aren't working and neither of us are used to the monitors and honestly, the size of the venue. It's one thing to belt out a song to a couple dozen people in a coffee shop or backyard party. It's entirely another to hear your voice echoing across six thousand empty seats and a massive, sloping lawn knowing soon enough the entire space will be filled with people who may or may not like your performance. And we still haven't worked out our set. With the alcove songs and "Don't You Want Me," we're at just over eleven minutes with eight minutes left to fill.

"We could each do one of our own originals," I say. "I'm sure you've got a five-minute jam band rocker up your sleeve, don't you?"

Kick doesn't respond so I look to Miguel and Mateo. They both shrug like they've never heard of original songs before.

"We could do another cover?" Kick says. "Maybe something to help transition from your alcove song to 'Don't You Want Me.'"

"Or we could do one of your songs?"

A look I don't understand zips through Kick. "We can do

another one of yours if you want. Or we could fill up the time with conversation."

"What, between you and me?"

It goes on like that until the sound guy kicks us off the stage and tells us to work it out by show time.

"Come with me," I say as we exit the stage.

We put our guitars in the guitar rack at side stage. Kick follows me as I stalk to the back row of seats, far enough away from the soundboard that no one will hear us. Thankfully, Miguel and Mateo don't follow.

"Your whole cool guy act is very convincing," I say, arms crossed, "but I know you know this is a complete disaster. You can't be okay with this."

"Spending more time with you? I'm very okay with that."

"Stop flirting and be real with me for five seconds. We're going to die up there!"

He worries his lips between his teeth, like he won't allow himself to say what needs to be said.

His whispered words from last night snake through my brain.

I didn't do this to hurt you.

That's not what this is.

"Why are you on this tour?" I ask. "And don't say something snarky or cute. Tell me the real reason. Why are you here?"

Kick rubs his clavicle tattoo and sighs. "It was this or work for H&E Moving Company. This seemed like the better option."

"You're a furniture mover?"

"That's where I met the guys. First day on the job, we got hired to move a house in Antioch for this session guitar player. We got to talking and he invited us to a party that night at some dude's house with a guitar-shaped pool. I didn't have anything else going on so I thought, why not?"

"You were at Jackson's party because the guy you moved happened to be a musician?"

He juts his chin out, scratches at the stubble. "Have you met anyone in Nashville who's *not* a musician? Aren't you the one who's dated them all?" He stares down at the concrete stair we're sharing and murmurs, "All but one."

"That doesn't explain why you're here."

"Why are *you* here?"

We watch each other like a dare, like an unsaid accusation, neither of us willing to say anything that might give us away. When he sees I'm not willing to go first, he continues on with his story.

"I worked with Miguel and Mateo at the movers for a couple weeks, wondering what happened to the girl from the alcove. Then one weekend we got called to this woman's house to move some heavy furniture around." He gives me a look. "Emily Wu."

"You moved Emily's furniture?"

"She wanted a piano moved from one room to another, wanted some couches rearranged. She asked me if I was a musician. I laughed because it reminded me of my first conversation with you."

"Please tell me you did not make out with Emily Wu in an alcove."

He chuckles at that. "She's the one who told me about the audition."

"Hang on. You're telling me she asked you to audition for the tour without ever seeing you play? You're seriously telling me you got the audition purely based on your face?"

"I did not say that."

"Did she hear you sing a single note?"

He blushes and looks away, caught.

"Was she trying to sleep with you?" I ask, terrified of the answer.

He shakes his head. "If she was, she didn't make it very clear. And just so *we're* clear, I wasn't and am not interested in Emily."

"I don't get it. You act like you don't care about any of this. You aren't pushing to play any of your songs, don't seem bothered by being paired up with me. It doesn't make sense. Tonight is supposed to be our big moment, our time to show the world who we are as artists. Despite your irritating nonchalance, I know deep down you want to be more than Mari Gold's guitar player who sings BGVs."

He lifts his eyes to mine, his expression somewhere between sad and terrified. "What if I don't."

"You do," I half-yell. "I know you do."

"Why does it matter to you. We can do the alcove songs, do the cover, do one of your songs, do all your songs for all I care. Can't that be enough?"

He steps across the aisle and sinks down into one of the stadium seats until it hits the back of his neck. His legs are too long to fit so he swings them up and over the seat in front of him. I sit next to him, equally slouched.

"Like it or not," I say, "we're in this together. For the next fifty shows, we're a duo. We have to be honest with each other if we're going to make this work."

Even though I'm not being honest with him. But my lie doesn't affect our performance. My lie doesn't matter. I don't know that he's lying, but he's definitely withholding something. No one on earth would be this cavalier about performing in front of thousands of people for the first time.

Kick shifts in his seat. He runs his hands down his face. He clears his throat. "I don't have any originals."

I keep my focus on the stage. "What do you mean?"

"I don't have any original songs. You keep pushing for us to do one of my songs but I don't have any. I've never…I'm not supposed to be here. I shouldn't be doing this."

"I don't understand. Your alcove song is so good."

He waits for me to look at him. "That's the only song I've ever written."

I'm completely stunned. "But…what were you going to do? Before they put us together, what were you planning to perform every night?"

He smiles a sad little smile. "I hadn't quite worked that out yet."

I turn in my seat to fully face him. "You're telling me you got on the bus last night not knowing what you were going to perform tonight?"

He shrugs.

"And Miguel and Mateo?"

"We figured we'd work it out today, which, we almost did." He pulls his legs down and sits up. "I'm assuming you handled it differently?"

"Are you kidding? I had a ten minute set rehearsed down to the second. I was locked in. I was *ready*. How the hell did you get on this tour and you've only ever written one song?"

"You're a really good songwriter by the way," he says. "How many have you written?"

"I am not exaggerating when I say hundreds."

"See? We could do your songs every single night and never run out."

I can't process any of the things he's saying. He's written exactly one song, a song about me, and yet managed to get on one of the biggest tours of the summer. I'd be mad about the unfairness but he looks so small right now, scared, like I've uncovered his most embarrassing moment and he's waiting for me to point and laugh.

"What about your brother? Your tattoo—you said you wrote that melody together. Do you not write songs with him?"

"No, I don't."

"Why not?"

He lets out a heavy sigh. "Can we not talk about my brother?"

"Family drama?" I say, stopping short of telling him my family drama runs deeper than I even know.

"I don't want to talk about my brother."

"You don't want to talk about the set, you don't want to talk about your brother. You have to give me something."

"He died." He says it quick. Quiet. Like I punched him in the stomach and that's the sound that came out.

My eyes go wide. "Oh my God, Kick. What happened?"

"It doesn't matter. He's gone."

Kick's words are laced with pain. I've unintentionally forced a confession he didn't want to make. I stupidly thought his reasons were surface-level, were ridiculous, that I'd be able to talk him out of whatever it was. But this is so much more. I need to say something, apologize for pushing, tell him I'm here if he wants to talk about it.

"We'll do the alcove songs and the cover tonight," Kick says. He's not looking at me. "We can figure out the rest later."

I want to argue but I've already pushed him enough.

Our set is in less than three hours. At this point, I don't see how we'll be ready.

NINETEEN
IRRECONCILABLE DIFFERENCES

IT'S an hour to showtime and I have a fleeting thought to call my mother. If I hired her as my manager, she'd have this whole thing sorted out so fast Emily Wu's head would spin right off her skinny neck. Before tonight's show she'd have me doing my own thirty-minute set and Kick demoted to checking tickets at the door.

I'm still debating whether or not to call her as I walk into catering. There's a long buffet set up with every kind of pasta dish known to man. I slide my phone into my back pocket, pick up a plate, and load it with baked ziti, lasagna, chicken fettuccini, a green salad and two large breadsticks. I'm too nervous to eat any of it but I want to have options in case the mood strikes.

I find an empty table and sit down. My loaded fork is halfway to my mouth when a shadow falls over me.

"There's not a rule against getting a second plate, Goldie." There he is, my karaoke king, smiling and pulling out the chair next to me. "Piling all your food together like that really disrupts the flavor intricacies."

"Can't a woman eat her feelings in peace?"

Kick points to his own double-plate situation. "Just pointing out something we have in common. The list is getting longer by the day."

He bites off a huge chunk of bread, talking while he chews. "Did you know that most performers don't eat before a show? Prefer to perform on an empty stomach."

"As a nervous puker, I'd think you'd follow their advice," Mateo says. He sits down next to Kick with a plate full of salad and nothing else.

"You're a nervous puker?" I ask.

Kick grins and shakes his head. "Nothing to be nervous about. We've got three killer songs ready to go."

I swirl my fork into my Italian mountain and shove a heaping bite of fett-sagna-ziti into my mouth. Half a ziti falls back onto my plate as I chew.

"So beautiful," Kick says, hand over his heart.

"Have you guys seen this?" Mateo turns his phone around to show us a TikTok video. It's from soundcheck, the four of us on stage running through "I Kissed Her In An Alcove." Over the video a girl is talking about us, about me and Kick.

Looks like Kick Raines and Mari Gold are gearing up for their first show tonight. And what's this? They're singing together? Be still our hearts. Who's planning on watching the livestream tonight? You know I'll be watching. Be sure and check back here for all the latest, juicy updates on our favorite duo. Marick fans unite!

"Who is this? How did she get this footage?" I ask.

Mateo shrugs. "My girlfriend saw it and sent it to me."

"Who was filming us while we were sound checking?" Kick asks.

We were so focused on getting through soundcheck none of us noticed anyone filming. And the girl in the video isn't someone on the tour.

We all three look around the room, assessing the crew, the merch team, even Cheddar as different groups sit huddled around their plates of food.

"You look sexy in that video," Kick says, giving me a heated look.

"Thanks, bro," Mateo says, head down, inhaling his salad.

I can't help it. I laugh the tiniest bit. And that feels so good I laugh some more. And then a little more until I'm full-on eyes-watering howling. Kick's laughing too.

"I'm gonna crack you yet, Goldie," Kick says, playfully punching me in the arm. "Every concrete layer."

"It's good to have goals." I pretend punch him on the chin right as Don Sparrow sits down at our table.

"Oh," I say, suddenly on my best behavior, "hi, Don."

"Mind if I join you? Wanted to catch y'all before the show tonight. See how it's going."

Kick and I give each other a look as Mateo says, "Rockin'."

Don laughs. "Good, good. Emily says they've got a livestream set up for tonight. Said they're expecting big numbers."

"Was it like this for you? Starting out?" I ask before I can help myself.

Don smiles and shakes his head. "Not quite, no. We worked hard for a long time before we ever made it to an arena stage."

"You and Deacon?"

I'm dancing too close to the edge, my father's name on the tip of my tongue. Don thinks about it for a moment, like he's considering how much to share. I want to shout at him that he should just say it, whatever it is. Just blurt it out and end my misery.

"We've had a few line-up changes over the years, but Joe and Randy have been with us for a long time."

Mateo points his fork in the air. "You guys used to be a trio, right? Like me and Miguel and Kick?"

I glare at Mateo, looking for any hint that he knows I'm a Lovejoy, but he just eats more salad and grins at Don like he learned this tidbit from Wikipedia.

"In the beginning, yeah. It was me and Deacon and a guy

named John. He left the band right as we were hitting it big, but he and I co-wrote some of our first hits. He's actually the one who wrote 'In A Dark Wood.' He was a great songwriter."

"Why'd he leave?" Mateo asks and wow, I might have to become Mateo's best friend. Without even knowing, he's casually peeling the onion that's plagued me my whole life. It's night one and it's happening. I'm about to find out what made my father leave the band.

Don waits a beat, another, before he says, "Irreconcilable differences."

"Just like my parents," Mateo jokes and we all laugh.

"Don," Nic calls from the doorway, "time to go."

Don pushes on the table to stand up. "The press awaits. Good talking with you." He looks right at me and smiles. "Have a great show tonight."

He waves at us as he leaves, like his heart's warmed from the time we spent together even though it lasted all of three minutes and left me with more questions than answers.

We eat our food in silence, me going over and over what Don said about my father. If I got this close to the truth tonight, it means I'll be able to get closer tomorrow. I thought it would be difficult to open the conversation but, thanks to Mateo, I'm halfway there.

I'm about to leave to go do my hair and make-up for the show when Mateo's eyes go wide as he scrolls through his phone.

"There's another one."

"Another what?"

He turns his phone around. It's open to TikTok and the same girl who posted the soundcheck video has another one up. This time she's talking over a photo.

Of me and Kick.

Sitting at the same table we're sitting at right now.

It's the moment from earlier, when Kick made me laugh, like

someone had been waiting for it to happen and captured it with intention. How did this girl even get a video up this fast?

I look back at the video as her head pops up over the image of me and Kick. She points up at my huge smile as she speaks.

Mari's looking pretty happy to be sitting next to Kick. I wonder what he said to make her smile that big? Hopefully we'll see that same energy at tonight's show. Don't forget to tune in to the livestream to watch Marick's performance and then come back here for a recap!

"How?" I say, unable to say anything else.

"It's obviously someone on the tour," Mateo says, "feeding her photos and videos."

"We should talk to Cheddar. He could probably find out who's doing it."

"Cheddar's not gonna care about any of this," Kick says. "It's free publicity as far as he's concerned, which is what he and Emily care about."

"Which means it's probably Emily," I say. "But why would she feed photos and videos to this person. What's the end game for trying to make us look like a couple?"

Kick's eyes dart around the room and I can see he's not about to say what he really wants to say. "We entered a fan voted contest. I don't think we can complain about fans being excited about what we're doing, on stage or not."

He's making a good point, but I don't *want* him to be making a good point.

"Is there nothing that bothers you?"

He chews, thinks, stalls. "I am very, very bothered by people with long toenails."

Mateo raises his fork in the air. "Word."

Fine, he's not bothered by the TikToker dissecting our every move. Maybe I shouldn't be either. But I can't shake the feeling something sinister is happening behind the scenes.

Mateo eats his last bite of salad and stands up with his plate in his hand. "I'm gonna go do my pre-show routine."

"And what's that?"

"One hundred push-ups, fifty pull-ups and one hundred squats. See y'all out there."

He walks away and I stare at Kick. "Tell me again where you found those two?"

"In a dark alley behind a moving truck," he jokes. "It's where all the best players hide."

TWENTY
NERVES AKIMBO

STANDING side stage in a packed amphitheater right before I'm about to go on is an entirely new sensation. And that sensation is unmitigated fear. Kind of like the moment right before the roller coaster sails over that first giant hill except my harness isn't buckled and I just ate four chili dogs.

I will not survive this show.

Thinking about it in the abstract I was all yeah, cool, I can totally get on stage in front of thousands of people and sing and play guitar on an arena tour. Easy. Now? My nerves have nerves that are shaking with nerves.

The show is sold out all the way to the very back of the lawn. It's minutes to show time, the sun is setting, people are finding their seats or spreading out their blankets. A decent portion of the seats are still empty, waiting for late-comers, but it's still more people than I've ever performed in front of total. A lot more.

Miguel's next to me, bouncing on the balls of his feet and swinging his arms wide. His solid black bass is slung over his back and he's dressed in all black. Mateo's leaning on a low concrete wall that separates a section of seats from the backstage area, tapping his drumsticks on his denim-clad thighs.

"Where's Kick?" I ask Miguel.

"He'll be here."

"We go in less than five minutes."

Miguel cracks the knuckles on both his hands. "He's getting ready. He'll be here."

What is there to get ready, an extra swipe of a hand through his hair? I spent a dedicated amount of time on my own hair, curling it into cascading waves and pulling the sides up into two braids that meet in the back. I'm wearing what I have now deemed my lucky plum lipstick, eyelashes and heavy black eyeliner, and the outfit Cass picked out for my first performance —black Doc Martens, a super-mini black dress covered in tiny white polka dots with a tight bodice and a twirly skirt and my cropped black leather jacket. It's too hot to be in a jacket but it's essential to complete the look. And it's only twenty minutes, right? I can do anything for twenty minutes.

Unless I pass out the second the spotlight hits me.

I trace my hand over the picture of my father taped to the back of my guitar, hoping having him with me, even just in a photo, will calm my rolling waves of doubt. I keep worrying I don't deserve to be here, that my real identity will be found out, that maybe Kick is better than me and should have been the winner, that I'll freeze on stage and ruin everything.

Nic hustles over, eyeballing the rows filling up with people.

"Full house tonight. Did you two work out a set?"

I lie and say yes right as Kick jogs up. He's white as a ghost and his face covered in a thin layer of sweat.

"Where've you been?" I say, low enough that Nic won't hear me.

Kick shakes his head too fast, lips sealed shut. He looks petrified. His breaths are pumping in and out in a hurried rhythm, like his lungs are trying to escape.

"Can't wait for 'Don't You Want Me,'" Nic says. "Chemistry on that song is off the charts. Hope the rest of your set is just as good."

He hurries into the darkness behind the stage and I look up at Kick. He is definitely on the verge of losing it. Specifically, the mountain of pasta he ate for dinner.

"You look like you're about to be sick."

"Too late," he mumbles, running a nervous hand over his stomach. He raises his other hand up to the collar of his shirt, to his clavicle tattoo, and rubs it back and forth with his thumb.

"Are you okay?" He doesn't answer me, just sways slightly. "What is going on with you?"

His eyes are watering. "I can't do this. I'm not this guy. I'm not the one who...this isn't. Me. I can't be. This."

I'm now less concerned about my own nerves and entirely freaked out that Kick's going to pass out before we even make it onto the stage. I grab both of his arms and turn him to face me.

"Kick, listen to me. You're a badass rockstar. When you get in front of that mic, you're totally electric. You're mesmerizing. It honestly makes me sick how good you are."

"Don't say sick."

I squeeze his arms. "I'll be right next to you the whole time. Just...keep your eyes on me. Forget about the crowd and focus on me. Okay? It's just you and me."

His cheeks puff out like he's going to puke directly on me, but he nods, his eyes wide. "You and me."

Deacon and Don Sparrow stroll up with easy smiles and casual confidence. They've done this a million times, maybe more. I doubt either of their dinners are threatening retreat.

"Cheddar says the fans can't wait to see you two play," Don says. "I know I'm personally excited to see what you're going to do."

"Us too," I say, too loud, all false bravado. My hands are trembling so much I have to smash them together to keep them from flying right off my arms.

"Just have fun, okay?" Deacon slaps Kick on the back and Kick swallows thickly. "The audience can sense when you're not in sync. Don't worry about how you're playing, just let the music move through you and stay in tune with each other and you'll kill it."

Helpful. Would have been a lot more helpful seven hours ago.

"Besides," he adds, waving to a group of twenty-something girls sitting right up front who all eagerly wave back, "looks like we've got a beautiful crowd tonight."

The arena lights go down. The cheers quickly swing from applause to an ear-splitting wall of sound when Deacon and Don jog up the stage stairs and the spotlight hits them. My heart jumps into my throat. I grab Kick's hand and squeeze.

This is it.

"Hello all you beautiful people!" Deacon waits for the applause to die down. "It's great to be in Indianapolis for the very first night of our Grand Total Tour!" Incredibly, the crowd gets even louder. Deacon waves his hands, motioning for quiet. "To celebrate, we've got a very special treat for you tonight. We decided to do something a little fun for this tour and let you, the fans, vote on who we brought out with us. We loved the idea of giving a young up-and-coming artist from Nashville a chance on the big stage." He throws his arms out. "And tonight's stage is pretty big isn't it?"

While he's talking, Kick and I and Miguel and Mateo get into position behind him and Don. The lights aren't on us yet, so anyone beyond the first few rows can't see us. I plug in my guitar and adjust my in-ear monitors, wipe my hands on my hips, stretch my fingers, adjust my hair, silently pray that I don't forget every lyric or break a guitar string or spontaneously start my period. When I look over at Kick, his eyes are on me.

"You and me," I mouth to him, even as my heart is about to vibrate right out of my chest.

Kick nods, a tiny movement of his head, letting me know he's with me.

"Now," Deacon says, his voice booming across the arena, "some of you, hopefully a lot of you, voted to see this very special opening act. How many of y'all voted?" A loud cheer rings out. "If you ask me, you voted right." Deacon looks at Don who silently nods in agreement. "I know you're gonna love 'em as much as we do. Please welcome, for their Sparrow debut, Kick Raines and Mari Gold."

Spotlights beam down on both me and Kick as Mateo hits eight beats on the kick drum. Kick and I watch each other, counting the beats, guitars at the ready. Miguel is to our right, set back behind us, on the bass.

On the ninth beat, we launch into the first notes of "I Kissed Her In An Alcove." We decided on Kick's high energy alcove song for the opener since it's full of driving chords and quick, shouting vocals. The crowd immediately gets into it, the amphitheater alive and moving, thousands joining us in this moment, this feeling.

Kick watches me as he sings the first measure, then looks out at the crowd, finally sliding into it. By the time we get to the chorus and I start singing with him, the color's back in his cheeks and he's smiling.

It's fast and fun, my adrenaline pumping, my heart racing. All my nerves leading up to this moment have faded into the darkness around the stage. It's only me, Kick, the song, the music.

As the song ends, we launch into my alcove song, the four of us totally in sync. I sense Kick relaxing into it, happy for me to take the lead. I'm sweating in my leather jacket, my legs are trembling and my heart is swelling up like a too-big balloon about to burst. Even though I'm wearing in-ear monitors, my voice sounds different, stronger, bigger as I sing out to the very last row of people at the top of the amphitheater. Singing to this many people is like sitting on the wing of an airplane, like parasailing off a speed boat. All I can do is hang on and hope I make it out alive.

We never did agree on any other songs to play so after my

alcove song ends, Kick straddles the microphone stand and smiles into the crowd.

"Hello, Indianapolis. Thank you so much for the incredible welcome." The crowd's energy, Kick's beaming face, my racing heart—it's more than I could have ever imagined. "I have an important question for you. Anyone here happen to see a little video of myself and the very beautiful Mari Gold doing some karaoke a few days back?"

There's enough applause to not be embarrassed but a group of women at the front of the lawn jump to their feet, screaming and whistling like Kick just told them they won backstage passes to his personal dressing room.

"Okay, okay," he laughs into the microphone and wow, you'd never know ten minutes ago he was puking his guts out from nerves, "I see you back there. For the rest of you who didn't happen to see it," he looks over at me conspiratorially, like we didn't already have this song queued up, like he's making a sexy suggestion in front of twenty thousand people, "maybe we should do it for them?"

"I think we could do that," I say, pulling my guitar over my head and handing it to the guitar tech who's scurried on stage to grab it along with Kick's.

"I don't know," Kick teases, "it's kind of a sexy little song. You sure you don't mind flirting with me in front of all these people?"

I know what he's doing. Killing time to fill out our set. Riling up the crowd. Setting up the song. Stoking the fire of the people who saw the video and are screaming for an encore. It's not about me and him, it's about the set, the crowd, the moment.

So why does it suddenly feel like my pelvic floor muscles have been dipped in molten lava?

"I'll flirt with you," a woman yells from the middle of the seats. A bunch of other people woo in response.

"Looks like you've got plenty of admirers here tonight," I say.

Kick keeps his eyes on me as he leans into the mic and says, "But I only wanna flirt with you." He looks back at the sound booth and shouts, "Hit it."

The track booms over the speakers, an electric pulse that pushes the entire crowd to its feet. Kick and I recreate our karaoke moment, singing to each other like we're longtime lovers, eyes only for each other. The excitement from the crowd ratchets our energy into the rafters of the amphitheater shell, our voices full and sure, like we wrote the lyrics for each other. We're loose, joyful, outrageous, dancing like we're the only two people in the entire world.

It's intoxicating. Soul-changing. I never want to do anything else as long as I'm alive.

TWENTY-ONE
THE CHEEK PAIN IS WORTH IT

AS SOON AS we step off stage, Cheddar and Emily are there, Emily talking a mile a minute. I haven't had time to catch my breath and they're already hustling us backstage.

"You were supposed to do twenty minutes but you only did fifteen. What happened?"

"It was good, right?" I ask Kick, dabbing the sweat from my face with a towel the guitar tech hands me. Kick's scrubbing his face and neck with his own towel. When he pulls it away, he's red-cheeked and radiant.

"That was incredible," he roars. "Wasn't it incredible?" He grabs me by my waist and lifts me into the air to spin me in a circle. "We just did that!"

When he sets me down I'm dizzy, but not from the spinning. Every second of our set was like riding on a rocket ship made of unicorns straight into a rainbow. We went beyond playing songs together. We transformed, became something new. Mixing our styles, our voices, each giving our best to compliment the other —it was magic.

Emily's still grumbling about our incomplete set and saying something about a meet and greet and photos and something else I can't hear over the roar of the crowd waiting for Sparrow.

Cheddar's happy-shouting stats at us—livestream numbers, Instagram likes, follows, TikToks—drowning us in numbers.

"You guys are on fire," he says. "Except for a couple of people who keep insisting Mari is related to LOVEJOY. Can you imagine?"

I pull away from Kick and freeze, unsure what to say.

"Don't worry," Cheddar says, "we're deleting them."

"I've got eight-by-tens," Emily says. "We're not going to make an announcement. We'll just head out there after the show. See how things go on the fly."

My heart starts beating again. The way Cheddar breezed right past the LOVEJOY comment, maybe it will be a non-issue?

"Wait," I say, my brain going in too many directions at once. "Out where?"

I just played the show of my life. People are commenting about me and my sister. And something's happening after the show? I need a minute to process.

Emily crosses her arms, all business. "We're going to have you both out by the exit to sign autographs for fans, take photos. We want to gage interest."

"Interest for what?"

"Interest for you." She's smiling like it's adorable I'm so clueless.

"According to socials, interest is off the charts," Cheddar says, glowing.

"Do I," I look at Kick who looks as shell-shocked as I feel, "should we change clothes?"

I'm sweaty and sticky and my heart's still pounding in my ears.

"No, keep these clothes on. We want people to recognize you from the set. Be in your dressing room at eleven and someone will escort you out."

Cheddar and Emily hurry off in opposite directions, Cheddar scanning his phone for more data, more numbers, leaving Kick and I to absorb the fact we're now meeting fans after the show.

"Is this happening?"

Kick scratches at the back of his neck. "I don't know anything about this meet and greet situation but what I do know is," his eyes find mine, "I've never had that much fun on stage. Ever."

I want to say yes, me too. Want to lunge at him, throw my arms around him, scream in his ear that we were incredible. We were incredible! But that would cross the invisible line we've drawn, would leave me vulnerable. I can't, especially now, give in to my basest desires and risk messing up our onstage chemistry.

A playful smile tugs at his lips. "Still worried about me stealing your spotlight, Goldie?"

I throw my chin in the air and return his smile. "I guess we can share."

"For now."

"Yeah, for now."

Emily guides us through the crush of people exiting the venue, lines of wide-eyed fans at the massive Sparrow merch displays buying shirts and posters and hats. A huge backdrop of me and Kick, probably nine feet high and just as wide, is set up near the main exit. It's one of the photos from the audition, the other contestants cropped out. The way Kick and I are standing together, angled towards each other, we look like a couple. Emily planned everything perfectly, down to the exact photo needed for a huge backdrop.

"Listen," Emily says as she hustles us over to the line, "if people ask if you're a couple, don't deny it. Keep 'em guessing."

My mouth drops open and I'm overly aware of hundreds of pairs of eyes watching me, watching Kick, watching every move we make. "Why would we do that?"

She gives me that look again, like I'm a clueless, adorable idiot. "To sell tickets, obviously. And livestream access. And t-shirts. And meet-and-greet passes."

Kick and I exchange a worried look as we get to the backdrop. Emily pushes us forward like a stage mom hungry for a crown. A line of people roped-off next to the backdrop clap and cheer as soon as we come into view. Kick's hand goes to my back, reaches to grip my waist. I look up at him and he's smiling at the crowd but there's a tightness in his eyes.

He leans in and whispers, "Let's just get through this. We'll figure it out later."

Figure what out? The overwhelming fish-out-of-water sensation of people lined up to meet us? That Emily wants us to pretend to be a couple? That all these people probably think we *are* a couple?

Emily positions us in the middle of the backdrop and turns her focus to the line.

"You get one photo and one signed eight-by-ten. Please don't linger, we need to keep the line moving. Thank you."

She motions for the first person to approach, a short woman wearing a Sparrow t-shirt and practically bouncing up and down with excitement. She hands her phone to Emily to have the photo taken and bounds over to us, grabbing our hands in hers.

"You guys are so ridiculously cute together, I mean, those songs? The sparks were flying on that stage tonight. Please tell me you're together." She's breathless when she says it, her face so hopeful. "I mean, if you're not then please give me your number."

I can't tell if she's asking for my number or for Kick's. I'm suspicious it's both.

"We do love performing together," Kick says. "We're..."

His voice drops off and my brain struggles to fill in the blank.

Just a duo?

Two people who perform together on stage because we were forced to?

Competitors?

Rivals?

...Friends?

"Well," the woman says, filling in the gap left hanging wide open, "it won't be long." She gives us an exaggerated wink and shimmies in between us for the photo.

Kick shoots me a quick look before we smile for the camera, like he's acknowledging an inside joke we have. Emily hands us Sharpies and we each sign an eight-by-ten photo of ourselves, the same photo Emily took at the audition, and thank the woman for coming.

The next person in line is pretty much the same. Wants to know if we're dating, thinks it's only a matter of time, thinks we're adorable together, wants to know when our version of "Don't You Want Me" and what are now known as The Alcove Songs will be available to stream.

The line goes on and on, which is equal parts thrilling and exhausting and shocking. All these people, here to see me, see us, when we've barely started the tour.

We're half-way through the line when a twenty-something wearing a micro-mini and a sheer tank top walks seductively up to Kick.

"Hi," she says while her body says ten times more.

"Hey there," he says. Friendly. Worried.

"Loved your set tonight," she says, angling her body so she's between me and Kick, her back to me. "I'm Bree. How long will you be in town?"

"Leaving right away I'm afraid," Kick says, reaching over to pull me closer. "Let's take this photo, yeah?"

She pulls a hotel key from her bra and pushes it into Kick's hand. "If there's time, I'll be waiting."

We take the photo, the girl never even noticing I'm there.

"If there's time, I'll be waiting," I mimic, slinging my arm across my eyes.

"You wish," Kick jokes.

The next guy in line heads straight for me when it's his turn. "What time were you born?"

"I'm sorry, what?"

"And your birthday? I was trying to do your birth chart and couldn't find any information about your birthday online. I found all your info," he says to Kick, thrusting a folded piece of paper into his hand, "but Mari here is a mystery."

"She was born right on time," Kick says, pulling the guy between us and facing him forward. "Say cheese!"

TWENTY-TWO
UGGOS NEED NOT APPLY

THE FRONT LOUNGE is crammed full of people. *Twilight* is playing on the TV which has sparked a lively debate about whether it qualifies as a vampire movie or not. The mood is light, people laughing, drinking beers and shouting if they're Team Edward or Team Jacob. I'm surprised to learn Emily is Team Edward and not surprised Mo is Team Alice. Jasmine declares she's Team Charlie which makes Emily throw popcorn at her head. Mateo argues that being Team Anything takes away from the vampire-ness of the movie and we should all shut-up.

Then there's me and Kick. We played the set of our lives. Our meet-and-greet was a wild success. What I thought would be a trainwreck was a full-blown Best Night Of My Life. It's confusing. It's not supposed to work, me and Kick. I'm supposed to be against the duo arrangement, supposed to push for being a solo act, doing my own songs. But singing with Kick was unlike any experience I've had on stage.

He keeps catching my eye every time I glance his way, a look on his face I can't pin down, like he's giving me everything while holding something back. Like he has a secret he's dying to tell me but swore on his grandma's grave he wouldn't.

Bella has just told Edward to put his seatbelt on when I nudge

Kick's foot from across the aisle. I cock my head toward the back of the bus and lift my eyebrows. His eyes light up. He leans forward, arms resting on his legs, his fingers grazing my knees. I shake my head no, letting him know all I want to do is talk.

I quirk an eyebrow and silently urge him to be subtle. If the two of us head for the back lounge at the same time we will never hear the end of it.

He bites his bottom lip and again, I shake my head no. Kick leans back against the couch and dips his head down, chin on his chest, an exaggerated frown tugging on his lips. In another world, I'd be sprinting to the back lounge to do exactly what's written all over his face. But I'm going to be good.

I stand up and stretch my arms over my head. My Tears For Fears t-shirt rides up and Kick stares. "I'm going to bed."

"No way," Mo says. "First night of tour we all stay up."

"I'm exhausted," I say, giving her a high five. "But I support your right to party."

I step through the tangle of legs in the aisle and slide open the door to the bunks.

"Where are you going?" Mateo says. "It's just getting good."

"I've seen it," I call over my shoulder. "Team Edward all the way."

"Charlie's hotter," Jasmine cries. "And alive."

Kick's crowding up behind me before I even reach the door to the back lounge. So much for subtlety.

"We're just going to talk," I say. "No funny business."

He flashes an unfair smile. "But we're so good at funny business."

Kick's feather-lite touch is on my lower back as I slide open the door. Rod the Stage Manager and Cheddar are sitting on the couch, drinking beers, a baseball game on the TV.

"Hey, guys," Kick says, plopping down next to Rod.

"What are you two doing back here?" Cheddar says.

"Escaping the bloodlust," I joke.

"That's not going to be a thing every night is it?" Rod asks.

"They do love their vampires," Kick says.

Rod tips his beer my way. "After they go to bed, I'll hide the remote."

"Cheers to that," Cheddar says, clinking his bottle against Rod's.

There's an awkward silence, Kick and I exchanging glances and Rod and Cheddar not getting the hint. Finally, after what feels like hours, Rod stands up.

"This game's a bust. I'm turning in."

"Yeah, me too. I've got some emails to send," Cheddar says.

"Y'all keep it PG back here," Rod jokes, "or at least PG-13. Nobody wants a tour baby."

"Whoa," Kick says as I say, "We're not…that isn't…"

"Calm down, kids, it's a joke. Get freaky if you want, no one cares."

I don't dare look at Kick, but I can hear his low chuckle.

Cheddar follows Rod out and turns around to wink at us as he slides the door closed behind them.

As soon as they leave, the unspoken tension between me and Kick jumps one hundred percent. The baseball game is still on, the commentators in the background seemingly narrating the two of us.

He's moving around the bases like he's on a mission.

This has been one wild season.

Everyone here can sense what's coming up next.

"You know they think we're gonna—"

"Yeah I think so."

I don't know what to say. This is the first time we've ever hung out without an agenda, or at least, an out loud agenda. I instigated us coming back here but now I've completely forgotten why.

"Seems wrong to disappoint them," Kick says. "I mean, you did ask me to come back here with you."

"We went through a lot today. I need to decompress about it away from teen vampires."

"Technically, Edward is not a teen. He's a very, very old man."

"Are you into that?"

He cocks an eyebrow. "Are you?"

"We're the same age, Kick."

He crosses his arms, a satisfied grin on his face. "Why am I the first person you thought of?"

I ignore that and motion to the TV. "You into baseball?"

He watches the game for a second before he says, "I'm more of a YouTube guy."

"What, like, videos of birds dancing to hip hop? A baby elephant sliding down a muddy embankment? A cat scared of its own meow in a microphone? Or wait, please tell me you don't watch those videos of other people playing video games."

"Cass is right. You are clueless about movies and TV."

"You've been talking to Cass?"

"You think you'd know more about YouTube since your manager runs a popular channel."

"What do you know about my manager?"

He doesn't answer, just smiles at the TV. "So, tonight's show get you all hot and bothered? You need to work out some tension?"

"There are ten different people who could walk through the door at any moment. It's not like I'm going to hop in your lap, yank off my top and let you motorboat my boobs while we watch baseball."

"It'd be a good start."

"Are you ever serious?"

It's not a real question. I saw a glimpse of his serious side after soundcheck, when he told me about his brother. But just as soon as it surfaced, he squirreled it away in favor of flirty, sexy Kick who doesn't have a care in the world.

"Okay, here's a serious question," he says. "Why are you on this tour?"

"Isn't it obvious?"

He feigns shock. "I thought we were being serious here? Tell me what deep emotional wound made living on a tour bus for the entire summer seem like a good idea."

As far as I can tell, he's being genuine. I remain suspicious, but decide to give him a portion of the truth.

"My father was an artist. He got his start in Nashville, playing gigs around town and writing songs with friends. I have his old songwriting journal and reading it feels like knowing him, if that makes sense. His songs are all so personal, which is probably why I write the way I do. Even though I don't remember him, he taught me how to be a songwriter."

"How did he die?"

"Heart attack. My mother says he got his heart broken and then it just gave out on him. We lived in L.A., I grew up there, but I came to Nashville three years ago to, I don't know, find him? Somehow? This tour sort of showed up at the right moment."

Kick nods. "I know what you mean."

We fall into a comfortable silence, the bus rocking back and forth in a soothing rhythm, vibrating us closer and closer. I consider telling him about Sparrow and my father, about the mystery I'm hoping to unravel, how my father's the one who wrote their first big hit, how he has the starting pieces of other hits in his songwriting journal, how none of this would be happening without him.

"What about you?" I ask. "What emotional wound brought you here?"

"My brother." He's not looking at me. "It's something he would have wanted." He blows out a long breath, eyes closed. "But that's a story for another night. When there's not so much sexual tension in the air."

I grab a pillow from the far end of the couch and throw it at him. He throws it right back at me.

"What was your brother's name?"

"Steven."

"How would Steven feel about you blatantly flirting with your...what are we? Song partners?"

"Duo bros?"

I laugh at that. "I will never be your duo bro."

"Give it time, Goldie."

We turn our attention back to the game, neither of us really watching it.

We keep drifting closer, inching toward one another, our bodies moving on their own accord. By the time a new inning starts in the game, we're practically nose to nose. All I have to do is reach a little further and my lips will be on his lips.

Kick reaches up and rubs his thumb softly underneath my eye. "You had a little mascara."

His hand is cradling my face. His eyes are soft, open. If I don't move, we're probably going to kiss. And if we kiss, it will absolutely go further. And if it goes further, it will change our dynamic. And if our dynamic changes, it might ruin our performance, which is too good to let go.

I know I have to be the one to move.

"It's pretty late," I say, backing away and faking a yawn that quickly turns into a real yawn. "I better get my beauty sleep."

Kick rolls onto his back and lets out a deep, dissatisfied sigh. "You should do that. I don't want to share the stage with an uggo."

"You're right. Only room for one uggo up there."

A smile crosses his lips. "See you in the morning, Goldie."

TWENTY-THREE
ROOM FOR TWO IN THE W

I'VE BARELY MADE it off the bus when Emily corners me by the open bay where my suitcase is stowed. She looks like she's been up for hours—full make-up, hair done, dark jeans and a baby blue silk tank top.

"There you are. I need you in hair and make-up right now."

I stare at her, my body still heavy with sleep. "Hair and who?"

She starts walking, expecting me to follow. I do.

"Didn't you get my email? We're doing a quick shoot this morning. I called in some favors. Everything's being set up now inside the venue."

"A shoot? This morning?"

She flashes me an irritated look over her shoulder. "We need photos of you and Kick for merch, a new background, eight-by-tens, the works. And we need them tout suite so yes, this morning."

"Will there be bagels? Maybe some fruit?"

Emily rolls her eyes and tugs on my arm so I'll walk faster. We make our way up a wide concrete ramp into the main backstage hallway of tonight's venue. It's big enough to drive a dump truck through it. A fleet of dump trucks. We follow the circle to an even wider section of the backstage concourse where a full-blown photo shoot is being set up. Two people dressed in all black are unrolling a pristine white infinity backdrop while two more set up huge light boxes on either side. A girl in a buttery yellow hat with a twelve-inch brim rolls in a rack of clothes with two more people rolling two more racks behind her. I'm still in my jammies with sleep crust in my eyes. My hair's twisted into a topknot with half of it falling out in chunks and there are people rolling in racks of clothes for me to try on.

"This way," Emily says and guides me into a side room. There's a long counter set-up with what looks like the entire contents of a Sephora along with rows of hair straighteners and wands and hair dryers and tools I've never even seen before. Two director's chairs are set up in front of the counter surrounded by four bright-eyed stylists ready and waiting to make me presentable.

"This is Mari Gold," Emily says. "I'll go find Kick."

"I'm here," Kick calls from the doorway.

My stomach swoops at the sight of him, obviously just back from another run in the morning humidity. We're in Charleston today and the heat is already ten degrees above favorable.

Emily scowls at his sweaty appearance before saying, "Go shower and then meet us back here ASAP. We're on a tight schedule. And don't shave."

"Can I shower too?" I ask hopefully.

"No. You need more work than he does. We'll," she leans into my shoulder and quickly straightens back up, "give you a few swipes of deodorant."

"Wow, harsh."

I plop down in one of the director's chairs and the glam squad immediately gets to work prepping my skin and combing out my hair while the girl in the hat holds up looks on hangers for Emily to approve. I'd offer to wear my own stage clothes but I can tell by Emily's clenched jaw this is her show and she is not open to anyone's opinion but her own.

"Mari," Emily calls, "how do you feel about booty shorts?"

The make-up artist is dabbing something onto my upper lip so I grunt out what I hope sounds like fine, whatever. I doubt Emily would listen if I said no.

"Hey," Kick says, easing into the chair next to me, his hair still dripping from the shower. He looks pointedly around the room. "Wild, right?"

"Did you know about this? Emily said she sent an email?"

"Heard about it this morning as I was leaving for my run."

"Who did your color?" the hairstylist interrupts, combing his fingers through my hair. He's got a bright red mini-goatee that's grown out to a point, a septum piercing, black winged eyeliner, and bright red hair to match the goatee. "It's stunning."

"My…manager."

"Your manager? I've never met a manger who does hair this good. Are they in Nashville by chance? Are they with a salon? If not do they want to work for a salon?"

"Actually, managing is sort of a part-time gig. Hair's the focus."

"Do you happen to have a photo of your manager? My salon is in East Nashville and we have a certain…look to maintain."

I slide my phone out of the front pocket of my hoodie and pull up a photo of Cass. He gasps. "Perfection."

"She does her own hair, too."

He fishes a card out of the bedazzled fanny pack around his hips. "I'm Gregry. Please have your talented manager-slash-hairstylist give me a call?"

"Sure," I say, already composing a text to Cass to tell her about it.

The stylists go quiet after that, focused on making us photo worthy within Emily's strict timetable. Every time I glance at Kick in the mirror, he's looking back at me which makes me blush and look away which makes him chuckle which makes me blush harder. I need to get control of my transparent face if I'm going to survive this tour.

Kick and I are released at the same time and hurried over to Hat Girl and her racks of clothes.

"You look hot," Kick whispers and I can't argue. Gregry styled my hair in long, spiral curls and then teased them out, pulling part of the sides up into an almost side-pony-knot situation. My make-up is severe but cool—dark eyes, dark lips, pronounced blush that would look clownish if I tried to do it myself. I look a little bit dangerous but somehow still like me.

Kick's fully rocked out, hair combed straight back and tucked behind his ears so the ends curl out around his neck, overnight stubble, enough eyeliner to make an impression, something smooth and inviting on his lips that I need to stop looking at right this second.

"I've pulled looks for them both to try on," Hat Girl says, thrusting several hangers-full at both of us but talking to Emily. "These should work to start. We're thinking three looks total, right?"

Kick and I stand there, holding the clothes, looking around like, *here*?

I wave my hand to interrupt Emily and Hat Girl. "Should we take these to the dressing rooms?"

"No time," Emily says, irritated we're not somehow already dressed, "we're ready to shoot."

Kick's eyebrows shoot up. "You want us to strip down right here?"

"In front of God and everybody?" I add.

Emily sighs. "We're on the clock and I don't have time for you two to be traipsing back and forth from the dressing rooms half a mile down the concourse. Let's go."

Is Emily seriously suggesting I strip down to my underwear in front of Kick? And thinking we'll all stand here while *he* strips down to *his* underwear? I look around the room and make a quick decision before draping my outfit over the back of the make-up chair.

"What are you doing?" Emily says, exasperated.

I start pulling the four long clothes racks into a sort of misshapen W. Kick figures out what I'm doing and jumps in to help. When we're done, we have two makeshift dressing rooms in between the clothes racks that will afford us at least the illusion of privacy.

"Fine," Emily says, "get dressed. Everyone's waiting."

I situate myself in my side of the W and peek over at Kick's side. There are enough cracks between the clothes that I can see him pull his t-shirt over his head. He does it in that movie-guy way, reaching one hand behind his head and pulling the t-shirt up and over. He's careful not to mess up his hair, which makes me giggle.

"You spying on me, Goldie?" His voice is low and teasing.

I bite my lip, taking in his long, sculpted arms. "Nothing I haven't seen before."

"Then why do you look so interested?" he says, bending over to pull off his shorts.

I can't see below his ribs, the clothes blocking my view. But I can imagine. I bet he's a boxer briefs guy. When I lean in closer to find out, he catches me and I quickly look away.

When I turn back around, his back is to me and he's bent over pulling on some black pants. I get my boxer briefs confirmation.

"I know you're looking," he whispers.

"Just making sure you don't need any help. Those pants look pretty tight."

He jumps as he tugs them up and over his very full and squeezable ass. Then he turns and looks me in the eye as he slowly, ridiculously, pulls the zipper up tooth by tooth.

God, this guy.

I shake my head and turn away, pulling my arms into my hoodie and lifting my hands up into the neck to spread it wide as I pull it off, careful of my hair. When I slip off my pajama pants, I hear a low noise and look up to see Kick, hands gripping the garment bar, eyebrows high, one corner of his mouth lifted in a knowing grin.

"Do you mind?' I say, pulling on the skirt I was given. The very, very short, black argyle skirt.

"Just wondering if you've got photos of your little doggie on your underwear."

"Perv," I say, but I'm smiling.

I should be embarrassed, I guess, but I like the look of open want on Kick's face. I like it a lot.

When I pull on the assigned paper thin white t-shirt, my black bra practically glows underneath. "Umm, excuse me?" I call out.

Emily and Hat Girl round the corner. Their expressions slide from worried to confused.

"My bra?"

"Bra?" Kick says, his nose sticking through the hangers. Emily pushes him back to his side.

"I love it," Hat Girl says. "It totally adds to the look." She pulls a boxy pink and black argyle cardigan off the hanger and helps me into it. Next come black knee socks with one wide, white stripe down the side and black combat boots that are taller and chunkier than my Docs. Hat Girl pulls me out of my see-through dressing room to a kit full of jewelry. She starts layering on necklaces and bracelets and rings until she's satisfied I'm camera ready.

"She's perfect," Emily says.

"Is the skirt too…short?" the stylist asks.

"Might as well give the people what they want," Kick says, rounding the corner in distressed black boots, skin-tight black slacks, a fitted black t-shirt and a black collar-less leather jacket covered in black zippers. Hat Girl gives him a chunky skull ring for his middle finger and ties a thin strip of leather around his throat. She stands back and stares at him, shaking her head.

"Something's missing."

Emily joins her and they both stare while Kick drums a

steady rhythm into his thighs with his thumbs, itchy from the scrutiny.

"I think we should lose the shirt," Hat Girl says. "Just go with the open jacket."

"Yes," Emily says.

Hat Girls starts pulling off Kick's jacket and he looks at me, helpless, which makes me laugh.

"Might as well give the people what they want," I parrot back to him.

He flips me the bird as he pulls his shirt over his head and puts the jacket back on, abs and pecs peeking through. My mouth fills with saliva.

"Good," Emily says. "Let's go."

Kick and I take an extra moment to give each other an obvious once over. We look good, separately and together. Like a duo. Like a couple.

Like sex.

I try not to think about that last part.

Kick's hand purposefully brushes mine as we walk out to the set but my attention is suddenly and entirely focused on the photographer walking toward us. The photographer who's photographed my sister on multiple occasions. The photographer who's been to my sister's house for dinner. The photographer who, by the pointed look on his face, knows exactly who I am.

Emily preens. "Kick, Mari, this is our photographer, T.O., a genius if I do say so myself. He's photographed all the greats and is doing us a massive favor by being here today." She turns to him. "I owe you my life."

"Promises, promises," T.O. says, his gaze focused on me.

"Mari Gold," I offer, sticking out my hand and hoping he'll take the hint.

He shakes my hand too long. "Yes, Mari Gold. I've heard so much about you. It's like I've...known you forever."

"And this is Kick Raines," I say, sliding my hand out of T.O.'s and trying to plan a way out of this situation.

T.O. has my mother on speed dial. Polly put him on the map when he shot her for *heartBREAK Magazine*. He was fairly well known before that shoot but after, he became one of the most sought-after photographers in the biz. I can't imagine what strings Emily had to pull to get him here on such short notice but here he is, staring at me like keeping my secret is going to cost me dearly.

"So, T.O.," Emily says, "we're needing some standard press shots and maybe a few posed live shots? We'll be using these for various marketing elements for the tour and socials, of course. Would be great to end up with eight to ten usable shots."

T.O. shifts his focus from me to Emily, sniffing at her like she's a bottle of wine he's considering. "Sounds simple enough." His piercing blue eyes find mine again. "You two ready?"

"Let's do this," Kick says, excitement in his voice. Shedding his shirt has given him a new level of confidence. He's practically bouncing.

T.O.'s two assistants guide us onto the set, a pristine white infinity backdrop that runs all the way out onto the floor without any corners or creases. We're situated next to each other, facing front, arms at our sides. Even though we look like we're posing for passport photos, I know T.O.'s eye. He'll make us look like superstars.

Everyone on set freezes as T.O. starts to shoot.

"Do we smile or play it cool or what?" Kick murmurs through mostly closed lips. "I feel naked over here."

I giggle and T.O. keeps shooting.

Kick and I are shoulder to shoulder, his shoulder higher than mine. I risk a quick side-eye and see he's side-eyeing me too.

"Good," T.O. says. "Good."

Click. Click. Click.

T.O. hands his camera to an assistant who hands him a different camera in one smooth motion.

"Forget I'm here," he says. "Just be with each other."

Kick chuckles to himself and faces me, bending down slightly so we're nose to nose. "You wanna be with me, Goldie?"

Click. Click. Click.

"I don't think that's exactly what he meant."

Kick walks a circle around me and I follow him with my eyes. "You know what they say about all work and no play." He boops my nose and T.O. captures it.

I'm about to argue, tell him to stop playing around, that this is serious, when Kick grabs me around the waist and tosses me over his shoulder, spinning me to face the camera. I can't help the wild laugh that shoots out of me, which T.O. practically salivates over. Kick's hand is gripping my naked thigh, his arm holding my legs in place so I don't fall and how, again, did I get here? How did that night in the alcove morph into us flirting in front of a camera so Emily can put our photo on a t-shirt?

Kick grins over his shoulder at the camera with me flailing in the air, one arm around my legs, his other arm flexing his bicep. When Kick sets me down, I shove him away from me but it's playful.

"Good, Polly, keep that up," T.O. says.

"It's Mari."

"Right." Click. "Mari." Click. Click. "Pardon my mistake. You just look so much like a girl I know named Polly." Click.

He's photographing my see-through face while dancing on the edge of outing me. Probably thinks he's capturing some sort of magic — me, desperate to stay hidden and him attempting to shed my mask in the name of art.

He captures a few more photos and we're sent back to change into our second looks.

I want to talk to T.O., explain my situation, but he's surrounded by a handful of assistants. Even if I had the chance, Emily hurries us along, keeping us on schedule. Hat Girl's on my side of the W holding up a new outfit for me. This time Kick practically knocks the rack over trying to peek at me. I throw a pair of jeans at his head and he ducks back behind the clothes.

My next outfit is a black party dress with a million layers of short black tulle and a bodice with such a deep-V it's more like two strips of fabric coming out of the skirt to cover my boobs. Gregry pulls my hair up in a slicked back ponytail and the make-up team adds more dark eye make-up. My look is finished with mid-calf cheetah print combat boots.

Kick's hair gets roughed up and he's in ripped black jeans and a white linen shirt with the sleeves rolled up, unbuttoned except for one lone button near his belly button.

We look...really good. The fans will go feral for these photos, which is probably Emily's goal.

We take some live shots on the stage, guitars in motion, singing to each other into unplugged mics. If I wasn't so stressed about T.O. spilling his guts to the entire tour, I might even say I'm having a great time. Because being with Kick is always a great time.

"What are you thinking about so hard over there?" Kick says, keeping his photo-ready smile on as he strums his guitar.

How I like you so much even though I shouldn't.

How hot you're going to look in these photos.

How terrified I am it's all about to come crashing down.

How much I'll miss you when this tour's over.

"Food," I say. "I'm really, really hungry."

"Emily," he hollers, "can we get some snacks up here for my better half?"

He is so not making this easy.

TWENTY-FOUR
K.O.'D BY T.O.

IT'S BARELY BEEN forty-eight hours since the shoot and, unsurprisingly, my mother's name is flashing across my phone screen. For half a second, I consider not answering. I'm twenty-four years old and am still not ready to incur the wrath of Candice Lovejoy Barton Moskowitz. But if I don't answer, she'll use her connections to go around me and that would be infinitely worse.

"Hello, Mother."

"Penny, good to hear your voice. Or should I say Ms. Gold?"

Right to the point, I see.

She follows up that revelation with a long, drawn-out silence that tells me exactly how mad she is that I'm on tour with Sparrow. It's a pointed silence, the kind I dare not interrupt lest I poke the already enraged bear.

"Imagine my surprise," she says, audibly drumming her nails, "when T.O. called to tell me he shot my daughter for a tour, only, maybe not my daughter? Some Mari Gold person? Honestly, Penny, are you that ashamed of your family?"

"No." Not ashamed, exactly.

"How you managed to get all the way onto a tour, *a tour with*

Sparrow I might add, without my knowledge is…I don't even have the words for it."

I roll out of my bunk and stumble into the empty front lounge.

"You know how Nashville can be. It just sort of happened."

And I'm an all-the-way adult who can make my own decisions, I don't say. I don't need your permission, I don't say. You're so uninvolved in my life I was able to get on a major tour without you knowing, I don't say.

"But why did it have to happen with Sparrow?" she asks, beyond irritated.

"This is something I wanted. Something I needed to do on my own."

"As Mari Gold."

"I thought, you know, given Sparrow's—"

The bunk door slides open and Mateo stumbles out rubbing his eyes.

"Hang on," I tell her. "Morning, Mateo."

"Morning," he murmurs before laying down on the couch, eyes closed.

"Mom, give me a second to get off the bus."

I go back to my bunk and fish my slides out from under my twisted comforter while she huffs with impatience. Out in the sunshine, I pace back and forth in the parking lot, phone to my ear, hand in my hair.

"When I heard Sparrow was auditioning people to open their tour, I was curious, sure. Given our family history, which I don't technically know by the way, I figured it would be best if I didn't use my real name."

"Deacon and Don recognized you, surely?"

"If they have, they haven't said anything."

I leave out the part that it was Don Sparrow who invited me to the audition.

"But you've talked to them? Spent time with them?"

I can hear it in her voice. She's scared I already know the

thing I still don't know. "Nothing more than short hellos. You know how tours go. The headliner never has time for the opener."

She pauses again, letting the moment simmer.

"Mom, just tell me about whatever happened between my father and the Sparrow brothers. Maybe it's not such a big deal. Besides, I'm proud of myself for earning my way onto this tour. Have you seen any of the livestreams? It's going really well."

She sighs deeply. "I'll have to rearrange some things but I'll get out to a show as soon as I can. Clear this up."

"There's nothing to clear up. I'm fine. Great, actually."

"You're on a major tour and you don't even have representation. Surely you know better than to sign anything that hasn't been read by our attorney."

"Mother."

"I can get some papers drawn up and sent over to Jasmine. Is she still running the show over there?"

"I don't—"

"I'm sure I still have her information."

"Mother."

"I'll have to hire another day-to-day person to cover you, but I think we can—"

"MOTHER."

She blows out a loud breath heavy with irritation. "What is it, Penny."

"I don't want you to manage me."

I've said this before, but never when it had real legs. Never when I was already on a national tour.

"Don't be ridiculous. You have to have representation. Who's looking out for your interests? Who's handling the details?"

"I have someone." I can't tell her it's Cass. She'll burst a blood vessel.

Another sigh, this one so laced with aggravation I can feel it seep through the phone and worm its way through my body, judging me. "So many secrets."

"Not secrets. Just…me living my life."

"A secret life. You're not even using your own name, a name that's highly respected in this industry might I remind you. I cannot for the life of me understand why you would create some ridiculous alter-ego when you have a path that's been laid out for you. You say you want to be an artist and yet you refuse to take advantage of all we've built."

"You built it for Polly, not me."

"I built it for all of us."

"Then why did you leave me alone all those years when I was a kid? If this was all for me, why did I grow up without a mother and a sister? You were gone, Mom. You left me to go tour the world with Polly. So forgive me if I don't buy that this was all for me. My entire life I've had to make it on my own, which is exactly what I'm doing now. It's the only thing I know how to do."

The line goes painfully quiet. I've never spoken so plainly about how she abandoned me to go make Polly a star. The unspoken expectation has been for me to show my support for Polly's career and ignore whatever damage it might have caused. But the truth is they left me. I was just a kid and had to grow up alone.

Now that I've said it, there's no taking it back.

It's a hot morning. I'm working up a sweat pacing around the parking lot and waiting for her to respond. She's quiet for so long I pull the phone away from my face to make sure she hasn't hung up.

Finally she says, "I'm getting another call. We'll talk about this later."

She's gone before I can say, again, that there's nothing to talk about. I'm doing this. I'm finding my own space, my own way.

I don't need her.

I haven't needed her for a long time.

"Hello superstar," Cass says, answering my video call on the first ring.

She's wearing sparkly purple eye make-up and has a bright purple streak in the front of her hair.

"Walk with me?" I'm taking a lap around the venue's main concourse, trying to walk off the call with my mother. "Love the purple. Is it theme night at the salon?"

She checks herself out in her phone's camera. "Mo said her favorite color is purple and I'm trying to make something happen. Too much?"

"You're always too much and never enough."

"I'm so getting Granny G to cross-stitch that on a throw pillow."

I'm walking past a massive merch display when Mo pops around the corner holding a headless body form wearing a Sparrow t-shirt.

"Hey, Mo," I call, turning my phone around so Cass can see her.

"Hey, Mari. Oh! Hey, Cass." Mo's face lights up when she sees Cass, which, adorable.

"Sorry I missed your call last night," Mo says to Cass. "It was a rager crowd and I crashed as soon as I crawled into my bunk."

"Oh, was that last night? I forgot all about it," Cass says, obviously blushing. "Got busy watching old seasons of America's Next Top Model while I did a client's rainbow balayage."

"I can see how that would be more appealing. Tyra does, after all, only have one photo in her hand."

"You two are gross," I tease. "Keep the phone. I'll take a lap and come back."

"Wait," Mo says, "did you hear? There's a laundry room down on the lower level."

"Are you serious?"

"Tons of machines. All free," she says with a huge grin.

"Mo, you're the best," I say, already running to my dressing room to get my suitcase. Stewing about my mother's call can wait. We've been on the road for fourteen days and I've been going commando for the last two.

I'm half-way to my dressing room when I pass Kick and Miguel.

"Laundry room," I shout, breathless. "Lower level."

Their eyes go wide and they run with me.

Turns out, the most exciting thing on a tour isn't the bright lights or the crowds or the long meet-and-greet lines. It's the possibility of clean underwear.

TWENTY-FIVE
SHOULD'VE GONE COMMANDO

I SCREECH when I find it. On the lower level of tonight's venue, just like Mo said, is a fully loaded laundry room. It has fifteen washing machines, fifteen dryers, free detergent, fabric softener, steamers, irons and ironing boards, the works.

I'm frozen, staring at the machines, when Kick and Miguel roll in with their suitcases.

"A laundry room in the venue is so metal," Miguel says, opening the lid of a washing machine and dumping the entire contents of his suitcase into it. It's a heaping pile of black fabric, probably too much for one load, but who am I to judge?

"Every venue should have one of these," Kick says. He's more delicate than Miguel, separating items methodically into two machines. I pick two machines next to Kick's and sort my own piles, my Chop pajama pants the last item to go in.

We're sitting on the machines, chatting about tonight's set, when Don Sparrow walks in with a duffle bag slung over his shoulder.

"Mind if I join y'all?"

Miguel claps his hands together. "As long as I can tell my mom I'm doing laundry with a Sparrow brother. She won't believe it. Mostly the laundry part."

"Even rockstars need clean clothes," Don jokes.

He works to get his laundry started while Kick, Miguel and I exchange glances. It's surreal for Don to be here, doing laundry with us. As much as I've wanted to talk to Don and Deacon and find out more about my father, they're never around, always off at a radio event or interview or whatever else they do all day. The guitar tech mentioned they find a golf course and play a round of golf most afternoons.

Don leans against the whirring machine with his arms crossed over his chest. "I've been enjoying your set every night. You'd never know you two didn't get together until this tour."

"Wow, thank you," I say, shocked. "It means so much that you'd check us out. I know you have a lot going on every night."

Don shrugs. "Never too busy to watch great music. Your alcove songs are really good. You two should think about writing more songs together."

"We didn't write those together," I say. "It was a…happy accident that we both wrote about the same night."

"The night you met, right?" Don asks. I'm surprised he knows so much, has paid attention. "I still think you should work on some songs together. Your chemistry on stage is really special. I bet that energy would translate into some killer new tunes. And you've both proven you're talented songwriters."

"I don't know if one song counts," Kick says.

His neck is tinged red and he's squeezing his thumbs into his palms. He catches my eye and I think back to our conversation before the first show, how he's never written anything but his alcove song.

"Is that what you had with John?" I ask, hoping to redirect the conversation. Don gives me a surprised look so I say, "You mentioned him the first night of the tour. At catering?"

"That's right, I did. John and I had great chemistry when it came to songwriting. He and I wrote 'Calm and Slow' together. If you're looking for advice, the biggest thing you need when writing a song with someone is trust. You have to trust your partner, be open to their input as well as their criticism."

"You should see the way these two argue," Miguel says, jamming his thumb in our direction. "I'd bet they'd write some bangers together."

"What about you," Don asks Miguel. "You ever write any songs?"

"Nah, not me. I'm all about the beat. I'm living my best life playing the low end for these two."

"What about after the tour?" Don asks. "Will y'all keep doing this together, the four of you?"

Kick and I stare at each other like Don just asked if we're planning on getting married after tonight's show. So far, *after the tour* hasn't existed between us. We haven't allowed ourselves to think that far. The tour is the only reality, a reality with no end as far as we're concerned.

"I think it would be rad if we stayed together," Miguel says. "We could keep the good times going."

"You should think about recording your alcove songs," Don says.

Kick nods. "Fans mention that every night in the signing line. They keep asking when the songs will be available to stream."

The washing machine I'm sitting on ends its cycle. I hop off to transfer my clothes into a dryer, grateful to have something to do. This conversation is teetering into territory I'm not ready to deal with yet.

"We have a few days off at home before the Nashville show," Don says, casual, like every word he's saying isn't raising my body temperature by ten degrees. "I have a studio at my house down in Franklin. I'd love for you to come check it out and record some demos. I'd be happy to produce."

Miguel lets out a loud whoop. "Seriously?"

"It's partly a selfish request," Don says. "I just built the studio and I'm dying to break it in."

A silent conversation passes between me and Kick. If we do

this, if we record our songs and put them out there, we'll be tied together for longer than this tour. A lot longer. We will no longer be a tour duo but an actual duo.

"Of course," Don says, "an added bonus is, if you have demos of your songs, you'll be able to shop them around town. I'm sure there are more than a few labels who'd love to work with you."

"Labels?" Miguel says excitedly.

Kick swallows, his eyes wide. He obviously hasn't thought about *after the tour* any more than I have. Recording our songs together? Labels? There are too many unanswered questions we'd have to face before ever getting to that level of commitment.

"What's your band name?" Don asks.

"We're not a band," I say.

Don looks surprised. "I know you weren't originally, but you're so great together."

"I'm down to be a band," Miguel says. "I know Mateo would be too." He raises his eyebrows at me and Kick. "Genre Explosion?"

"My advice," Don says, "capitalize on what works. And what works is the four of you together. Get some more songs under your belt and you'll really have something."

Kick's washing machine beeps. He starts to unload it and then Miguel's beeps. It's a welcome pause in conversation.

Kick and Miguel load their clothes into dryers and come back to our little huddle.

"It's a really generous offer, Don," Kick says, "and we can't thank you enough. Seriously. But," he looks at me, "can we think about it and get back to you?"

I'm sure he's mostly worried about having to write new songs, but I'm glad he's not eagerly accepting Don's offer. Even though Don didn't mention any strings attached, there will be strings. My mother taught me that. Right now, the most obvious one is the decision for the four of us to move forward as a band. Miguel and Mateo are all in, but am I? Is Kick?

Don smiles, not at all worried. "Even if you decide to do it after the tour, my offer stands. I'd be happy to produce some songs for you whenever you're ready."

"That's so incredibly kind," I say.

"We wouldn't be where we are today if others hadn't offered us a hand when we were starting out," he says. "If you decide you wanna record your songs, you know where to find me."

"Don't worry, Don," Miguel says. "I'll talk them into it. I can be a very persuasive person when I need to be. Just ask my mom."

Don laughs and he and Miguel start chatting about Miguel's mother. I can't hear them over the sounds of my heart pounding in my ears. Kick's looking at me like he's hearing the same thing. We've been thriving in the little tour world we've built for ourselves. The outside world hasn't existed. But Don's right, the tour won't last forever. Sooner or later, we'll have to decide how, and if, we're moving forward together.

TWENTY-SIX
DESPITE ALL MY RAGE

AFTER PUTTING my suitcase full of clean clothes back in my dressing room, I slip inside the arena and watch the crew as they finish setting up the stage. Mornings and most afternoons are bustling with activity inside the arena — crew assembling the stage, hanging the light trusses, setting up speakers and the soundboard, the merch team assembling an army of merch booths around the concourse. But there's a lull an hour or two before the doors open when everything's quiet, everyone scattered to the buses or dressing rooms or catering.

I don't know how to think about the conversation with Don, don't know how to categorize my feelings. Part of me thrills at the idea of the four of us becoming a band and doing music together for real. We have great chemistry. We're already growing a fanbase. There are a lot of pros in the pro/con list.

But I never envisioned myself in a band. I'm a singer songwriter. I'm a solo artist. I'm supposed to do this on my own, right?

The bigger question is how long can I keep my real identity out of the spotlight? How long until the Mari Gold facade is uncovered and I become the sister of the famous pop star who went on the Sparrow tour that one time. I jumped into this tour so quickly, I didn't think through what would happen if it worked, what would happen next.

Then there's Kick.

I am definitely not ready to think about Kick.

My brain is too full, too crammed with scenarios and maybes and what ifs. That's when it hits me. I know exactly how to work through my confusing feelings about Kick and the band and Don Sparrow and all of it.

Once I'm sure all the crew members have left and the venue's empty, I slip through the backstage curtains and climb up on stage. There's a huge black banner with the Sparrow logo on it that hangs in front of Sparrow's gear and stage set-up. Kick and I and the twins play in front of it every night. When it's time for Sparrow's set, the banner drops to reveal their staging.

I look around the empty venue and listen for any activity, but it's row after row of empty seats. For half a second, I worry if I'll get in trouble for playing, but decide just as quickly I don't care. I have too much pent-up aggression and rage drumming is the best way to get it out.

One advantage to growing up with a rich pop star sister is the entire studio set-up we had in our house. With my mother and Polly gone so much, I had plenty of time to myself in the studio with a top-of-the-line drum kit. I could rage drum my little heart out until all hours of the night. Whenever I got particularly lonely, which was often, I played guitar 'til my fingers went numb and then drummed until my shoulders and forearms went numb. Music's been the one constant in my life. The only thing that's never left me, the only thing that's ever been mine.

I sit down behind Mateo's kit and get a feel for it, adjusting the stool up for my height. I pull out a pair of drumsticks from the slim bag hanging from the snare and twirl them both in the air. As soon as I stomp the peddle for the kick drum, everything else melts away. It's just me and the beat. No questions, no pressure, no fear, just the steady rhythm of my foot on the kick drum pedal, my arms flying over the snare, the floor tom, the crash cymbal.

I play with my eyes closed, my hands powered by a mix of frustration and want, pouring all of my emotions from the last few weeks into the beat. It feels good. Feels like belonging. And belonging is the only thing I've ever wanted.

As I'm getting out of the shower, my phone's buzzing on the counter. Mo must have left it for me after chatting with Cass.

Cass: Have you seen this?

The next text is a link to a TikTok video. I click the link and there I am, rage drumming for all the world to see. The all-too-familiar face pops onto the screen. She's already posted a dozen videos from the T.O. photo shoot, including photos that weren't officially released, theorizing every smile and glance between me and Kick.

Looks like tour stress might be getting to our Mari Gold. She was caught on camera earlier today playing the drums with enough energy to set the stage on fire. If you ask me, tonight's performance will be straight up explosive. Kick Raines better bring the heat because it's obvious Mari Gold will be.

Me: The arena was empty. How did they get this footage?

Cass: No idea. But you look amazing.

Cass: Like a beast with drumsticks for hands.

Cass: That came out weird but it's a compliment.

Cass: Every drummer wishes they could be a beast with drumsticks for hands.

All I can think about is the comments Kick will definitely make if he sees this.

Hey, Goldie, nice sticks.

Hey, Goldie, if you need to work out some tension, I have some ideas.

Hey, Goldie, do you always get that sweaty when you're…exerting yourself?

Me: If Kick sees this…

Cass: Sorry if he can't handle performing next to an artist who can kick his ass from here to Canada.

Cass: Bottom line, people are seeing you totally rule on the drums. That's a good thing.

Me: Is it? Drumming has always been like, my private thing. I don't love that it's out there for the world to scrutinize.

Me: Because they're not talking about me as an artist. I'm just Kick's maybe-girlfriend, a PR sideshow who happens to rage drum in empty arenas.

Cass: All the great ones are.

"Knock, knock," a voice calls from the door. "It's Cheddar."

"Getting dressed," I call back.

"I need to talk to you. It's important."

The tone of his voice tells me whatever he has to say is the last thing I want to hear. "Give me one second."

I hurry to throw on some clothes and run a towel through my hair before opening the door for Cheddar. I flop down on a worn leather couch against the wall and he sits on the opposite end.

"What's up?" I ask, worried.

He takes a deep breath, like he has to work up the nerve to deliver the news. "We've been getting a lot of comments."

"That's good right? Engagement and whatever?"

"We've been getting a lot of comments about you." He stares at me for a beat. "About you being Polly Lovejoy's sister."

The hairs on the back of my neck stand up. My ears ring. I involuntarily ball my hands into fists.

Here it is, the moment I've been dreading since the audition.

All the rage drumming in the world isn't going to get me out of this. The only way out is to flat out lie, which I don't want to do. Cheddar's been nothing but nice to me.

"What do the comments say?"

I can see it in his face. He already knows.

"Someone posted a photo from when LOVEJOY first started out. She's with her little sister. Her little sister who looks a lot like you."

He taps his phone a few times and spins it around to show me the incriminating photo. There I am, six years old, beaming a toothless grin next to my much older, much cooler sister.

"My team has been deleting everything as it comes in, so it hasn't spread too far. But, Mari, I have to ask. Is it true? Is this you in the photo?"

What happens when I say yes? Will he go to Deacon and Don? Will they reveal they hate my family as much as my family hates them? Will I be kicked off the tour? The next thought in my head surprises me. *Will I ever be able to perform with Kick again?*

Us becoming a band won't matter if I can't even make it through this tour.

Still, I can't say no. It's obviously me in the photo. And I'll need Cheddar on my side if we're going to try and fight the rumors.

"It's me."

He blows out a long breath while shaking his head. "Why didn't you say anything?"

"If your sister was a massive pop star and you wanted to make music in your own way, on your own talent, and not just be known as someone's sister, would you use her famous name?"

He smiles at that. "No, I guess I wouldn't."

"It's not that it's a secret. I mean, it is, hopefully. It's just that I wanted to be on this tour as me, not as LOVEJOY's sister. If people know the truth it's all they'll think of. Not my songs. Not my voice. Just, oh hey, there goes LOVEJOY's sister."

He nods like he gets it. "Does anyone else know?"

"Jasmine knows, but she promised she'd keep my secret. I know it's a lot to ask, but I'd love it if you could too?"

"But we could leverage this. You're already here on your own volition. We could make an announcement, use this to your advantage. I bet twice as many people would stream your set if they knew who you were."

"That's exactly what I don't want."

"But think about how much it would benefit you. And the tour."

Screw the tour, I think.

"I get where you're coming from," I say, "but I have twenty-four years of experience with this. It will not benefit me, or anyone, to announce that I'm Polly's sister."

He's quiet, still thinking about it, trying to decide how to convince me, how to make my personal drama a benefit for the tour.

"I don't want Deacon and Don to know," I say.

He makes a face. "They wouldn't care."

"Trust me. They would."

Don would rescind his offer to produce our songs, that's for sure. Which means it affects Kick and Miguel and Mateo too.

Cheddar goes quiet again. He doesn't have a reason not to tell them other than me asking him not to. I'm sure all he can see are dollar signs and engagement numbers.

"Cheddar, please. I'm asking you, begging you, not to tell anyone. Please. It's really, really important to me. More important than anything."

He sags against the couch. "You really should reconsider." He's quiet for a long, uncomfortable moment before he starts typing on his phone. "I'll make sure my team shuts it down. Any comments or videos or posts will be deleted. But, let me just say again that I think you're making a big mistake."

No, the big mistake I made was thinking I could make it through this tour without anyone finding out I'm a Lovejoy.

TWENTY-SEVEN
WAIT UNTIL THE TIKTOKER HEARS ABOUT THIS

KICK and I are backstage tuning our guitars and getting ready for tonight's show when Deacon Sparrow shows up.

"Hey, you two." He pats us both on the shoulder. "Wanted to say you guys have been killing it on this tour. I'm hearing nothing but good things."

"Thanks," Kick and I say at the same time.

I search Deacon's eyes for any hint that he's learned the truth, if my mother called him or if Cheddar's broken my trust and told him I'm a Lovejoy. He's hard to read, just like Don. Even though we've seen Don a handful of times, we never see Deacon except right before we go on. Sparrow doesn't do their own soundchecks and Deacon never comes to catering.

"Have you had a chance to catch our set?" I dare to ask.

Before he can answer, Nic shows up and calls him away.

"What do you think he would have said?" Kick asks.

"Nothing we'd want to hear." I strum my guitar half-heartedly. "It's like we're on two different tours."

He pauses, waits for me to meet his gaze before he says, "I'm glad I'm on the one you're on."

He keeps saying things like this, things that border on sincerity instead of shameless flirting. Things that will eventually need to be dealt with. Between my mother's threats to blow up the tour and Cheddar's knowledge of the truth about me and Don's suggestion that we become a legitimate band, I have more than enough things to deal with. I can't handle Kick's puppy dog eyes.

"Kick," I murmur, unsure what I should say next.

A familiar screech echoes down the hall, interrupting us. I squint into the distance and my mouth falls open in surprise as my pretend manager flys straight toward me. I pull my strap over my head and shove my guitar at Kick just in time to grab Cass in a huge embrace. Cass, who is very much smaller than me, picks me up off the ground with the force of her hug.

"What are you doing here?"

"Came to see rising star Mari Gold," calls a familiar voice behind Cass.

It's none other than Jackson Lord.

"It's so good to see you, babe," he says, wrapping his arms around both me and Cass. I feel Kick's eyes on me as Jackson spins the three of us in a half-circle.

I pull away and grab them both by their shoulders. "What is happening right now?"

"You think I wasn't going to come see my best girl on her big tour?" Jackson swings his All Access pass around his neck like *ta da*.

"Best girl?" Kick says.

"Jackson Lord," Jackson says, holding his hand out to Kick, "Nashville screenwriter and filmmaker."

Cass and I exchange a look. We've never heard him introduce himself as a screenwriter or a filmmaker.

Kick takes his hand but his expression looks like he wants to commit a backstage murder.

"Seriously, what are you two doing here?" I say. "I had no idea you were coming, but I'm so happy to see you!"

Jackson winks at me and turns to Kick. "I've been watching

your livestreams. Y'all are hot shit together. I'd love to film you sometime."

Kick side-eyes me. "Thanks?"

"Give it a rest, Jackson," Cass says.

Jackson catches on, but only five percent. "My dad starred in a video for Sparrow a few years back and is friendly with the band. Since my best girl was out on the tour, I thought I'd come check it out. Cass begged me to bring her along."

"I remember meeting you at your house," Kick says. "At a party last April?"

"That's right," Jackson says, dragging out the words. "Y'all's cute little alcove songs. I love that this all happened because of my party. Didn't I tell you Pen…Mari? I said my party would be worth coming to, didn't I?" He looks at Kick. "You're welcome, by the way."

He and Kick share a look like they're daring the other to make the next move. Jackson's trying to take credit for me and Kick and Kick's looking at Jackson like he might grab my acoustic and swing it directly at his face.

"I can't wait to watch you live and up close," Cass interjects. "And maybe peruse the merch stand. Check out the… merchandise."

"So you didn't just come to see me?" I joke.

"I'll *buy* your merch," she says. "If that merch happens to be sold by a beautiful merch goddess named Mo I am definitely hoping to kiss? All the better."

Rod finds us and circles his finger in the air like a propeller. "Time to roll."

"You can get in this way," Kick says, motioning for everyone to follow him.

Cass and Jackson have tickets so they go find their seats while Kick and I wait side stage.

"So. That guy. Not a musician, huh."

Kick's face is a mask of torment. He's working so hard to hide it it's doing nothing but shining a bright light on how bothered he is. Does he actually think something's going on with me and Jackson? That I've been hiding it this entire time?

Then I remember Jackson's snide comment about his connection to Sparrow.

"Just so we're clear, Jackson's supposed 'in' with the band has nothing to do with me. I promise you I got that audition on my own."

Kick shakes his head and opens his mouth, closes it again. Puts his hands on his hips. Puts them on his head. Turns around in a circle, his guitar nearly knocking into me. "You're dating that guy?"

I can't help the laugh that bursts out of me.

"He called you his best girl," Kick says. "Twice."

The look on Kick's face can't be anything other than jealousy. I can't stop laughing because Kick Raines, America's Most Desirable, the guy people drool over every single night, the guy whose pockets are stuffed full of phone numbers after every meet and greet, is jealous.

"Are you serious?"

Kick cocks his head, waiting. "You haven't answered the question. Are you two a…thing?"

"Jackson Lord believes the world exists for him to reign supreme over. He's one hundred percent about making connections, knowing people, and being known by people. He's only here to flex that he has access to the band."

"So, you're not dating him."

If I could stuff the look on Kick's face into a jar and keep it on a shelf, I would. His normally confident veneer has cracked, part of his heart peeking through. I look him in the eye as Deacon and Don hop up onto the stage steps in front of us, waiting for us to follow.

"Why does it matter?" I flip my hair when I say it and his eyes go hilariously wide.

Kick grits his teeth but follows me up on stage. We plug in as the Sparrow brothers introduce us and rev up the crowd. I can hear Cass screaming from the third row and it fills me to the brim with joy. I look over at Kick and his eyes are boring into me, waiting for confirmation to his question. The Jackson possibility has punched Kick's energy into overdrive. I flash him my brightest, sweetest smile and he bites his lower lip and closes his eyes.

This is going to be so good.

As soon as the spotlights hit us, we're all fire and spirit, throwing everything we've got at each other as we launch into "I Kissed Her In An Alcove." Kick's singing like he has something to prove, like he's singing straight to me, to Jackson, letting us both know exactly how it went down that night in Jackson's backyard. The crowd is giving it right back, the entire venue a giant ball of crackling energy. We sing like we haven't sung before, play like we haven't played before. Miguel and Mateo are giving it just as hard.

When the song ends, we're both out of breath, watching each other, our faces glowing in the bright stage lights. It's the perfect moment to let my guard down and show Kick what I'm made of.

I lean into the mic, still watching Kick, and drop a bomb big enough to rattle the internet. "I can't believe you wrote that song about me."

The screams are so loud I can't hear my own laughter. Kick's face goes from surprise to something downright dirty. We've never admitted this online, never in a meet and greet line, never on stage. I don't know why we've been avoiding it since everyone already assumes, but saying it out loud tightens my stomach in the most delicious way. I'm standing in front of twenty-three thousand people confessing I made out with Kick Raines in a tiny alcove.

And I liked it.

Kick leans into the mic and shakes his head. "I can't believe you'd tell on me like that in front of all these nice people."

The giant screen behind him projects his face all the way to the back row of the third balcony. He's beaming so bright the screen's in danger of cracking down the middle.

"What, like you told on me in that song? The alcove was our thing and then you made it everybody's thing."

My flirty mouth is running away with me and I'm happy to watch it go. Maybe Kick's jealousy over Jackson is a good thing because suddenly I have nothing to lose.

"If I recall," Kick says, eyes on me, his sparkle gaze piercing my soul, "you wrote a song about the alcove too." He looks out across the audience as they gulp down every word we're saying. "Hey, Chicago, would you like to hear the song Mari Gold wrote about kissing me in an alcove?"

The roof shakes with their cheers and applause.

"Good God, woman. I've never seen you play like that, ever," Cass says once we're offstage and in the back hallway.

I pull her away from anyone who might be listening, namely Kick. "Was it too much?"

"Smoke'll be coming out of the internet tonight but no, I don't think it was too much. I think you and Kick are the greatest duo since Joey and Chandler."

"So you think we're good as a duo?"

"Mari, we've been over this a million times, but since you're a moody artist who cannot absorb actual facts, I'll say it again. Today is not forever. Being the opener for one act, for one summer, even as a duo, doesn't define your entire career. This is only the beginning. A massive, incredible beginning. I'm your manager. I should know. And you can't tell me that wasn't fun."

"It was fun, yes, more than fun. But what if this is like when an actor gets a big role right out of the gate and then can't ever play anything else ever again because they're always known as that first character. Like the Luke Skywalker guy."

"First of all, Mark Hamill is an actual cinnamon roll human and we will only speak of him with glowing praise. Second, you are not Mark Hamill."

"I could be Mark Hamill."

"No. You're Mari Gold, Manipulator of Melodies and Crafter of Words. White Hot Performer. Stage Vixen. One summer as a duo can't change that."

"What if it's more than one summer?"

She pauses, stunned. "What do you mean?"

"Don Sparrow told us he'd produce our songs so we could shop them around town. As a band. Like, that we'd do this for real. Be a band. The four of us. Me and Kick and the guys."

Her eyes go impossibly wide. "I love that so much. So much! What did you say? What did Kick say?"

"Kick said we'd think about it."

She grins and lovingly squeezes my shoulders. "Everything's coming up Mari Gold. You, my love, are a star."

"Who's a star?" Kick says. His cheeks are flushed and he's still breathing hard.

"You two," Cass says. "And if you're asking, my vote is yes to the band, yes to recording with Don, yes to all of it. You should definitely, definitely do it."

Kick's shit-eating grin takes over his whole face. "I've been telling Goldie that since the night we met."

I roll my eyes as dramatically as I can. "Would you shut-up? She means we should be a band."

"Oh wow," Cass says, catching on. "He really is as bad as you said he is."

He's still grinning. "You told her I'm a bad boy?"

"I told her you're a dumbass. Now go away so I can talk to my manager in private."

Kick throws his hands up in surrender. "Fine. Wouldn't want to interrupt your conversation about me being a bad boy."

I watch him walk away and Cass shakes her head. "There is no way the two of you haven't ripped each other's clothes off."

"We haven't and we won't. We're professionals."

She looks down the hall at Kick who's still walking backwards, smiling at us. "It's only a matter of time."

TWENTY-EIGHT
WE CAN'T HAVE THINGS IN COMMON. THAT WOULD RUIN THE VIBE.

I'VE STARTED DRUMMING, not always in a rage-y way, every afternoon before doors. Some of the crew have seen me, but no one seems too bothered by it. It levels me out in a way nothing else does. Some people do yoga. Some meditate. I drum.

Today when I walk out onto the stage, two drum kits are set up in front of the Sparrow backdrop. The new one is a Yamaha set which isn't used for shows since Sparrow has an endorsement with Pearl. I can't imagine why the crew would set out two drum sets but figure they'll be taking it away soon enough.

I sit down at Mateo's kit and pull out some sticks. Before I can hit the first downbeat, I sense someone else on stage with me.

"What's up, Goldie."

Kick's sitting at the Yamaha kit, sticks in hand, close-lipped grin on his face.

I rest my chin on the tip of a drumstick and attempt a glare that is definitely coming off as me fighting a giant smile. "What are you doing up here?"

We haven't really talked about anything that's happened the last few shows—Don's offer, the possibility of becoming a band, the way we brazenly flirted with each other in front of thousands of people at the Chicago show.

Cass was right, smoke did come out of the internet. Cheddar nearly had a fit screaming about numbers and trends and growth percentages. Our signing line has grown longer every single night. We've kept the flirting routine going on stage, but off stage, maintained our friendly rivalry.

Kick shrugs. "Thought I'd come see what you're made of."

I sit up straighter, ready for the challenge he's obviously proposing.

"This is supposed to be my private drum time. I mean, do you even play?"

"Oh, come on. You're not scared of a little competition, are you?"

He's bouncing on his stool like he just instigated a round of chicken in the swimming pool, not a drum-off on an arena stage. No matter. I'm ready. I'm always ready.

I throw my chin in the air, a subtle acceptance of his challenge.

"I won't go easy on you."

"You never do."

Without preamble I launch into my favorite drum fill—a complicated rhythm with triplet-fills and double kick flourishes. It's technical and precise and, for someone who doesn't really play, very, very difficult. When I'm done, I point one of my sticks at Kick in challenge.

He throws me a big toothy smile and proceeds to play the same fill. Beat for beat. Perfectly. I can't decide if I'm more irritated or impressed.

I play another fill, a showy number that's all drama with big swings and stick spins and an abundance of cymbal crashes, hoping Kick is more of a technical drummer than a showboat.

By the end, my heart's racing and beads of sweat have popped up across my forehead.

Kick rolls his shoulders and spends a few seconds in concentration before launching into the combination, playing it like a pro, his arms flying over the high tom and the floor tom, his cymbal crashes powerful and dramatic.

When he finishes, he takes his time looking at me, slowly rolling his head to the side, like he's sure I'll be irritated.

"Where'd you learn to play like that?" I'm doing my best to hide how impressed I am but feel sure it's written all over my transparent face.

"I could ask you the same thing. You're badass."

We're both breathing heavy and sweating, glowing from the inside out.

"You have some earbuds?"

He leans back and fishes a pair out of his front jeans pocket. I connect his pair to my phone so we can listen to the same song.

"Do you know Nirvana's 'Smells Like Teen Spirit?'"

He squints at me. "Would I be allowed to call myself a musician if I didn't?"

I queue up the song and as soon as I hit the downbeat, he's right there with me, drumming in sync. Together, we plow through the song, our duet rocketing through the entire arena. We keep checking in with each other during the song, watching each other, staying in sync. Playing beside Kick, my beats hit harder, my timing perfect.

We play through all my rage drum favorites—Metallica "Enter Sandman" and Black Sabbath "Paranoid" and Foo Fighters "Everlong"—completely aligned on each song. I can't stop watching him, his arms flying, his shoulders flexing under his tight t-shirt. He looks like a fantasy, like a poster teenage me would hang on her wall of a sweaty, sexy drummer going all out.

I half-wonder if I look like he does. If Kick finds me posterworthy.

At the end of "Everlong," we notice we've drawn a crowd. A handful of crew guys are watching from Kick's side of the stage and clap when we stop playing. Emily's there too, phone up, recording us, a satisfied smile on her face.

"Show's over," I say, getting up from Mateo's kit and bending over to wipe my sweaty face on the bottom of my Celine Dion t-shirt.

"Hey," Kick touches my forearm softly as I move past him. His skin is hot, his fingertips searing into my skin. "That was really fun."

My eyes drift from his face to his shoulders to his lips to his eyes. "Maybe we can do it again sometime."

He holds my gaze, saying absolutely yes with his eyes.

Emily smirks at me as I'm coming down the stairs. "You two make my job so easy."

"You're the one who's been feeding photos and videos to that TikToker."

"Just doing my job, Mari."

I stare at her, looking for the hidden meaning. "But why be so secretive about it? Think about how I feel, seeing videos of myself I didn't even know were being filmed."

She's tapping out a message on her phone as she says, "A good lesson to learn as early as possible is you have to feed the machine what it wants. I'm helping you do that."

"Helping me or helping yourself?"

She shakes her head, done with the conversation. "The sooner you stop resisting, the better off you'll be. Look at Kick," she says, motioning behind me where he's happily chatting with the crew guys, "you don't hear him complaining, do you?"

When I look back at her, she's typing on her phone, probably sending the video of me and Kick drumming to her TikTok contact. Even though she says she's doing this for me and Kick, I know there's more she's not saying. There's no way the end game doesn't somehow benefit her.

TWENTY-NINE
ROCK, PAPER, SCISSORS, SHIT

KICK bumps hips with me as I'm bent over pulling my suitcase out from the bay underneath the bus. I look up at him over my shoulder with a question.

"I can't eat one more deli tray lunch from catering," he says with a groan.

"Sliced cheese finally lost its appeal, huh?"

"What do you say we see what St. Louis has to offer?"

It's a loaded question. Even though we spend every day together, sleep three feet apart, eat every meal together and flirt relentlessly on stage every night, Kick and I don't hang out. It's easier to avoid The Big Questions when we don't allow room for them to materialize.

"Where would we go?"

There's a twinkle in his eye. "Somewhere that isn't a venue."

His offer *does* sound pretty great. I'm beyond tired of cold cuts and potato salad. I shove my suitcase back into the bay and gesture to myself. I'm wearing denim cut-offs and a hot pink sports bra under a stretched out Weezer t-shirt. "This okay?" I say, gathering my hair into a haphazard knot at the crown of my head.

"You're perfect." He holds his phone out in front of him,

moving right past the perfect comment. "I found this site that has all the fun things to do in downtown St. Louis. I say we scroll, stop on something random and go do that."

"I thought you said we could get lunch. Sushi?"

He squints at me. "I don't trust sushi in a landlocked state."

"Fair, but doesn't a spicy tuna roll sound so good right now?"

I know he likes spicy tuna rolls from a conversation I overheard between him and the Vampire Twins talking about desert island foods. He said he loved spicy tuna rolls but didn't think they qualified since raw fish would be plentiful in an island situation.

"A loaded burger bigger than my face sounds so good right now," he counters.

"How about we rock paper scissors for it? I win, we find some non-suspicious sushi. You win, we find a sports bar and you can get the biggest, greasiest burger of your dreams with an extra side of mayo."

"How do you know I like mayo on my burgers?"

"Don't you?"

Kick rolls his eyes and tucks his phone under his arm. He places his left fist in his right hand. I match him, counting down.

"Rock, paper, scissors, shoot."

He shoots a rock and I shoot scissors.

"Burger it is," I say as he cries, "yes!"

I follow him around the buses and back into the venue.

"Shouldn't we be going the other direction?" I ask. "St. Louis is that way."

"We're a mile or so from the action. A tour runner can take us over there and drop us off."

So, this wasn't a spontaneous lunch invite. He thought about it.

"What were you going to do if I'd said no?"

"Go with Miguel and Mateo."

I can't help the twinge of disappointment that shoots through my chest. "You'd really choose to spend the day listening to their theories about why Kiefer Sutherland's vampire is far superior to Brad Pitt's vampire?"

"Personally, I prefer Ian Somerhalder."

"Who's that?"

He startles, stopping in his tracks. "You've never watched *The Vampire Diaries*?"

"Cass claims I am pop culture illiterate when it comes to film and TV. She keeps a list on her phone of shows and movies I need to watch before I die. Anyway, why do you have a favorite vampire? Don't tell me one of your hidden talents is cosplaying as a fanged creature of the night at ComicCon."

He shrugs. "I went through an Ian Somerhalder phase."

I'm about to ask him to expound on that multi-layered answer when we find Freddy, one of the runners for today's show.

"Hey, man," Kick says, shaking his hand. "Would you be able to give us a ride to lunch?"

"Absolutely. You need a recommendation?"

"Kick needs a burger," I say.

"Yeah, burger's good. Love burgers," Freddy says with a nod. "You like video games?"

"Sure," I say, assuming Kick does because come on, video games.

Freddy snaps his fingers in the air. "I know the perfect place."

We follow Freddy out to a black SUV parked in the lot behind the loading bay. I expect Kick to get in the back seat with me, but he climbs into the front. It's a six-minute drive and Kick and Freddy chat the whole way about St. Louis, Freddy talking a mile a minute about the St. Louis Cardinals and how he's lived here his whole life and how his parents were both from St. Louis and their parents too. He pulls the SUV to a stop in front of a red brick building on a downtown corner.

"You'll love this place. Tons of vintage video games, pinball machines, burgers, the works."

"Thanks, man," Kick says, opening his car door.

Freddy hands him a card with his number on it. "You guys have fun. Call me when you need a ride back."

We cross the sidewalk and step inside. A blast of cold air hits us as we walk through the door. It's more arcade than bar, dozens of vintage arcade consoles lining the walls on the three sides not taken up by the bar. Down the middle, flanked by tall tables and chairs, are rows of back-to-back pinball machines. The lights are low but it's still bright, the bar glowing from within by millions of blinking lights.

"You should know," Kick says, "I am amazing at pinball."

"That sounds like a challenge."

"It could be, Goldie," he leans down so we're nose to nose, "if you think you can handle me."

There's no other way to say it. I have a sudden and overwhelming urge to get it on with Kick Raines, fully, like a sex-crazed wildcat prowling for fresh meat. Just grab him in the middle of a St. Louis video game bar and go to town. It's the same invisible force that's been pushing me toward him for weeks, whispering in my ear to *do it already*. Fighting my inner-horndog is a daily struggle, especially when he blatantly flirts with me and bats his ridiculous eyelashes and practically offers himself to me in every subtle way a person can. Cass says it's inevitable, wonders what I'm waiting for. I'm having more and more trouble coming up with a believable answer.

I wonder if he can see it on my face, how much I want to give in. If he does, he's hiding it well. I shove the wildcat down, *again*, and push past him into the bar.

There are a few people scattered around but the place is fairly empty. We find a table and I avoid looking at him, which I've decided is the key to the whole wanting-to-jump-him problem. If I don't look at him, I can remember that we're partners, that the on-stage chemistry is working too well to mess it up, that the likelihood he wants to be with me in a real way is too unlikely to risk everything else. He just likes the chase, the innocent flirt. He's never said anything substantial to insinuate he really wants to go deep with me. A momentary release isn't worth screwing up everything else we have together no matter how great it might be.

And I bet it would be *so* great.

"Goldie," he says, waving a hand in front of my face.

"Sorry. What?"

"I was saying there's a Star Wars pinball machine over there that's calling my name. Care to make a wager?"

I look over and see the machine he's talking about. It has a huge image of Luke Skywalker waving a lightsaber. I can't help but think, *what would Mark Hamill do*? "What's the wager?"

He takes his time deciding, his eyes never leaving my face. I keep looking away, acting interested in the games, the menu, the building, anything but him.

"I got it," he says, forcing me to focus on him. "I win, you have to ask Deacon Sparrow for his autograph. Not Don. Deacon."

"On a scale of one to ten, ten being the most, I am a solid one hundred no way am I doing that." I've heard the things my sister has muttered under her breath about hangers-on who ask for an autograph. Drivers who want one for their kid. Servers who want one for their friend. As the opener of the tour, it would be the ultimate kiss of death if I acted like a fan, which, is probably why Kick's making it the wager.

"You win," he says, "we switch bunks."

I cross my arms and lean back in my chair. "You would seriously give up your back middle bunk, arguably the best bunk on the bus, over a pinball game I am definitely going to win?"

He shrugs and purses his lips like he isn't scared of me in the slightest.

"You don't even know if I'm good at pinball or not. I could be, like, the Pinball Champion of Nashville. Of America. I could have competed in international pinball competitions. I could have an entire shelf lined with pinball trophies at my house."

"Then you shouldn't be worried about a friendly little wager."

He's either truly amazing at pinball or is certain I could never beat him, because no way would he willingly give up his bunk.

"You're on."

We find the token machine and Kick slides a five-dollar bill into the slot. We rock, paper, scissors to decide who plays first. I win and settle myself in front of the machine. I've played a few times, but definitely inflated my capabilities. Still, it's pinball. How hard can it be?

When I pull back on the plunger, I'm completely in the zone. There's a second set of flippers on the upper level, which I hit, and immediately get fifty thousand bonus points.

Kick's standing close to me, eyes on the machine, lighting up my nervous system like he just hit *my* second set of flippers. My ball pings against the Luke Skywalker stand-up and Mark Hamill's voice rings out. *Use the force.* I play so well I get an extra ball, which I can sense worries Kick. By the time my game is over, I've scored over ten million points. 10,457,992 to be exact. I pull out my phone and take a photo of my score, just to be safe.

"Your turn, big talker."

Kick hip checks me out of the way and assumes the position.

He loses a ball immediately and my confidence shoots through the roof. No more sleeping on rolling tires! No more bathroom smells! I will finally have the middle bunk of my dreams!

He keeps his second ball going for a while and eventually hits the top flippers, scoring his own fifty thousand bonus points. His broad hands are cupped around the machine, his middle fingers jamming the flipper buttons lightning fast. It makes my toes curl and the back of my neck burn.

I watch his score climb higher and higher, my dreams of a middle bunk slowly fading away. He ends his game with a score of 10,543,710. I am defeated.

"Best two out of three?" I ask, hopefully.

Kick slings his arm around my neck and pulls me into him. "Let's get those burgers. You need to load up on protein before you humiliate yourself asking Deacon for his autograph."

"I am never going to do that."

My heart thrums as my cheek rubs against his neck. He's not usually this loose with me, this tactile. He's always flirty, but not in a physical way.

He keeps his arm around me as we walk back to the table and I wonder if this is a date. Could it be a date? Does Kick think it's a date? We're alone, having a meal, touching and flirting. My stomach flips. I shouldn't be on a date with Kick Raines. We're professionals. Co-workers, essentially. We're supposed to keep it about the music, the performance, the show.

But. If I'm already *on* a date with Kick Raines, I may as well make the best of it, right?

THIRTY
WE'RE WRITING THIS ONE IN PERMANENT INK

"SO, when are you going to tell me more about that tattoo?" I ask, biting a fry in half.

Kick's been worrying his thumb over his clavicle tattoo a lot today, usually when he thinks I'm not looking. I've noticed his hand absentmindedly goes to it every few minutes.

"What about you?" he asks, redirecting. "You have any tattoos?"

"Not any you're allowed to see."

His eyebrows go up. "I've seen quite a bit, if you recall."

I decide to let that go. For now. "There is one I've always wanted to get."

He takes a huge bite of his loaded burger with mayo and motions for me to go on.

"I have this photo of my father."

"The songwriter, right?"

I pause and pull the photo up on my phone. I saved a screenshot of the original in case the print got damaged. I turn my phone around to show Kick. "I've always wanted to get an orange flower, like the ones on his shirt."

"I've seen this photo. It's on your guitar."

I shrug, embarrassed. "I know it's weird, since I didn't

know him, but I like having him close to me when I play. The guitar I play, it's his. There's some part of me that thinks playing it will give me some of his talent by osmosis or something. Like I can be, maybe not as good as him, but some version of it."

He studies the photo, expanding it with his fingers to look closer at my father's shirt. "The flowers on his shirt, they're marigolds."

My cheeks burn. I never thought he'd notice.

"And your name is Mari Gold," he says.

"I...when I...yes. Those are marigolds on his shirt."

I'm trying to come up with a better response when the server comes over to check on us.

"How's everything tasting?"

"Could I get some more water, please?" My voice cracks.

I've wanted to tell Kick the truth, should have told him, but I've been so afraid. I made the mistake of getting too close, letting him in enough to matter. Losing him now would break me.

The server is back at our table with a pitcher of water, refilling my glass, and Kick's still staring me down.

"I hope you guys don't mind me asking but, you're Kick and Mari, aren't you?"

"That's us," Kick says.

The server pumps their fist up in victory. "I am *such* a huge fan of you guys, you don't even know. Those alcove songs? I've watched like, three of your livestreams."

"That's so cool, thank you," I say.

"Are you coming to the show tonight?" Kick asks.

"No, which is the biggest bummer of my life. When I tried to get tickets, the show was already sold out."

Kick pulls out his phone. "What's your name? I'll get you on the comp list."

The server's eyes pop open so wide I can't help but laugh. "Are you serious?"

"I'm completely serious. But I'll need you to do something for me, if you don't mind."

"Anything. I'll do absolutely anything."

"Could you direct us to a good tattoo shop? Preferably walking distance from here?"

"Rowdy's is two doors down. Opens at one, I think? He did this one for me." The server turns their forearm out and shows us their arm-sized tattoo of a wolf howling at the moon.

Kick's foot finds mine under the table. "Looks like Mari Gold's getting a tattoo today."

The server, Ez, is delighted. "I'll be back in a bit to check on you."

After they leave, Kick's still rubbing his foot against mine under the table.

"Mari Gold is my stage name," I say. My pulse pounds in my neck.

"Because of your dad's marigolds."

"I don't, um, I don't really tell people my real name."

His gaze is intense. "Do you want to tell me?"

"I do, but…it's complicated."

"Life would be pretty boring if it wasn't complicated."

I blow out a long breath and rest my chin in my hand. It's the easiest thing in the world, introducing yourself to someone, but the words are stuck in my throat. Despite the kindness in his eyes and everything I know to be true about him, this might be the moment I lose him.

"I'm Penny Lovejoy." Saying it out loud feels like a punch to my stomach. "Polly Lovejoy is my sister."

"Wow. Okay."

"And my father, John Lovejoy, was one of the original members of Sparrow. He's the one who wrote 'In A Dark Wood.'"

He scrunches his eyebrows together in confusion.

"They don't know," I say. "I never met them before this tour and my mother hasn't been in contact with them since before I was born. There was some falling out between my father and the Sparrow brothers."

"Which is why you're Mari Gold instead of Penny Lovejoy."

"Exactly. My mother always refused to give me details. She went apoplectic when she found out I was on the tour."

He sits back, hand on his chin. "And no one on the tour knows?"

"Jasmine knows. And Cheddar found out."

"Cheddar?"

"He, of course, thinks I should shout if from the rooftops so more people will tune in to the livestreams. I tried to explain that's the exact thing I don't want. I want to be here because of me, not because I'm someone's sister."

"And Mari Gold isn't anyone's sister."

I hold my breath and wait for him to ask me about Polly, ask when she'll be coming out to the tour, tell me he'd love to meet her.

He takes a bite of his burger. He swallows it. He takes a long drink of water.

"Your sister is really talented." My stomach sinks. Here it comes. Or more accurately, here it all goes. Everything we've built together on this tour is about to evaporate on the next words that come out of his mouth.

"And judging by Sparrow's songs, your father was too. But it doesn't matter what your name is. It doesn't matter who your sister is or who your father was. I know you. *You.* You're like this…pain in the ass miracle of a person. You drive me absolutely crazy and make every day better with your sassy mouth and your big brown eyes. And your talent." He shakes his head. "You're scared about people knowing you're Penny Lovejoy but you could call yourself Spacesuit Susan and you'd still be most incredible artist I've ever seen."

Tears spring to my eyes. His words are like water to my thirsty soul. I just gave him the one thing that could hurt me the most and instead of driving the knife deeper, he's saying everything I've been longing to hear.

"So you're…you don't care that I'm LOVEJOY's sister?" My voice shakes, giving me away.

Kick sets his burger onto his plate and reaches across the table to take my hand in his. He looks deep into my eyes and says, "I care about you."

I want to believe him. I'm trying to believe him.

"Thank you for telling me," he says.

I search for any sign that he's like all the others. That he'll betray me the first chance he gets. All I see is sincerity. Kindness. Something more I don't dare name.

"Thank you for being someone I trust enough to tell."

And please, please, please, *don't make me regret it.*

Thirty minutes later I'm on what looks like a massage table, my arm turned out with a light beaming on it. Rowdy the Tattoo Artist is pressing a stencil of the marigold he drew onto my arm so I can approve it before he does the ink.

"I can't believe you're making me do this," I say to Kick. He's practically rubbing his hands together in glee.

"This is the best way to memorialize your dad. And this tour. This summer…all of it."

We lock eyes while Rowdy peels off the paper covering the marigold design. Right in the crook of my left arm is a delicate, tiny orange flower, exactly like the ones from my father's shirt. It's perfect. A piece of him I'll always have with me, close to me. Even though I don't remember him, I've always felt closer to him than my mother or Polly. Like him, I'm a songwriter. Like him, I'm emotionally connected to the music. Polly and my mother have always been about the fame, the money, the spectacle. That's never been me. I want to create like my father did, want to make moments with music, give people something to hold on to, relate to. From everything I've learned about my father, he was the same way. And now he'll be with me permanently.

"I love it, thank you," I say.

Rowdy gets to work and I look over at Kick. "I'm getting a needle jammed into my arm. It's only fair you distract me and tell me about your tattoo."

"I already told you. It's a melody Steven and I made up when we were little."

"But there has to be more to it."

"This is about you, not me."

"Come on. Take my mind off what's happening to my arm right now."

He shakes his head but he's smiling. "When Steven was about eight and I was five, we decided to write a song for our parents." He rubs his tattoo. "We sat side-by-side at the piano, which was our first mistake. We only got through three measures before we started fighting and got in trouble. We never finished the song."

"What were the lyrics?"

"We never made it that far. The plan was to write it about snacks. Being eight and five, our lives pretty much revolved around snacks."

I can't help but giggle. "I'm twenty-four and my life revolves around snacks."

"After he died, the little melody we'd written came back to me one night when I was trying to sleep. I thought this way I'd never forget it."

"You know, you light up when you talk about him," I say.

He smiles a sad little smile. "I haven't been able to talk about him much since...everything. But you're so damn pushy."

"One of my many talents. And hey, I don't think I can explain what it means to be getting this tattoo, but it means a lot. More than you know. Thank you for your forceful suggestion."

I expect him to say something flirty, something to break the tension. Instead, he reaches over and takes my right hand, pulls it to his lips and softly kisses my knuckles. "You're welcome."

I want so much to believe he means it, that his sparkle gaze is just for me. That it's not all a put-on for the show or the fans or the gimmick of the whole Marick song-and-dance. No one who's ever treated me this way has meant it, has wanted me for me. And as scared as I am to find out if he feels something real for me, I'm even more terrified to admit how hard I'm falling for him.

THIRTY-ONE
BANJO BY SIX

WE DECIDE to walk back to the venue instead of calling Freddy for a pick-up. Neither one of us is ready for the time away together to be over. It means we'll be late for soundcheck, which means we'll get a lecture from Rod.

Totally worth it.

"So, I was thinking," Kick says as we walk down the busy sidewalk.

"Uh-oh."

He elbows me playfully. "Since you shared a scary truth about yourself, I figured it's only fair I share one too."

"Your name's not really Kick?" I say with a laugh. The look on his face tells me I'm totally right. "I *have* been wondering. No way your parents named your brother Steven and then named you Kick. If your name's really Kick your brother would have been named, like, Stretch or Truckstop or Pants."

"You think my mom would name her son Pants?"

I arch my eyebrow. "If she named her son Kick then yes, I do."

He pulls his lower lip into his mouth. Something tells me this isn't a secret he shares with many people, and if he shares it with me, we'll be one step closer to identifying the invisible string that's keeping us tethered together.

We dodge a group of men in business suits taking up the entire sidewalk before he says, "My legal name is Willard Joel Raines."

I gasp like a scandalized church lady and pull him against the window of a Starbucks. "Your name is *not* Willard." He nods, embarrassed. "No way your name is *Willard*. I'd expect like, Colby or Graham or Cash. Austin maybe. Even Keanu. Not Willard."

"It's a family name. And I would have gone by Will, obviously, but Mom said I kicked the shit out of her when I was still cooking. She started calling me Kick and the name stuck. It's the only thing anyone's ever called me. You are now one of a handful of people who know my real name."

"Miguel and Mateo?"

He shakes his head, chuckling to himself. "You're the only one who's ever pinned me down about it."

"I hardly pinned you down."

His eyes find mine. "You've been pinning me down since the moment we met."

I'm not sure how to do this, how to flirt with someone I made-out with and then sort of resented and now perform with every night and maybe want to kiss again. And then some. We've done everything out of order. I'm not sure which step this is supposed to be. Today has been so awkwardly wonderful but it feels like a blip, like as soon as we step back into the venue it will all go back to our version of normal.

"What are you doing on this tour, Willard Joel Raines?"

"Sparking internet rumors about me and Mari Gold and hoping they'll eventually come true."

"I know there's more hiding in there," I say, poking his chest. "When we're on stage, it's like you were born to do this, like it's the destiny of your whole life. But then we get backstage or on the bus or rehearsing a song and you're all jokes and bravado. I can't figure out what's important to you, what motivated you to come on this tour."

Kick wipes a hand across his face and looks down the street with that same far away look he always gets when he rubs his tattoo. I've challenged him and he's deciding what he wants to do about it. I wait for the smartass comment, wait for him to call me Goldie, wait for the innuendo.

He takes my hand and we start back down the sidewalk.

"My family was really into music growing up." He says it with a sigh, like he's glad to finally get the words out. "My dad is a studio musician. He has a whole studio set-up so he can record. He's played on tons of albums. My mom traveled as an indie artist for a while in her twenties. She was a lot like you, singer-songwriter, great voice, great guitar player. Naturally, my brother and I grew up singing and playing. My dad had every kind of instrument and would let us experiment. I was playing banjo by the time I was six.

"When we got older, Steven and I used to perform together all the time. He was the talented one, the songwriter, the driving force behind the whole thing. Even though he pitched us as a duo, I was really his drummer. We'd play anywhere he could get us a gig. One time we even played this guy's sixtieth birthday party. His wife rented out an Olive Garden in the suburbs."

He smiles at the memory.

"After high school, Steven was determined for us to get a record deal, do the whole thing, you know? He was always pushing my dad to use his contacts to help us, which Dad wasn't thrilled about. He thought we should earn it. 'Play the gigs and the rest will come,' he'd say.

"Steven and I used to fight constantly, like siblings do. I loved him but he drove me crazy half the time, always pushing, always working an angle to get us a show or meet some A&R person, stuff like that. I loved playing, but I wasn't sure music was what I wanted to do with my life. I never felt like it clicked with us, doing the whole artist thing together. But he'd decided, basically didn't give me a choice."

"All brothers fight, sure, but we could really get into it sometimes, like, really get angry with each other. And over nothing, usually. We'd fight about music stuff but also about dumb things." We're waiting at a corner to cross the street. He goes quiet, gathering himself. "Three years ago we were driving to a gig down in Franklin, arguing about something. I honestly don't remember what it was about." His mouth turns down into a small frown. "I was driving. I was irritated with Steven and wasn't paying attention and I…" He swallows, looks at me for a fraction of a second. "I didn't see the stop sign. Or the truck going through the intersection. I woke up in the hospital with a broken clavicle and a brutal concussion."

His scar. It's from the accident.

"What happened to Steven?"

His head bobs to the side, answering the question. "He died at the scene."

He pulls his hand away from mine and scrubs it down his face, wiping his eyes in the process. When he looks back at me, he's still brimming with emotion. When I asked him what his deal was, I had no idea it ran so deep, so painful.

I loop my arm through his. "Kick. I'm so sorry."

The light turns and we cross the street.

"After the accident, I ran from music for a while. I didn't know how to do it without Steven, didn't think I could. But then at that party at Jackson's house, there was something about the way you were teasing me about being a musician. Whatever it was you saw in me, it was like Steven was waving it in front of my face. I knew Miguel and Mateo played and they let me go out on a couple gigs with them. Then Emily told us about the audition and it seemed like the right move. If you break it all down, I guess I'm here because of you and your smart mouth."

His comment breaks the tension and we both smile.

"I auditioned for the tour because I was trying to honor

Steven's wishes. He always believed in my talent, would have been all over something like this. Of course, I never thought I'd get this far."

"He'd be so proud of you. Your parents must be so proud that you're doing this in his memory."

Kick shakes his head causing a single tear to shake loose and slide down the side of his nose. I crowd closer to him, shielding him as much as I can from prying eyes.

"My mom blames me for the accident, says I should have been paying attention, that I never take things seriously. She freaked out when I told her about the tour, said I was 'dishonoring my brother's memory,'" His eyes spill over. His chin quivers. "She said I killed her talented son. That she's stuck with me when he's the one who should be here."

I pull him under the awning of an office building as he buries his face in his hands and lets out a quiet sob. I wrap my arms around his waist and squeeze.

I stand on my tiptoes and whisper in his ear. "It's not your fault." I know it's not enough, but I say it again. Over and over. I kiss his temple and hold him tighter. I can't imagine the pain he's feeling, the underserved guilt.

He pulls away from me and wipes his face on the sleeve of his t-shirt.

"I'm sorry." He's not looking at me. "I probably could have picked a better place to have a breakdown than a busy sidewalk in St. Louis."

"Nothing to be sorry for. You went through a shitty thing. You're still *going* through a shitty thing. And forgive me for saying so, but what your mom said is the shittiest thing of all. If I ever meet her, I might punch her right in the face."

That makes him laugh, hard, which makes me laugh.

"You know, I give you a hard time because, well, it's fun to get you riled up," he says. "But I think I've also been a little jealous."

"Jealous?"

"You're so sure." He wipes his eyes and nose with the back of his hand. "You know exactly who you want to be, what you want to do, and damn anyone who gets in your way. Meanwhile I'm over here trying so hard to fulfill my brother's dream, having no clue what I should really be doing with my life."

It kills me he can't see how good he is, how special and magnetic.

"Why not this?"

He shakes his head. "I'm not a front man."

"You, infuriatingly, are an amazing front man."

He shifts closer, like his body is on autopilot. "I'm amazing with you."

His bright eyes pour into me and as much as I want to look away, I can't. He's laid himself bare, showing me so much, trusting me with it all.

"When all this started, I never imagined I'd be paired up with someone like you," I say.

"Someone like me?"

"You know, irritating and gorgeous."

He hides his face in my shoulder, faking embarrassment.

"Does singing with me remind you of Steven?" I hope it's okay to ask.

"Singing with you is nothing like performing with Steven. With him it was more like a job, like something I was required to do to keep the peace in my family. I was never…being a front man wasn't something I was interested in. All I wanted to do was play drums." He chuckles to himself. "I was scared shitless at that first audition."

I remember the way he walked in that day, bravado personified, like he'd already won and was just humoring the rest of us.

"I…do not believe you."

"It was such a relief when I saw you there. I don't know if I could have gone through with it otherwise. I was late coming in because I'd been puking in the parking lot." He reaches for my hand. "Performing with you…it's not like anything I've ever experienced. It fills me with this energy, like lighting a sparkler and painting the sky while it burns."

My heart leaps inside my chest, straining towards Kick. "I know exactly what you mean."

"I still don't understand how I ended up here, and if I'm honest, every day I feel like I'm auditioning to stay. Like at any moment they'll figure out I'm a fraud and kick me off the bus in the middle of the night."

"I feel the same way."

I remember the first time I ever mentioned wanting to be an artist in front of Polly. She laughed and told me I didn't have the personality for it, like because I wasn't exactly like her, I had no chance. Looking back, it was more of a sisterly jab than a poisoned arrow, but it stabbed me in the heart just the same. As much as I want this, want to be here, there's a part of me that's still worried she's right. I don't have what it takes.

"But you're so good," he says.

I shake my head. "I'm better with you."

We walk a full block in silence, my hand in his. My mind is a buzzing torrent of happy/scared thoughts, too many to concentrate on anything specific. All I can do is feel—Kick's hand wrapped around mine, my heart beating in my chest, how being this close to him rights something inside me that's been off-center for as long as I can remember.

"Thank you for telling me about Steven," I say. "I had no idea you were carrying something so painful."

He shrugs. "My therapist says I flirt with you as a way to cope."

"Hold on. You told your therapist about me?"

"Don't get a big head about it," he says with a smile. "I'm supposed to tell her about all the things that irritate the hell out of me."

I playfully punch him in the shoulder. "You love me."

He catches my wrist, pulls my hand to his chest. "You have no idea."

THIRTY-TWO
BETTER A WILT THAN A WITHER

WHEN THE SPOTLIGHT HITS, Kick and I are grinning at each other as Mateo plays a beat. Normally we go right into "I Kissed Her In An Alcove," but I'm holding his gaze, drawing it out.

"Hey there, Kick."

Bum, bum, bum, bum.

"Hey there, Mari."

Bum, bum, bum, bum.

"It's a beautiful night tonight, isn't it?"

Bum, bum, bum, bum.

"It is. I love St. Louis, don't you?"

The crowd's cheers drown out the drumbeats, but we stay in rhythm, watching each other.

"What song do you think the lovely people of St. Louis would like to hear tonight?"

Bum, bum, bum, bum.

The crowd shouts out song titles while Kick and I keep smiling at each other, ignoring them, working them into a frenzy. A guy in the front row screams "Freebird."

"We could do 'Don't You Want Me.' People seem to love that one."

The crowd's enthusiasm washes over me. My marigold tattoo is wrapped in plastic underneath my jacket, reminding me it's there, reminding me of my father, of why I'm here. For maybe the first time in my entire life, I feel like I truly belong here in the spotlight. "I don't know. We met a new friend today, right here in St. Louis, named Ez. They said they really loved The Alcove Songs."

Bum, bum, bum, bum.

"Do it," a girl to our left screams. I wonder if she means the song or something else. Me too, girl. Me too.

"The Alcove Songs," Kick says. "Do you mean the songs we wrote about each other, about that night at the party, when I kissed you in an alcove?"

Bum, bum, bum, bum.

I look out at the crowd. "Do any of you believe I'd actually let Kick Raines kiss me?" I shoot him a look. "I mean, I do have standards."

Bum, bum, bum, bum.

"Oh, I kissed you all right. Question is," he says, "when are you gonna let me kiss you again?"

He throws his guitar up, strumming the first chords and launching into the song. He sings the first line to me, not the audience, and my knees nearly give out. After this afternoon's confessions our energy on stage has exploded. Everything is happening at once—Kick's eyes, full of heat, focused on me, the ear-splitting cheers from the crowd, all four of us absolutely killing every beat, every note, every word.

"Isn't she something?" Kick hollers into the microphone at the end of the second song.

The roar of approval is deafening. To be fair, Kick and I are both milking it for all it's worth. There's a new, unspoken understanding between us, like our confessions tore down an invisible wall and now we can see each other all the way. We still talk shit to each other, but there's a softness behind it that wasn't there before. I keep catching him watching me when he thinks I'm not looking, a new heat in his eyes.

The guitar tech runs on stage to grab our guitars as the opening strains of "Don't You Want Me" boom over the sound system. Thousands of people jump to their feet to dance with us, but Kick only has eyes for me. We flirt and dance and sing to each other and it feels real. The words we're singing to each other are real. He wants me. And I want him. The way he's singing to me squeezes my ribcage like a too tight hug. We've been sitting on simmer since that first audition and now that we've bared our souls, things are threatening to boil over.

When the song ends, he pulls me into an engulfing hug in front of everyone, lifting my feet off the ground. A row of girls on the front row squeal loud enough to break glass. When he sets me down, we take a bow, him never letting go of my hand.

We're both giddy as we exit the stage, caught up in the music and the moment. The guitar tech hands us each a towel. I peel off my leather jacket and hold it between my knees while I pat my face and neck.

Kick's face is buried in his towel when he says, "Can you believe—"

When he pulls the towel away, his voice halts as his face turns to stone.

"Believe what?" I ask.

He's staring at someone behind me. I turn around and see a tall man wearing an All Access badge who looks just like Kick only thirty years older. Same hair but laced with grey, same eyes, same chin.

"Son," he says.

Kick doesn't move, his towel still raised to his face like a terry cloth beard.

Kick's dad walks over, slowly, his whole body moving in painful hesitation. When he's finally standing in front of us, his eyes are filled with tears.

"Mari," Kick says. He pauses, clears his throat. "This is my dad, Art Raines."

We spent the whole day in the city, talked about his brother, about the accident, and Kick never mentioned his parents lived here.

"Nice to meet you," I say.

Art reaches out for Kick, his hand resting lightly on Kick's shoulder. "You were really, really good, Son. Really good. I've never been more proud of you."

The moment is charged, like any sudden movement will trip an irreversible explosion. Kick's mouth is working back and forth, trying to get the words out. "I didn't think you'd come."

"Your mother," his dad says, pausing to swallow, to look toward the stage where Sparrow is playing their first song, to put his hands in his front pockets and then take them out again. "She wanted to be here."

Kick deflates next to me, turns into himself, his face etched in pain. Instinctively, I reach out for his hand. He pulls away from me and crosses his arms over his chest. He's locked in a stare down with his dad, the two of them having a silent conversation.

"I'll give you some privacy," I say.

"You were really wonderful," Art says as I start to walk away. "We didn't, uh, well, thank you for…for playing with Kick. It means so much."

It's obvious the punch those words carry. Kick's wilted even more in the last ten seconds and it squeezes my heart. I wait to see if he wants me to stay, but he keeps his eyes on the floor.

"It's me who should be thankful," I say. "Kick's wildly talented. The fans love him. But more than that, he's such a generous artist. You don't see that very often in situations like ours. Honestly, I've never met anyone like him. He's exceptional. I'm lucky I get to play with him every night."

Kick's eyes jerk to mine, his expression a mixture of surprise and something more, something like adoration. I reach out and touch his arm, run my hand up to his shoulder.

"I'll be in my dressing room if you need me."

He reaches up and grips my hand, the unspoken tether between us pulling tighter.

"*Thank you.*" His words are silent as a breath, a whispered declaration.

I squeeze his hand one more time before walking away.

THIRTY-THREE
WHAT GOOD IS AN ALMOST

AS WE MAKE our way to our meet and greet line, I slip my arm around Kick's waist.

"You okay?"

Jasmine and Emily are walking in front of us. Emily doesn't know to catch our private moment and send it to her TikTok contact.

"I'm here," I whisper.

Kick's eyes tell me thank you, that he's glad I'm here, but he doesn't offer anything more. And that's okay. I know he'll tell me more if he needs to.

Our signing line is longer than ever, everyone wanting to know if the hug meant we're official. We dodge, telling fans we were just caught up in the moment. I doubt they believe us. I certainly don't.

After we've signed the last autograph and the venue is mostly cleared out, we follow Jasmine and Emily to the elevator that goes down to the backstage concourse. The doors open and we all four get on, Emily standing between me and Kick. She prattles on about the success of tonight's show and how long the signing line was and how much merch we're selling and how we're her little superstars. I don't see how Emily and Jasmine don't notice the electric current running between me and Kick. It's as tangible as a burst streamer cannon, waves of crepe paper floating all around us.

All during the signing line we kept catching each other's eye, our hands grazing, Kick touching me every chance he could. It's obvious the unanswered question that's hovered over us since the start of the tour is about to be answered.

Back underground, Cheddar sees us in the hall and raises his hand for a high-five. "What a set tonight, guys. We need to respond while things are hot. Why don't y'all go to one of your dressing rooms and shoot a video together about tonight's show. Fans'll love it. Send it to me when you're done. I'll make sure it's posted to both your socials."

Various crew members and tour people congratulate us on our set as we make our way down the hall.

"Great show tonight, y'all."

"Killer tonight!"

"You two are solid. Respect."

We walk into Kick's dressing room as the Vampire Twins are on their way out, suitcases in hand.

"What's on for tonight?" I ask.

"*Lost Boys,*" Miguel says, pumping his fist in the air. "Epic eighties fashion and Kiefer Sutherland is a vamp. You coming?"

"Wouldn't miss it. We'll be there as soon as we film this video thing for Cheddar."

A Bluetooth speaker is playing a familiar song as they leave, but I can't quite place it.

"What's this song? I feel like I've heard it before."

Kick's eyes are shining. "It's 'Heaven' from Bryan Adams. It's...this is the cover I did. For the competition video submission."

It's an eighties power ballad, Bryan Adams' voice raspy and emotional and a lot like Kick's.

"We should add this to our set. I bet you sound incredible on it."

Kick holds out his hand. "Dance with me, Goldie."

"We need to film this video and get on the bus."

He reaches out further and takes my hand. "Dance with me."

I let him pull me in. We don't look at each other, just sway to the music, our feet shuffling against each other's as we circle, slowly. My heart revs into high gear with Kick's breath hot against my ear, his eyelashes brushing against my temple, his nose in my hair. The song fades out, the signal from Mateo's phone no doubt out of reach. But we keep dancing. Kick hums the remainder of the song softly in my ear, the sound washing over me like warm water. Kick cradles our joined hands, resting mine over his heart. His other hand is on my lower back, pulling me into him. I willingly go.

His voice is low in my ear as he sings about waiting for love to come along. How I'm all he wants. All he needs.

It feels like an unraveling, the layers I've wrapped tightly around my heart slowly peeling away. I close my eyes and let my arm snake around his shoulder, let my hand rest on the back of his neck as he hums into my ear.

Our bodies, so close, radiate heat. If attraction is a flame, I am burning hot enough to set the entire arena ablaze. I look up at him and his smile is wide and happy.

"What's that look?" I say, even though I know.

"It's just...you normally look like you want to murder me or pants me or spit in my water bottle."

"I do not."

"But right now, you look really happy."

I press my lips together, still scared to let him see how being with him lights me up inside. How he's right. I *am* happy.

"Tell me," he says, "what's the happiest you've ever been. Your whole life. What's your best, most perfect happy moment."

I can't say the thing that immediately pops into my head. I'm scared about what it could mean, what he would say, of all the things that could go wrong. Of getting hurt again. Being used. Stepped over. Forgotten.

But he shared a huge truth with me today, which I'm sure was a big risk for him. And he learned my truth and he's still here, still looking at me like I'm the only girl in the whole world. My gut and my heart are telling me I can trust him, that we're good together. He's good. That has to mean something.

I slide my hand down his chest and around his waist. It feels natural, like we've always done this. Like we've always been us.

"The happiest I've ever been is when I'm on stage with you."

Kick's mouth pops open. "Yeah?"

My gigantic smile is answer enough but I still say yes. "It's hard for me to admit. I've never been able to trust anyone or, when I have, they've always let me down."

He squeezes my waist. "I'm scared too. If I'm honest, I don't know what the hell we're doing or what's going to happen or how we even got here. Every day on this tour is like a fever dream. The only real thing I know is this." He pulls me impossibly closer. "I've wanted you since the second I laid eyes on you. Now that I know you, I want you even more. Everything else we can figure out."

He reaches his hands up to gently caress my face. My body knows what it wants, and it wants Kick. My brain rages reality so loud I'm sure he can hear it, but I don't pull away. Because I want it, want him. So much.

I angle my face up, our lips so close, the moment so alive I can touch it. Kick leans in and presses his lips against mine.

"You guys got the video?" Cheddar calls, walking into the room.

Kick and I fly apart like we've been struck by lightning.

"We were just about to…do it," Kick says and I cough into my elbow.

"I can film it, since I'm here," Cheddar offers, oblivious.

"What, uh." Words fail me. My legs are trembling. "What is it? You wanted us to say?"

"Thank people for coming to the show, talk about the

upcoming shows, remind everyone to tune in to the livestream, follow you on socials, all the usual stuff."

Cheddar holds up his phone and motions for us to start talking. Kick pulls me in, his arm slung casually around my shoulder. We paste on our practiced we're-a-duo smiles for the camera and say all the things Cheddar's commanded us to say. We do a couple of takes and once he's satisfied with our performance, Cheddar walks out, tapping his phone as he goes.

"Better get moving, bus is rolling in five. I'll post this for you both."

When I move to follow him, Kick pulls me back.

"Wait." His eyes on me are branding irons.

"The bus is leaving."

He grabs my hand. "Not for five minutes."

"It's not enough time," I say, shaking my head.

His eyebrow curves up. "Enough time for what?"

I take a few steps away from him, attempting to step outside his magnetic pull. "Time to go, Willard."

He laughs, chasing after me. "That's low, Goldie. Real low."

THIRTY-FOUR
ALCOVE, BUNK, WHATEVER IT TAKES

I CAN'T SLEEP. It's been hours and my skin's still warm, my heart still thumping against my rib cage like morse code—you want him…you want him…you want him.

I hid in my bunk as soon as the bus rolled out. I knew if I hung out with everyone in the front lounge, my feelings would be painted across my face like a neon sign. Not that they don't already know. Not that we aren't practically shouting our feelings at each other every night on stage.

But that's all for the act, right? For the fans.

That's what I keep repeating to myself over and over, because the thought of letting this go any further terrifies me. When I was with Brad the Bass Player, I thought things were perfect. He was charming and attentive, said all the right things. I trusted him. Then as soon as he learned the truth about me, everything changed.

But Kick isn't someone who'd step over me to get to someone else, not even someone like Polly. I don't know everything, but I do know that. I believe in my heart I can trust him. I just have to take the leap.

I'm torturing myself, replaying every moment we've had

together, trying to convince myself it's okay to let go, to let him in, when my phone buzzes with a text.

Do Not Kiss: knock knock

Even seeing his text on my screen makes my thighs clench.

Me: Sleep texting again?

Do Not Kiss: Check your curtain, Goldie. You've got a visitor.

I pull my curtain back a fraction of an inch and see a sliver of his soft brown waves before shutting it back tight.

Me: We're closed for the evening.

Do Not Kiss: You'd really leave me out here laying on the gross bus floor all by myself?

I reach my hand underneath the curtain and grab his arm, pulling him to me. He rolls inside my bunk with a loud huff. There's barely enough room in here for one person, definitely not for two, especially when one has legs like a giraffe. He's nose-to-nose with me, sparkle eyes on full display, the air around our faces tinged with the smell of minty toothpaste.

My heart jerks in my chest, like Kick's found our shared tether and given it a hard yank.

"Is it always so loud and rumbly in the bottom bunks? How do you even sleep down here?"

"Infrequently."

I can see over his shoulder that my bunk curtain is curved out in the middle, his ass hanging out into the aisle.

"If someone walks by, you're going to get your ass kicked with it hanging out like that."

"Are you inviting me to come closer?" he says, moving his hips against mine to try and fit more of his long legs into my space.

"What are you doing in here, Kick?"

I try to keep my voice flat, despite the heat churning in my belly.

His teasing smile fades, his pupils blown wide. "We didn't finish our conversation."

"Oh? Was there something else you wanted to say to me?"

We're both lying on our sides and Kick's hand goes to my waist. His touch is soft, hesitant, but it might as well be a blowtorch. I swallow so he won't hear my breath pick up.

"Just one thing." His hand moves around to my lower back, his fingers looping in a lazy pattern. He snakes a leg around me, tangling us together. "Something I've been trying to say for a while now." His fingers trace up from my lower back to cup my neck under my hair. "I think maybe you've been thinking about it too."

His eyes, full of want, swim over me. But he's waiting, giving me space to move things forward or stop them.

"I've been thinking about it too," I say. "I've been thinking about it since that night. In the alcove."

Look at me, hurtling past the edge of my self-imposed edge of reason. I told myself Kick was off-limits, but here I am, hitching a leg over the barbed wire fence and lunging straight for him.

"You were wearing those tiny little shorts and a Spice Girls t-shirt, grumbling about ice for some reason."

"You remember what I was wearing?"

He rubs his nose against mine. "It's imprinted on my brain. You kept telling me how you weren't interested in me even though you so obviously were."

We're giggling now, remembering that night.

"I couldn't figure you out, which is what I liked about you. It's still what I like about you."

He presses us closer, our hips aligned, evidence of how much he wants me hard against my thigh. "Don't you know what I want?"

"I'm getting an idea."

"Do you remember what you said to me that night?" Kick says, his lips brushing my eyebrow, the edge of my eye.

"I said a lot of things that night."

"You said I couldn't kiss you unless it was my birthday."

I lift my chin, our lips so close. "I was dying to kiss you."

"Mari," he whispers.

I pull him to me and press my lips against his. It's better than the alcove, better than the tease. We take our time, learning each other again. There's a sweet tenderness in his touch, his mouth claiming mine over and over.

My hand slips under his shirt and I scratch across his back as he kisses my neck, my jaw, whispers in my ear, "I've wanted you for so long."

I open my lips willingly as his tongue slips inside, every part of my body responding with a resounding and enthusiastic Yes. I push away every thought but Kick's lips, Kick's heavy sighs, Kick's fingertips beneath my hoodie, on my ribs, higher.

I'm craving more, need him closer, but there's no room in here, our range of movement limited to small, intentional touches.

Kick moves his hand lower, teasing the band of my sleep shorts.

"I want to touch you," he says. "Can I touch you?"

"Kick," I breathe out, pulling at his shirt.

We both jump as my curtain is yanked back and a water bottle smacks Kick in the head. Mateo's hand reaches down from the bunk above mine, his middle finger pointed down but sending a clear message.

"Can you two stop moaning like cats in heat? Some of us are trying to sleep."

"Thank you," an irritated voice pings from across the aisle.

I stifle an embarrassed laugh in the crook of Kick's neck, which quickly turns into kissing his neck.

"I guess I should go back to my bunk," he whispers, "before we wake up the whole bus."

I trace his lips with my fingers, trace his jaw, his ear. His lips find mine again and I sigh into him, believing, even if it's just for now, that I've finally found someone who sees me for me. And wants to stay.

"Raincheck?" He kisses my chin.

I kiss his mouth. Again. One more time. "Raincheck."

He kisses me again, deep and long, his big hands sinking into my hair. We're both breathless when he pulls away.

"Goodnight, Goldie."

"Goodnight, Willard."

He smacks my butt and rolls out of my bunk.

Me: Kick just left my bunk.

Cass: It is almost 4am.

Me: You answered!

Cass: It's Pavlovian.

Cass: Wait, did you say in your BUNK? Like, horizontal? You did horizontal things?

Me: It was............

Cass: Please finish that sentence.

Me: More tomorrow. Good night.

Cass: You wake me from my precious slumber, get me all riled up and now you're going to sleep?????????????

Cass: Wake up right now. I need details.

Cass: MARI LORRAINE GOLD PENNY LOVEJOY YOU TELL ME EVERYTHING RIGHT NOW

Cass: You suck.

Cass: I'm happy for you.

Cass: Really, really happy for you

Cass: But you suck

THIRTY-FIVE
BULLSEYE

KICK'S been gone all day. I haven't seen him since this morning when he pinned me to the side of the bus and kissed me soundly.

"I have a surprise," he said. "I'll be gone today getting it ready. I'll see you tonight?"

"You'll be gone all day?"

"Trust me," he said. "It will be worth it."

I really hope so because I've been pacing the venue all day, still keyed up from our time in my bunk last night. We crossed a bridge, told the truth, and now I'm ready to make good on our unspoken promise. I'm still scared it will affect our performance, our on stage chemistry, but not enough to deny my overwhelming need to get him alone as soon as possible.

It's thirty minutes until showtime. We're in Dallas tonight. I'm in the bathroom of my dressing room putting the finishing touches on my hair when I hear Emily and Cheddar come in. The bathroom door's cracked open. I start to kick it wider with my foot but something in their voices makes me pause.

"We can use this room," Emily says.

I peak through the crack in the door and see a third person

with Emily and Cheddar. It's not someone from the tour and no one I recognize.

"As I was saying earlier," Emily chirps, "with our collective experience it was pretty easy to set it up. We had Sparrow's blessing for the contest. They trusted our experience to choose who would be the best fit for the tour."

"After we made sure they both got the votes, it was smooth sailing after that," Cheddar adds.

"But why both of them?' the third person asks.

"Honestly, we were pretty set on Kick Raines, but the Sparrow brothers wanted Mari Gold. Don was adamant about it. It could have derailed things but, lucky for us, Kick and Mari tee'd themselves up with those alcove songs. It was a no-brainer after that."

What the hell?

"Who should have won?" the third person says.

"That grey band," Emily laughs, "if you can believe it. But look, fans don't always know what they want. We made sure they got the right artists, the best ones for the slot. And as you can see from the numbers, we were right about those two. You wouldn't believe the lines of fans waiting to meet them after every show. It's grown every single night. Fans can't get enough of them!"

"And we've shown you the livestream numbers," Cheddar says.

My skin, already hot, bursts into flames. Emily and Cheddar manipulated the votes. *Shades of Grey was supposed to win.* This entire time, every city, every show, Emily and Cheddar have been pulling the strings. Even with a different name, a different identity, I didn't win this spot. Kick didn't either. None of it is real. We aren't supposed to be on this tour.

"After we made sure Kick and Mari got the votes, it wasn't hard to generate the social chatter," Cheddar says. "My team is plugged into hundreds of different accounts. I told them what to post to get the chatter going. A lot of it happened organically, too, but we definitely got the ball rolling. Using our dummy accounts helped make sure the narrative went the way we wanted it to."

My legs are trembling so hard I have to lean against the wall. The Instagram polls. The TikTok videos. The hashtag. The fanbase I thought was growing by leaps and bounds—it's all fake.

"So, you see," Emily says, "if you invest in our new label, it's a sure win. We'll launch with Kick Raines, who'll come with a built-in fanbase from Cheddar's social plan and this tour. Word of mouth is happening exactly how we planned. Once we launch Kick, we can pretty much repeat the process again with the next artist until it's no longer needed. All you have to do is sit back and let the money roll in."

There's a pause, Emily's words hanging in the air.

"Kick's really the star, here," she says, like she's trying to reassure the other person.

"But they're so great together. Why split them up?"

"The novelty of the little flirty thing they've got going will wear thin by the end of this tour. It's great for now because it ups Kick's desirability which, let's be honest, is already pretty damn high. Their relationship opens the door for Kick to release a break-up album fans will die for. It's the perfect set-up."

They all three laugh, ha ha ha, like they're in a TV writer's room talking about a couple's inevitable demise.

"We think it's smart to launch with a solid solo act that can go the distance. Kick's got everything we're looking for, plus he's easy to work with. He's not a great songwriter, but we can feed him songs. Better to leave that part to the professionals anyway, right?"

"A break-up album," the third person says. "That's really interesting. And the girl?"

"Mari's expendable," Emily says, her voice smooth as glass. "It shouldn't be a problem."

Expendable? Seriously? I nearly storm in and blow the entire meeting to smithereens. I've done everything that's been asked of me, which, now makes me feel like a fool. I should have pushed harder against the duo thing, should have refused. Although, the way they're talking about Kick, they would have just kicked me off the tour entirely.

"I don't know," the stranger says, a question in his voice, "I really do love them together."

"Until they break up, which they will," Cheddar says. "We can't launch a label with an act that hinges on twenty-four-year-olds staying committed."

Emily sighs. "Isn't Harry Styles better since going solo? Beyonce? I could name a dozen more."

"We believe the set-up on this tour will catapult…is catapulting Kick Raines to stardom," Cheddar says. "We could go with them both, but it's our belief that we'll have more success, more *financial success*, with Kick as a solo."

Another long pause.

"What does Kick think about this plan?"

I strain my neck to hear every word because, yes, what *does* Kick think about this plan?

"He's on board," Cheddar says right as Emily says, "He's in."

"Kick's a team player," Emily adds. "He knows what he has to do to make this work."

More silence. More of the new life I thought I was building sailing over the edge of a cliff. More confirmation I never should have let Kick in, never should have let my guard down, never should have believed I could make it on this tour on my own.

"Sounds like you've both thought this through," the mystery voice says. "I'd love to invest."

I slump behind the door, unable to process a single thing I just heard. After everything Kick and I have been through, everything he said, once again I'm just a stepping-stone, a way for someone to get to the thing they really want. And the thing they want is never me.

I'm just the easy target.

THIRTY-SIX
ZERO OUT OF TEN

"YOU OKAY?" Kick shouts over the noise of the crowd.

We're side stage, about to go on, and I can't stand still, can't stop walking in circles and rubbing my hands up and down my arms. Emily's words keep running through my mind. *Kick's got everything we're looking for, plus he's easy to work with. Mari's expendable.*

"Hey," Kick says, reaching out for me.

I shake him off and bite back, "I'm fine."

He recoils, confused, but I can't care. Because Kick is the one who's fine. Kick is the one getting a record deal. Kick's the star. Kick has everything they're looking for. I'm just the empty-headed side piece here to sell tickets until my charm runs out.

Deacon Sparrow comes over to tell us to have a good show but immediately senses something's off. "You kids okay?"

Kick stares at me, the same question in his eyes. I have nothing to say. They win. I lose.

"You guys ready?" Don says, coming up behind us. "Full house tonight."

I turn away from him, unable to look any of them in the eye after what I overheard. Are Deacon and Don in on the whole label deal? Have they known this entire time that I'm just a pawn? Emily said they insisted on me winning. But why? Do they know I'm a Lovejoy and let me win as some sort of peace offering for the past? Is that why Don offered to record our songs?

Don squeezes my shoulder before he and Deacon run up on stage to do their nightly intro. Kick and I and the guys follow them and get into our spots. I plug in my guitar and look out into the audience. I feel sick, drained of all my energy. I need to focus, need to think of the show, the crowd, all the people watching the livestream. I can't fall apart on stage.

Not that it would matter.

I could leave the tour. Let Kick have his spotlight. Run back to California and let my mother manage me, broker me a record deal as the new and improved LOVEJOY. That would make everyone happy, for me to be in my proper place.

I'm frozen on stage, aware of nothing and no one but Emily's voice in my head. *Kick's got everything we're looking for, plus he's easy to work with. Mari's expendable.*

Kick and the band launch into "I Kissed Her In An Alcove." Kick sings lead and I do my best to fade into the shadows.

By the time the song's over, it's obvious we're off. The whole set's off. I know it. Kick knows it. Miguel and Mateo know it. Even the audience knows it. But I can't fake it, can't play the role of the doe-eyed songstress enamored with her handsome musical partner. Because we aren't partners. He's been competing with me this entire time, setting me up to be something he knew I never wanted to be. He played the unaffected cool guy, not in it for the acclaim, only here to fulfill the wish of his brother. But he's been strategizing, moving the pieces, playing me.

We stumble through the next song, my heart no longer in it. I'm going through the motions, singing the notes I'm supposed to sing and playing the chords I'm supposed to play, but it's empty. All the magic's been snuffed out like a blown candle.

It's our last song, "Don't You Want Me." My stomach twists

into a knot. I don't know how I'm going to get through it. My voice barely works and now I'm expected to sing and flirt and dance around the stage with someone who lied to me, whose every word has most likely been a lie.

Maybe my mother was right. I can't do this on my own. One hiccup and I'm falling flat on my face like a first timer. I've been running around this tour acting like I belong here when really I have no idea what I'm doing, no idea how to be this person I've convinced everyone I am.

The microphone shakes in my trembling hand and I'm waiting for the track to start, to force myself to smile and shimmy.

Kick motions to the sound engineer to hold the track. He gives me an indiscernible look before smiling into the audience. He's still wearing his guitar.

"Dallas, you've been such a great crowd tonight, I was wondering if I could change things up a bit."

Cheers rise from the crowd, but they don't mean anything. They'd be captivated by anything he said. His sexy grin reaches all the way to the back of the arena.

"I wrote a new song today." A loud whoop from the lower section on the left, probably full of Kick fans. He looks over at me, nervous. "It's about this sizzler of a girl over here. Y'all give it up for Mari Gold."

My body goes numb. He wrote a song? Kick doesn't write songs. Even if he did, he would never play something he'd just written in front of this many people. Something's off.

"You already know how talented she is, what an amazing singer she is. But if you'd be so kind, I'd like to share a song with you about who she is behind the scenes."

I glance at Miguel and Mateo. They're clearly in on whatever is about to happen.

The guitar tech comes out on stage, hands Kick an acoustic guitar and takes his electric. Kick pulls the acoustic strap over his head and plugs in. A hush falls over the crowd, everyone waiting to hear what he'll say, especially me.

"Truth is, I never expected to meet someone like her, someone who's made me better just by standing next to her on this stage every night. It wasn't easy trying to put her brilliance into a song, but I gave it my best shot. This is 'She's A Ten.'"

Oh my God. Oh my *God*.

He strums something melodic and lilting before he starts to sing.

Met her, liked her, kissed her
Then I got to know her
Found out she's so much more
More than funny, more than cool
Made my wounded heart unspool
For her
Just her
This complicated, dedicated, understated girl

He's singing to me, but I can't hear the words. This isn't what I want, being manipulated in front of a packed arena. Did he even write this song? Or did Emily and Cheddar put him up to it, give him a swoony ballad to sing the night their investor is in the audience so he could show off?

Bile climbs up my throat, twenty-two thousand pairs of eyes waiting to see what I'll do.

He gets to the chorus, his voice filled with emotion. He should really go into acting. His dopey, hopelessly-in-love expression is very convincing.

I may be a star
But she's a constellation
I may be the moon
But she's the one I orbit
If I'm five out of five

She's a ten

I have to get out of here. Right now.

Even though it won't look good for Sparrow, even though Emily and Cheddar will screech about responsibility and following orders, even though I might be blowing up my future career on the spot, I walk off stage in the middle of Kick's song.

I walk right past Nic, who calls my name, past the crew, past Rod, past the crowd of random All Access pass holders who gather side stage at every show, and head out to the loading dock. Once I'm outside, the stifling heat seers into me but I don't care. I can't be inside anymore. I can't listen to Kick's swoony love song full of meaningless words.

Every experience from my sister's career should have prepared me for this moment. I've seen with my own eyes how it's all a con, artists doing anything they have to do to make the audience fall in love with them. And spend money. I should have seen this coming a mile away. I've been so caught up in the Kick swirl I completely lost sight of why I'm here in the first place.

Pausing between the buses, I bang my shoulders and head back against the side of our bus and will myself not to cry. Because if I start, I may never stop.

My phone rings in my boot and I ignore it. As soon it stops ringing, it buzzes with a text. I pull it out and see it's Cass.

Cass: What just happened?

Cass: I'm doing highlights and watching the livestream and you just walked off stage.

Cass: Are you okay?

Cass: Answer your phone.

I can't talk to her right now, can't admit my humiliating failure in out loud words.

Me: I'm okay. Will call soon.

Cass: I will fly to Texas so help me. Just say the word.

THIRTY-SEVEN
WHEN TRUST GOES BUST

IT ISN'T long before Kick finds me. He walks over slowly, hands shoved deep into the front pockets of his jeans. It shows off the definition of his arms and I curse myself for noticing when my whole life is imploding.

"Mari," he says, his voice tinged with confusion, a little desperate. The fact that he's not calling me Goldie only amps up the tension. I wonder if he's figured out what I know.

"I don't want to talk to you."

I can't look at him, can't believe I've been put in this position, can't believe everything I thought was finally right has gone so completely wrong.

My arms are crossed over my chest and I'm biting my bottom lip so hard I'll probably leave teeth marks.

Kick paces in a slow, tight line in front of me. He's probably worried about the performance, upset I left the stage, wondering if this will mess up his chances with Emily and Cheddar's new label, hoping the investor doesn't back out because I'm *expendable*.

"I don't know what I did," he says, "but I know it must be bad for you not to be taking shots at me right now."

He leaves space for me to make a snarky comment. I don't take it.

"I thought I was doing something good, with the song. I thought...honestly, I need some context here. I can't make things right if I don't know what's going on."

There's obvious sincerity in his voice, but it's too late. I need to let myself spiral and he's an easy target.

"You thought you were doing something good with that song?" My words spit out of me, angry and hurt. "That wasn't for me. I know I'm just now catching up to what's going on but give me a little credit."

He stares, confused. "Going on?"

"Kick, the entire arena was eating out of the palm of your hand. You had them all yearning for you, which, great job, right on schedule. But that song wasn't about me. It was about you being Kick Raines." I do air quotes around his name. "Super charming sexy guy whose special talent is eye-fucking the back row through the giant LED screens. You making a big show about how that song was for me was...humiliating. You humiliated me."

He shakes his head, his eyebrows drawn together. "How are you...what are you saying right now?"

"It's all been about setting you up, hasn't it?" My eyes flash up to his. "All of it, the flirting on stage, the songs, the signing lines, the photos, all the social media posts." I pause, not wanting to say it. "Last night in my bunk. That will feed right into the new Kick Raines single, right?"

Kick pulls at his hair and takes a step closer.

"How can you say that to me?"

"Did you even write that song? Or did Emily and Cheddar have it written for you knowing it would make the audience love you?"

A shadow of confusion passes over his face and his jaw tightens.

"I don't know why you're being so mean right now," he

pauses, swallows, "but I wrote that song myself. I thought you understood what a big deal that is for me." He throws his hands out to his sides and lets them fall, slapping against his thighs. "I was trying to tell you how I feel about you. How you dazzle me every single day. How performing with you is the most fun I've ever had in my entire life. And now you're just, I don't know. I don't know what's happening right now."

Either he's the best liar that ever lied or he really doesn't know the whole thing, me and him and all of it, was manufactured from the start. And if that's true, he thinks our chemistry is real. Earned. But we've just been playing into a script written for us. How can he know how he feels about me when we haven't been real the entire time we've known each other?

"You don't know what you're saying."

He grabs my hand and pulls me to him, holds my hand over his heart. "Yes, I do."

I could do it. I could give in to this moment, let him woo me, kiss me, hold me. I could pretend not to know about Emily and Cheddar's plan to dump me as soon as I'm no longer useful to them. To Kick. But I'd know it was a lie.

"I thought we were building something," I say. "I thought I could trust you. All my life, all I've ever wanted was for someone to see me. It's always been Polly or my mother, never me. I've been invisible. Then when I met you, when we got on this tour, I thought," I push him away, "but you used me, just like everyone else."

"Please explain to me how I've been using you." His expression shifts "You think I give a rat's ass about your sister? I've known who you are since the day we met, Mari. I knew the whole time and I never cared. After everything we've been through, how can you say I've been using you?"

I stare at him, fuming. This cannot be happening.

"You knew?"

"I was waiting for you to tell me, to *trust* me. When you

finally told me I thought it meant something. I thought we were finally—"

"You knew the whole time."

He blows out a long breath. "That's the point, isn't it? I don't care. I never did. I care about you, period. No one else."

I am going to throw up. "You knew I was Polly's sister and you never said anything."

"You never said anything either."

Visions of Kick and Emily and Cheddar laughing it up at my expense flash through my mind. Have they all three talked about it? How I'm using a stupid stage name when everyone on planet earth knows the truth? Have I been a joke this entire tour?

"Who told you?"

"You're not listening to me. I. Don't. Care."

"Who told you, Kick?"

He sighs, defeated. "It was at the party, at Jackson's. When you left with Cass, some guy, a producer I think, came up to me wondering if I knew you. He wanted an in with you."

Tears finally fall from my eyes as the knife to my heart plunges so deep it disappears entirely

"I can't believe this," I say.

"I don't understand what's happening here. You walked off stage in the middle of my song, which, thanks for that by the way."

"You lied to me."

He hangs his head, hands on his hips, and talks to the pavement. "I never lied to you. Not once. I didn't tell you I knew your name, but I didn't lie."

"I knew this would happen," I say, my heart splintering like shattered glass. "I knew the second I let my guard down I'd be disappointed. I am so sick of feeling this way, of being overlooked and thrown away like I don't matter."

"That's not—"

"I'm not done." I glare at him. "I let you in. How could you do this to me?"

He glares right back. "The thing I'm trying to understand is how you accuse me of being flirty and unserious all the time when you're the one who runs away the second things start getting real."

"I don't do that."

"You've been running from me since the second we met. You said you dated half of Nashville but did you ever have any real feelings for anyone? Did you ever let anyone in? You write these open, honest songs and yet you can't let your guard down for a single second with me."

"That's not fair."

"I'm here, Mari. I'm ready. I'm in this for you, to be with you. You're the one who keeps pushing me away. All I've done is care about you."

Sounds like the perfect song title for his debut album about The Big Breakup.

"If that's what you think you're doing, you're a bigger asshole than I thought you were."

He wraps his hands around my arms, his eyes on fire. "You know what this is, what we are to each other. You know how I feel about you and, despite how hard you deny it, I know how you feel about me. You're running so hard from something you're sure will be bad, you're missing the good right in front of you."

Nice words, but he lied to me, manipulated me. He's been scheming with Cheddar and Emily behind my back. I was right not to trust him. I never should have let him in.

"You two."

We startle as Emily's shrill voice bounces off the side of the bus. She and Cheddar are standing a few feet away, arms crossed.

"We need to talk," she says. "Now."

THIRTY-EIGHT
COINCIDENTAL CATASTROPHE

"FOLLOW US," Emily commands.

I can't look at Kick as we trail after her. Cheddar brings up the rear like he's making sure one of us doesn't escape. Tonight's venue has a huge production office right across from the backstage entrance and Emily barges through the door. Nic's sitting on a long, brown leather couch with two men I haven't seen before.

"May we have the room?" Emily says. She's sweetened her tone, but there's still an edge to her voice.

Nic studies her for a moment before saying, "Is there a problem?"

"No problem. We just need to go over some things with Kick and Mari."

"And you can't find someplace else to do it?"

They stare at each other, neither one willing to back down. Their stand-off goes on longer than the rest of us are comfortable with until Cheddar finally says, "We can find another spot."

I follow him back through the door and Emily stomps out after us as we head to Kick's dressing room. It's a locker room lined with wooden benches and Emily sighs heavily before perching on the edge of the bench closest to the door.

"Sit," she says.

Kick and I sit across from her, enough space between us to fit three other people.

"What is going on with you two?" Cheddar says.

"Tonight's set was off," Emily huffs, "way off."

"Numbers are down," Cheddar says, as if his social numbers are the one and only reason for us to exist.

I have no idea how to respond. I don't want Emily and Cheddar to know I overheard their little plan to make Kick a superstar while I fade into expendable oblivion. Somehow admitting I know would make things even more embarrassing for me.

I glance over to Kick. He's watching me, waiting, hoping I'll say something to knock a hole in the wall I've erected between us. But I can't. I won't.

Emily's eyes narrow in on me. "I'm sure you don't want to blow this opportunity."

A laugh bubbles up my throat and I swallow it down. Of course I don't want to blow this opportunity. I'm not the one who *is* blowing this opportunity. The opportunity is being pried out of my too-tight grasp.

"Is there something y'all need to share with the team?" Cheddar asks Kick. "Because whatever interpersonal drama you have going on, you can't bring it to the stage."

"We're fine," Kick says unconvincingly.

I know I should say something, should fight for my space, should convince everyone that despite the rigged contest I deserve to be here. But my voice won't work. My mouth won't move.

"Mari? Do you have anything you'd like to say?" Emily asks.

I look down at my feet and shake my head.

"This is unbelievable," she says to Cheddar. "They're ruining everything. *She's* ruining everything."

"Is this about your sister?" Cheddar says.

My head snaps up in shock.

"What sister?" Emily asks and wow, I'm surprised he hasn't told her yet.

"That has nothing to do with this," Kick says.

"What sister?" Emily insists.

Cheddar stares me down. "Do you want to tell her or should I?"

"Go ahead," I say, "it's obvious you're dying to share."

Cheddar straightens up, a gotcha smile on his face.

"Her name isn't Mari Gold. It's Penny Lovejoy. She's LOVEJOY's sister."

Emily screeches a word somewhere between *what* and *huh*. "How did I not know this?" She points at Cheddar. "How did you know this and not tell me? How is this happening right now?"

"Why does it matter?" Kick asks.

"You don't think that I, the tour publicist, should know that the artist I'm killing myself to promote is the sister of one of the biggest pop stars in the world? I cannot believe this. Who else knows? We need to put out a statement. We need to—"

"I don't want anyone to know," I say.

Emily laughs like a villain who's just been told they're not allowed to throw a puppy down a well. "That's not your decision to make."

"It's my life," I say.

"And right now, your life belongs to me."

She's about to say more when Cheddar holds his hand up to silence her. He looks at us, at me, before he says, "We're going home tonight. We have four days off from the tour. I suggest you use that time to get your shit together." His eyes burn into mine with a warning. "Both of you."

"I won't perform as Penny Lovejoy."

"Then you'll be off the tour," Emily says.

I let out a sarcastic laugh. "So you'll be getting what you wanted. Great plan."

Emily asks what I mean by that but I'm already off the bench and out the door, her screeching voice chasing after me.

I practically run into the arena. The only safe space on this tour right now is the sound booth, watching Sparrow's set, where no one can talk to me about why I'm not being the good little artist they want me to be.

When I get back to the booth the sound tech waves and motions to some chairs set up behind him. I flop into one right as Sparrow starts a new song. I hunch over, elbows on my knees, my head in my hands. I'm not going to make it to the Nashville show. This break will be my break-up, with the tour, with Kick, with all of Nashville. I'm as good as done.

When I look up at the band, the spotlight is on Don as he plays a guitar solo. A close-up of him flashes on the LED screen and I stand up so fast I knock my chair backwards. My vision goes wavy for a second as I stare at the screen. I close my eyes as tight as I can and lean against the soundboard. When I open them, the same impossible image is on the screen. The cameras pull wide and what I see shreds my already damaged heart into a thousand pieces. Because unbelievably, undeniably, Don Sparrow is wearing a cowboy shirt.

A cowboy shirt with orange flowers.

Marigolds.

And he's playing a mint green Les Paul.

It can't possibly be the same cowboy shirt with marigolds and mint green Les Paul from the photo of my father but also, it has to be the same cowboy shirt with marigolds and mint green Les Paul.

I grip my arm and cover my new tattoo. The tattoo I got in memory of my father. Because that shirt is supposed to be his.

It doesn't make sense, how Don could be wearing that same shirt, playing that same guitar, my father's shirt and my father's guitar.

I run out of the sound booth and down the aisle, flashing my All Access pass at security before I slip side stage. I pull my acoustic from the guitar rack to look at the photo of my father taped to the back. I hold it up to the lights and there's no mistaking the shirt, the guitar. They're the same.

THIRTY-NINE
NOT EVEN BRYAN ADAMS CAN FIX THIS MESS

WE HAVE four days off from the tour. Four days for me to figure out how to fix the downward spiral that is my life. I know I need to confront my mother about Don Sparrow, but I'm not sure I'm ready to hear it. Especially if the truth she finally reveals is the person I believed to be my father my entire life is in fact not my father.

I spent the drive back to Nashville hiding in my bunk, staring at the photo of what I now believe to be Don Sparrow, my maybe-father, questioning my entire existence. There's no way he doesn't know who I am. Emily's ominous words to their mystery investor keep rolling through me: *We wanted Kick, but the Sparrow brothers wanted Mari. Don was adamant about it.* Does that mean Don Sparrow knows who I am? And that's why he asked me to audition for the tour? And if he knows who I am, why hasn't he said anything? Why hasn't my mother said anything? Why is everyone walking around acting like everything is completely normal when the entirety of my life just blew up in my face? Did Don Sparrow think getting me on the tour would make up for never being in my life? Did he think reassuring pats on the back before going on stage every night, offering to record a demo for us, would make up for a lifetime without him? Does Jasmine know? Have she and Don been talking about it behind my back the whole tour?

I'm sitting on the couch at Granny G's eating pork potstickers Cass made in the air fryer. We're half-watching a show from Cass's Essential Viewing List.

When I got home, I told Cass the whole sordid tale about Emily and Cheddar's plan. She was horrified, worried for me, ready to fight Emily and burn down the tour, all the essential emotions. When I moaned *what's the point of going back out on the tour*, she ranted for a full hour about how I deserve to be there no matter what evil scheme Emily and Cheddar cooked up. That I should take advantage of their insidious motivations. That I should continue to kill it every night and then convince their investor to spend all of their money on my career instead of Kick's.

I haven't told her about Don Sparrow. About the cowboy shirt with the orange flowers. Saying the words out loud would make them true, and I'm not ready for it to be true.

Instead of thinking oh-my-God-Don-Sparrow-is-probably-my-father on an infinite loop, I'm trying to decide if Cass is right about Emily and Cheddar. But that feels too hard to think about. I could think about Kick, but he's impossible to think about. Instead of thinking, I'm wallowing. I haven't showered and my hair is in a messy knot, no make-up, Chop pants and Kick's vintage Bryan Adams t-shirt. He left it in the front lounge one night and I...took it. I didn't know why at the time, but now I'm glad to have it. It feels like he's here with me even though I don't want him to be here with me. As strong as my feelings are for him, I also question every moment we've had together, if any of it was genuine or if we just blindly played into Emily and Cheddar's carefully structured narrative. I want to believe things between us are real. I want to believe the song he wrote for me was real. But it's too convenient, too perfectly timed, too much. A part of me believes I should shut him out forever, should protect myself from falling any further. Should burn this t-shirt.

But it's crazy soft and smells like Kick. So.

The doorbell rings and Cass and I eye each other.

"I didn't order anything."

"I'm not communicating with the outside world so you know it wasn't me," I say.

Cass jumps up to find out who it is and I hear him before I see him. Kick Raines at my door. I lean forward and see he's filling up the doorframe like a hero sent to save the damsel in distress. He's wearing loose sweatpants cut off above the knee and an oversized black t-shirt, running shoes on his feet. He's effortlessly cool and so beautiful it makes my teeth ache. But I don't want to see him.

I sink lower into the couch, hoping Cass will adios him right as I hear her say, "Come on in."

Traitor.

When Kick walks into the living room, Chop hobbles over to him, sniffs his shoe, barks once, and hobbles away.

"It's Chop," Kick says, "from your pants."

I ignore him and make a big show of putting a huge bite of potsticker into my mouth.

"I'll just," Cass says, leaning her body towards the hallway, "go see if Granny G needs anything."

"No," I mumble, mouth full, pointing my chopsticks at her, "you stay."

Cass slides down into her favorite armchair, her butt making an exaggerated fart noise against the worn leather on her way down. It does nothing to break the tension. Kick hesitates longer than is comfortable, but eventually sits on the couch, scooting as close to the opposite end as he can.

Granny G sweeps into the room. She's in a hot pink muumuu, giant gold hoops and bright pink lipstick. "Girls, has anyone seen my, oh, hello." She bats her eyes at Kick. "You're the handsome young man from Mari's concerts."

"Yes ma'am," Kick says. He stands up to shake her hand and

towers over her. "I'm Kick Raines. It's a pleasure to meet you. I've heard many wonderful things."

Granny G smiles at me, her tiny hand still in Kick's massive grip. "I like him."

She excuses herself to the kitchen where she will inevitably eavesdrop.

"Looks like you're having a great day off," he says, sitting back down and motioning to *The Vampire Diaries* on the TV. When I saw it on Cass's list, I remembered Kick's comment about loving Ian Somerhalder which made me want to watch it to somehow feel closer to Kick. Pathetic.

"How did you know where I live?"

Kick's cheeks go red and he glances at Cass.

"You told him?" I bark at her.

She's defiant when she says, "You two need to talk about… things. I thought this would be a good place to do that."

This time I say it out loud. "Traitor."

Kick rests his long arm across the back of the couch. "I wanted to explain why I never said I knew you were LOVEJOY's sister. I thought in person would be the best way to do that."

I eat another potsticker and keep my focus on the TV. Out of the corner of my eye, I see Cass motion to him like, *go on*.

"When that guy at Jackson's party mentioned you were Polly Lovejoy's sister, my very first thought was wow, Polly's lucky to have a sister like her." I don't react so he keeps talking. "I also laughed because of the way you turned your nose up when we heard her song." His fingers tentatively graze my shoulder. "But it meant nothing to me that you were her sister. All I cared about was seeing you again."

I risk glancing at him. His eyes are puppy dog soft, which is totally unfair, and I wonder for the millionth time how I got mixed up with a guy like Kick Raines.

"Then when you introduced yourself as Mari Gold at the audition, I figured you didn't want anyone to know who you were. So I waited for you to tell me on your own."

"Why didn't you tell me?"

"Because I thought it might hurt you that I knew. And I'm going to keep saying this until you believe me but, I don't care that your legal name is Penny Lovejoy or who your sister is." He waits until I look at him and says, "I am not using you to get to someone else or whatever else it is you think I could be doing. I never was."

If I tell him what I know about the record deal, it will confirm whether or not he's lying. If he's telling the truth, maybe we can find a way out of this whole mess. If he's not, goodbye Kick Raines and goodbye my heart.

"I found out," I start, quickly losing my words. I'm scared to take this step, scared to put it all out there. Scared of finding out something I don't want to know. Scared of losing him. I bite my lips and keep going. "I overheard some things at the Dallas show. Things I'm hoping you don't already know. Because if you do..." I let that hang in the air for a moment. Kick doesn't say anything and I wonder if it means he does know. I eat another potsticker, take my time chewing, stare at the TV. Kick's right. Ian Somerhalder makes a sexy vampire. I swallow my bite and take a long drink of water before I look back at Kick.

"Emily and Cheddar are starting their own record label."

I wait a beat to see if he'll say he knew. He doesn't.

"I overheard them meeting with an investor. They," I swallow, not wanting to say it out loud, "manipulated the votes from the audition. Neither one of us won. We didn't get the most votes. Cheddar manufactured the posts on socials talking us up, which means the momentum we thought we had isn't real."

Kick looks shellshocked. A good sign, at least for me.

"They told the investor they wanted to go with just you, make you the winner of the competition, but the Sparrow brothers wanted me, so they thought up the duo. They planned to make us popular as a couple with their fake social posts and meet and greets and, just, all of it. They believe fans will buy into you because of the couple thing and then at the end of the tour they're planning to announce you as their first artist, as a solo act. Without me. It's all been a lie, the contest, us, the whole thing. It was just a ploy for them to get what they wanted. Which was you, apparently."

Kick's taking it all in, his lips parted in shock. It's quiet, the low murmur of sexy-vampires-who-are-brothers on the TV. Cass and I look at each other and wait. Kick's quiet long enough for me to come up with a plan to suggest we watch this every night on the bus instead of vampire movies.

"Who won?" he asks.

I almost laugh because that's the exact question I would have asked if the roles were reversed.

"Shades of Grey."

"Fuuuuuuuuck." He takes a long, deep breath and scrubs his hands down his face, pulling the corners of his lips down with his fingertips. "You're sure?"

"I heard all of it. They were in my dressing room right before our set. In Dallas." I repeat that part, waiting for him to put it together.

He drops his head to his chest and takes another deep breath before looking at me. "So when I did that song for you."

I hold his gaze. "Yeah, when you did that song."

"I didn't know." He looks over at Cass and then back to me, emotion all over his face. "About any of it, I didn't know. I had no idea. Mari," he reaches out and wraps his hand around my arm so gently I nearly whimper out loud, "I didn't know."

The tightness I've been carrying in my chest since hearing the whole sordid plan loosens like the pulled end of a Christmas bow. I've been so worried I was being played by everyone, including Kick, that I haven't taken a full breath in days.

Kick lets go of my arm and leans forward, elbows on his knees, fingers raking through his hair. He gives me a sideways glance. "I feel like an idiot."

I raise a chopstick full of potsticker in salute. He eyes my plate, hesitating for a yes. I nod. He grabs a potsticker and nearly swallows it whole and wow, I might be in love with him.

I clear my throat and brace myself. "I believe, now, your intentions were good. With the song. And it was really good. Like, really, really good."

"You liked it?" He looks so hopeful I might burst into tears.

"Kick, I loved it."

Cass played the song for me when I got home from tour. She'd been recording every livestream in case there were any I wanted to watch back or use clips to post online. I hadn't really heard the song when he'd sung it, too in my head with everything else going on.

"It wasn't fair of me to get so angry with you," I say. "I thought winning the spot on the tour was this life-defining moment for me, something I'd achieved on my own when for so long I haven't…" I pause, not ready to fully spill it all. "My life hasn't been my own for a long time. Maybe ever. And winning the competition—that was mine."

Kick nods. He gets it.

"Then I heard Emily and Cheddar's plan and realized I hadn't achieved anything at all, that I'd been stepped over once again by people in pursuit of their own agenda. And in that moment, it felt like, like maybe you'd been playing me too." He starts to butt in but I stop him. "And then that song. It was like I didn't have a choice, that you'd decided we were going to go public for the spectacle of it, like you were doing that song for the investor and not for me. That maybe it was all part of the plan to charm people into buying your debut record."

"Mari, I could never, ever…would never—"

"I know. Now, I do. But you can see how it would feel that way to me, right?"

His eyes go soft, his voice even softer. "Yes."

"It felt like every other person was pulling the strings of my life and that I had no say in anything that was happening or was going to happen. It wasn't at all what I wanted. And then…"

Kick scoots closer to me, trails his fingers on the back of my neck. "There's more?"

Cass quirks an eyebrow, curious.

I cup my hand over my marigold tattoo and squeeze.

"Last night. Don Sparrow. On stage he was…he was wearing a cowboy shirt with orange flowers. And he was playing a mint green Les Paul. I'm pretty sure it's the same shirt and the same guitar from the photo I have of my father."

Cass inhales a loud breath and Kick pulls his hand away from me, shocked.

There's a muffled cry from Granny G in the kitchen.

I set my plate on the coffee table and pull my legs up underneath me. Kick leans forward again, elbows on his knees. He leans back, his head against the back of the couch. Leans forward. He's a seesaw of shock.

"You think Don Sparrow might be your father?" he asks.

"The shirt and the guitar could be a massive coincidence, but there's something Emily said when she and Cheddar were talking to that investor." I look at Kick. "She said they only wanted you, but the Sparrow brothers insisted on me winning too. Don specifically. She said he was adamant. That has to mean something, right?"

"Damn," Cass says.

"Just to review," Kick says, "you're Polly Lovejoy's sister. And Don Sparrow is your dad, maybe. Probably. And we didn't win the contest. And Emily and Cheddar are…I don't even know."

We all three stare at the TV, unseeing, absorbing the mountain of info I've just unleashed. Granny G walks back through the living room shaking her head in disbelief. All of us are stunned speechless.

Elena's invited Damon Salvatore into her house by the time I find my words again.

"What do I do? If Don Sparrow is my father? What do I do with the fact that we've been on tour together for weeks and weeks and he's never said anything to me. If he knows who I am, why wouldn't he say something?"

"Maybe he doesn't know," Kick says.

"Or maybe you're right and the shirt is a coincidence," Cass offers. "I mean, how many cowboy shirts with marigolds are there in the world? Gotta be what, at least a few hundred? He and your dad used to be friends. Maybe they bought them at the same time."

"I thought about that. But it all lines up so neatly, doesn't it? My father had a huge falling out with the band. Mom said he died of a broken heart. The shirt. The guitar. The fact that Don wanted me on the tour. But how do I confirm it? It's not like I can climb onto his bus and say, hey, I noticed your shirt the other night. I think you might be my father."

"We could get a DNA sample," Cass says, "send it to be tested."

"Sure, I'll just run on stage and swab his cheek when he's singing 'Meltdown.'"

"Emily would pass out if you did that," Kick says with a laugh.

Cass scoffs. "I would honestly love to tell her the girl she's manipulating to ultimately reject is actually Don Sparrow's daughter."

"I bet she'd suddenly find a way to release two artists instead of one," I say.

Kick and I look at each other, both of us thinking about what comes next.

"So, you'll sign with them?" I ask.

Kick sinks back into the couch and crosses his arms over his chest. He blows out a long breath and closes his eyes. When he opens them, his face is twisted in conflict.

"It's never been the dream, never been *my* dream. I thought this tour would be this one amazing experience, you know? That I'd fulfill Steven's long-held passion and move on. I'm not a frontman, not a solo act. And it feels wrong, how it all came about, how they're using us for their little plan. I've never had a problem with Emily and Cheddar, but the sneaky way they're putting this whole thing together." He shakes his head. "Besides, if they don't want us both, I don't want them." His eyes fall on me. "You're what makes me good."

A sharp pain pinches inside my chest and the future dances in front of my eyes—me and Kick on stage as headliners, singing together every night. It's not something I've truly considered a possibility until now. But what if we could keep the magic going?

"Mari," Cass says. "You said you feel like you haven't been able to make any of your own choices. And Emily and Cheddar are both massive dicks, obviously. So, speaking as your pretend manager, I think the important question to ask yourself is, what do you want?"

"What do you mean?"

"If you had the choice, the ability to make the next step happen, whatever that is, what would you want it to be?"

This feels like a trick. "Like, anything?"

"Everything."

It's such a simple question but it lights my brain up like a string of spotlights. I haul myself off the couch, needing to move. I circle the living room, Kick and Cass's eyes on me and each other.

What do I want?

What do I *want?*

What do *I* want?

I used to be so sure. I wanted to write songs that connected with people, like my father did, or, the man I thought was my father. I wanted my mother to take me seriously as an artist, not just another opportunity-maker for her to use at her own discretion. I wanted to someday find someone who wanted me for me, one hundred percent. After everything that's happened, my foundation has shifted, but the roots of those wants are still there.

"I want to write and perform my own songs and make it in the industry, but on my own terms. I want to know for sure if Don Sparrow is my father and if he is, I want to figure out a way to have a relationship with him. I want to find a way to heal what's broken between me and my mother and my sister."

I stop in front of them, hands on my hips.

"I want Cass to be my manager, but not pretend. For real." She makes a face like *no way*. "You're the smartest person I know and can talk to anyone about anything. That's essentially what a manager is, right?"

"Could I still do hair?"

"Obviously."

Her face scrunches up, skeptical. "You'd seriously want me?"

"I wouldn't trust anyone else."

"Me too," Kick says. "I want you to be my manager."

Cass, for once, can't think of a single thing to say.

My eyes move to Kick. If I say this next thing, it's me taking the biggest risk of all. It's me throwing the doors of my heart wide open and finally inviting him all the way in.

"I never thought I'd ever want to be anything other than a solo artist. But singing with you every night is my most favorite thing, the best thing I've ever done. You bring out something in me that's special and powerful and so, so good. We're good together. Great. I can't imagine ever doing this without you. I don't want …"

I'm about to say *to do it without you* but Kick leaps off the couch and envelops me in a hug before I can get the words out. He's pressing close, fully engulfing me in his arms. The way he's holding me erases the last few days and sets everything right again.

"Well," Cass says, a smile in her voice, "my first decision as acting Real Manager is going to the store to get ingredients. The three of us are going to film a new Sapphic Sammies video."

FORTY

RIGHT HERE. THE WHOLE TIME.

ONCE CASS LEAVES, Kick follows me into the kitchen as I put my empty plate into the sink.

"Is it bad to admit I'm really excited to be in one of Cass's videos?" he says, giddy.

"You should consider it a high privilege. She's never had a dude in one of her videos before."

"Wait, you think I'm a dude?"

"Okay," I say, rolling my eyes, "she's never had a *guy* in one of her videos. If she thinks you're worthy, that means you've reached a whole new level of guy-ness."

"You know, I've been trying to level-up my guy-ness for some time. Been stuck at bro since high school."

I blanch at that. "Never, ever be a bro."

"Not now, at least. Now I'm gonna be a guy in a Sapphic Sammies video."

I get us both a glass of water and hand him one. He leans back against the island all long limbs and casual confidence. He's looking at me over the top of his glass, the same way he looked at me over his cup of ice in Jackson's outdoor kitchen. I'm just as spellbound now as I was then. Only this time, I know more than his face. I know his heart. I know his pain. I know what makes him laugh, know what it feels like to be in his arms. I wasted too much time lying to myself that he didn't matter, wasted too much time pretending I didn't care.

"I'm sorry I was so horrible to you in Dallas."

"When you walked off stage in the middle of my song, I almost threw the guitar down and ran after you. I was so confused about what was happening."

"I am truly, truly sorry I did that to you. I know I explained my reason but that's doesn't make it okay. I'm sorry. I'll apologize forever if I need to."

The mention of forever pings between us. It's the closest I've come to conveying how I really feel.

"You've been so patient with me," I say. "Most guys wouldn't do that."

"It helps I've had a lot of therapy. Turns out, learning to be patient with yourself spills over onto other people."

I keep thinking about what he said in Dallas, how I was so busy running from something that might be bad, I was missing what was right in front of me. But I'm done running, done denying myself something that has only ever proven to be good. He is good.

"I really want to kiss you right now."

He takes a long drink of water, his eyes never leaving mine. "Why?"

It's a challenge, but I'm ready.

"I don't know if you know this, but you have ridiculously beautiful eyelashes." He chuckles at that. "But you're also kind. You're generous. You're not afraid of your feelings. You've been telling me how you felt about me since we met even though I refused to hear it. But you kept telling me anyway. And you're funny and fun and so, so special. And your voice makes me weak in the knees. And you have incredible hands." I pause. "You want me to keep going?"

He stares at me long enough to make things uncomfortable in the best way.

"Be honest, Goldie. Are you saying you want to climb me like a tree?"

"Oh, I wanted to climb you like a tree that first night. The overwhelming desire to put my body against your body has never been the problem."

His eyes darken. "Then come over here and do it."

I set my glass down and take two big steps to jump into his waiting arms. I wrap my legs around him, my hands on his neck, and kiss him with my whole heart. It's a promise, a declaration, me telling him with my lips and hands how deeply into him I am. More than that. How much I love him.

"I think it might be obvious at this point, but I need to say it." I frame his face with my hands. "I am so in love with you, Kick Raines."

He spins us around and sits me on the island. His smile is so big, so bright, it makes my eyes water.

"I am crazy in love with you, Mari Gold."

My heart explodes. Never did I imagine finding someone like him, someone who loves me for me.

"Tell me this is real," I say. "Tell me I'm not dreaming."

"You're awake" he says, his hands on me, his voice deep and rumbling, his smile so wide. "You're in love with me. And you still owe me one more confession."

I tilt my chin up at him, confused.

"All the other confessions were pretty big, sure—you're a Lovejoy, we didn't win, you might be Don Sparrow's daughter, you're obsessed with my eyelashes—"

I kiss him. Then I kiss him some more.

He smiles against my lips. "—but the biggest confession is still out there. It's time for you to come clean."

"If you're insinuating I have another tattoo in a secret place you haven't seen yet…"

He grips my hips and runs his hands slowly up my waist, over my ribs, thumbs grazing the sides of my breasts. "You have something of mine. I need it back."

Oh, right. His Bryan Adams t-shirt.

He pushes his hands under the shirt like he's going to take it off.

"I'm not wearing a bra," I say, my voice a teasing warning.

"I can tell." He cocks an eyebrow. "But would you mind if I check for myself?"

I cock my own eyebrow in response. He bites his bottom lip and slides his hands higher to cup my breasts under my shirt. He lets out a slow breath as his thumbs graze my nipples. "I knew you'd be more than a handful."

His lips find mine, hot and urgent. We're close to getting carried away when I pull back.

"As much as I like where this is going, and I *really* like where this is going, Granny G could come in here at any moment." What Kick doesn't know is, if Granny G walked in on a topless make-out situation, she'd probably cheer us on. "But I'd be happy to give you your shirt back. Later. After we make Cass's video."

He growls low in his throat and nuzzles into my neck as his hands move down to squeeze my ass. "When I get you alone, Goldie."

"Aren't you scared?"

He pulls back to pin me with a look. "I've been dreaming of getting you naked for months."

"Obviously," I say with a laugh. "You weren't exactly subtle. But I meant giving in to this." I motion between us. "Aren't you scared we'll lose our magic on stage?"

His hands sweep up to my neck, his touch feather lite. "If loving each other makes us lose the magic, then it's not really love and it was never really magic."

My heart jolts before finally clicking into place.

Because he's right. We can love each other and still be who we are, be what we've created together. Because it's him. It's this.

We can be us and be magic.

When Cass gets back, Kick and I are still wrapped up in each other against the countertop.

"Do I need to disinfect the kitchen of hetero hormones?" she says, shoving us aside and setting her grocery bags on the counter.

Kick and I pull apart, laughing. "What sandwich are we making?" I ask.

"I had an idea while I was at the store. You both want to do this your own way, right?"

We nod, interested.

"Then let's do it your own way. Your next show is the Nashville show. Let's invite label people out to see you play. You don't need Emily and Cheddar. We can make it happen ourselves."

I look at Kick, a question in my eyes.

"Hell yes," he says.

"You really think we can get label people to come to the show?"

Cass shrugs. "Why not? You two are white hot right now. Yes, it's partly thanks to Emily and Cheddar's scheming, but let's use that to our advantage. They may have manufactured the initial hype, but you kept it going with your real talent. People are screaming for you every night, not some Instagram post Cheddar made up." Cass pauses unloading her bags and spreads her arms out wide. "We want to exude power, right? Show that you're in charge? Show that you know what you want and you have the talent to back it up?"

"While also sticking it to Emily and Cheddar?" I say. "Yes, absolutely."

"That's why we're making the Rachel Maddow Power Sandwich. Roast beef on rye with onions and Dijon mustard."

"Killer," Kick says and I elbow him in the ribs.

"Only bros say killer. Remember, you're a guy now."

"What do guys say? Righteous? Rad? Amazing?"

Cass sighs. "Are you two going to be gross or are you going to shut-up and slice the onions."

"We'll slice," I say right as Kick says, "Rad."

I find a knife and cutting board for Kick and start arranging the roast beef slices on a platter.

"You know, Mari," Cass says, "if we want to reach out to label people, there's one person we know who could really help us out. He's got the contacts. Or can at least get them for us. It'd be better than cold-emailing everyone and getting buried in an in-box."

"Who're we talking about," Kick asks, his eyes teary from the onion. "Not that douchey Jackson guy I hope."

Cass and I nervously laugh and Kick waves his knife in the air. "No. No way."

"Don't worry," I say, bumping my hip into his, "he'll only hold it over our heads for the next five years or so."

FORTY-ONE
SEEN

IT'S LATE. We're at Kick's apartment, finally alone. As soon as we walked through the door I expected things to be frantic. I expected us to tear at each other's clothes and scream the walls down. I expected him to take me against the door, neither of us able to make it to his bed. I expected it to be physical and tactile, an unhinged release that's been building for months.

But Kick, once again, surprises me in the best way.

He wordlessly takes my hand and guides me to his room. He shuts the door and crowds me against the wall, bracketing me in with his arms. He's close, but purposefully not touching me.

We stay like that for what feels like forever, cocooned in our own tiny world. I can't do anything but breathe and look at him, this man who pried open the door to my heart.

"I want you to know," his sandpaper voice is low, just for me, "really know, what this is about for me. I see you, Mari."

Instinctively, I wait for him to look past me, look through me, for the moment to be about sex and nothing more. The way it's always been. People have always looked past me for something better.

But my battered heart can't deny the truth all over his face. His open, unguarded gaze fills me like a long, slow pour. His voice, the way he's holding me without touching me, it's almost too much.

"I see you," he says. "And I want you. I'd give up everything else, the fame, the tour, all of it. You're what I want. The rest of it only matters if you're there with me."

I want to touch him, reach for him, but I can't break the spell.

"As much as I want you, Mari, I can't move forward until you believe and understand what this is. Why we're here." He's so close, but still not close enough. "I know you're scared. I know it's hard for you to trust your feelings. I know you've been hurt. But I'm here, right now, in this moment, because I see you and I know you. Because I love you."

"Even when—"

He touches my lips with his finger. "Yes, even then."

I nod, unable to respond with words, held in by his eyes, the way he's putting his entire heart on display.

The world could burn down around us and I would stay here, bound by the truth that this man, this wonderful, incredible man, loves me. *Me.*

I swallow. My body is covered in goosebumps, heat pooling low in my belly. I want him so badly, in every way you can want a person, his body, his mind, his talent, his heart. I want all of it, all the moments that make up who he is and who he'll be.

He cups my face with his hand. "I want to take things slow."

"Kick, I—"

My words are cut off by a searing kiss.

I let go, let him lead. I believe I can trust him.

He's true to his word about taking things slow. He takes his time undressing me, mapping my skin as he goes. With his lips and tongue and fingertips he learns every surface, every curve. He revels in it, in me, drawing me out of my protective shell with each kiss, each intentional touch. Kick whispers praises across my skin like a gift, showers me in awe, telling me over and over how incredible I am, how beautiful, how good I feel under his hands.

He's kissing the curve of my waist when I grab at his shirt, pull him to stand and tug at his pants, urging him to shed every layer still left between us. Naked, he presses me into the wall and my body sings with desire.

"Kick."

I can't say anything else. My thoughts are wordless pictures of him, this, every moment we've shared.

He kisses my lips as he picks me up and carries me to his bed. In between kisses, his touch urgent and perfect, he keeps up his praise.

"You are the most incredible person I've ever met."

"I can't believe you're mine."

"I'm going to love you forever."

It leaves me raw, like an exposed nerve. I'm not sure how to respond, how to allow myself to be taken so entirely, so sweetly and with so much reverence.

We hold each other, our bodies intertwined. When he enters me, I cling to him and will myself to stay present, to be in the moment, saying yes over and over. We ride it out together, hands clasped, eyes open, coming together and coming apart.

The whole night is one long intro to a song we haven't written yet. Sex with Kick is like singing with Kick. We watch each other, move together, give and take in a practiced rhythm. It's surprising and fun and good, so good, my legs wrapped around him, his hands in my hair, our eyes on each other as we fall deeper and deeper into the all-encompassing, heart-changing love we've made.

It's early, still dark, but I'm awake. Kick's a breath away. He's sleeping on his side, hands tucked under his pillow, lips parted in a dreamy expression. I can't believe I'm here, next to this man, in his bed. I can't remember the last time I felt so relaxed, so at peace. Since the start of the tour my mind's been a spinning carousel of self-doubt and worry and the need to keep everything under control by myself. But being here with Kick in the sleepy pre-dawn settles the chaos, blurs the worry. Being here with Kick eases the longing that's hummed beneath my skin for as long as I can remember.

I slip out of the bed and pad lightly to the bathroom. When I catch my reflection in the mirror, the night flashes through my mind, sending me spinning all over again. I've never experienced this kind of connection, this kind of completion. I've never been so full, so loved, so wildly happy. I might need to tie a weighted rope around my ankle so I don't float away.

As I'm walking back to Kick's bed, his eyes open and land on me.

"Stop right there."

I stop, standing naked in a beam of moonlight shining through the window. I resist the urge to cover myself and let him look, let him linger.

Kick's voice is gravelly from sleep when he says, "You are so unbelievably beautiful."

I squeeze my hands into fists at my sides and look up and away. His words, the choked emotion in his voice, crack something open inside my chest. A warmth spreads through my center and out to my arms and legs, down to my fingers and toes. Even after everything we've shared over the last few hours, his words make me ache for him.

"Come here," he says.

I climb into his bed, into Kick's waiting embrace, into a place so new that already feels like home.

FORTY-TWO
THAT TIME EMILY GRITS HER TEETH SO HARD SHE CHIPS A TOOTH

JACKSON, thrilled to be asked, helps us invite eight different label people out to the Nashville show. Five said they'd come, but we put everyone on the comp list just to be sure.

We're playing Bridgestone Arena and the show's sold out. I'm as nervous as I was for the very first show, scared to see Don, anxious to play for the label people we invited, worried they'll tell us we aren't as great as we think we are.

I made what might be a rash decision and finished out one of the songs in my father's songwriting journal, one he wrote with Don. I'm hoping Don will hear it and, I don't know, do something? Say something? I'm not sure what I want to happen, I just know it needs to happen.

We're all in Kick's dressing room going over our set for tonight's show. We've been practicing the new song for the last day and a half, wanting it to be perfect. We're also adding the Bryan Adams cover, "Heaven." Kick sounds so dreamy on it my knees nearly buckle every time he sings it. With this many songs, we'll probably go over our allotted twenty minutes but we don't care.

We're running through "She's A Ten" when Emily and Cheddar burst into the room.

"Did you two add all these names to the comp list for tonight?" Emily growls, a copy of the list in her hand.

"Oh hey, Emily. How was your time off?" I am not and will never again give her the satisfaction.

"You do know," she says, her eyes doing their best to pierce into my soul, "you can't just invite label people out to a show like it's your birthday party at the roller rink. This is Nashville. There are rules."

"Roller rink parties are rad," Kick says, which makes me laugh, "and I helped submit the names so if you want to yell, yell at us both."

Cass stands up, shoulders back, chin up. "I sent the list to Nic. And we didn't go over our allotted comp tickets so I don't see what the problem is?"

"Look, Kick," Cheddar says, casual, like he's about to man-to-man the situation, "you need to leave things like labels and record deals and all that other stuff up to the pros. I'd be happy to sit down with you to go over your options. In fact, Emily and I have a proposal I bet you'd be interested to hear."

"Mari too, right?" Kick smiles, wide and wicked. "I can't imagine you'd offer me something and not her. After all, wasn't it your idea to make us a duo?"

"And I'm now representing Kick, so any offers can come to me," Cass says.

Cheddar side-eyes Emily who's now crumpling the comp list in her tight fist.

"You think this is some kind of game?" She says it to all of us, but her anger is directed at me. "You think you can come on this tour, pretend to be someone you're not, and get away with it?"

"It's you who thinks it's a game," I say, "playing with our careers like we're chess pieces you get to move around wherever you want to."

"What are you talking about?" She spits the question out.

Miguel and Mateo, normally so chill, are stone-faced. When we told them about Emily and Cheddar's backdoor deal, they offered to handle the situation the Diaz way, but we convinced them violence wasn't the answer.

"I overheard your little meeting," I say. "In Dallas? With your investor? We know what you're trying to do."

Emily cackles. "And what, you think you can get your two-bit manager, who I've never heard of by the way, to email a few label people and do better on your own? You're delusional. You have no idea how any of this works, which, given your family history is surprising."

"If what we're doing is so delusional, why has seeing those names on the comp list worked you into such a frothy lather?" Cass asks.

I resist high-fiving Cass as Emily narrows her eyes and presses her red lips together in a firm line. "I'll take this to Deacon and Don."

"Cool, tell them we said hi," Kick says. "And could you shut the door on your way out? We're trying to rehearse for our set."

Emily storms out but Cheddar stays behind a second longer to glare at us. "We can have you both off this tour. Tonight."

I think about Don, how he fought for me to be here in the first place. "No," I say, "I don't think you can."

Cheddar leaves in a huff and we happily watch him go. Kick and I were already amps turned to eleven for tonight's show but now we're absolutely levitating. I'm about to lean over and kiss him when the door opens again and Jackson Lord walks in.

"Right in here," he says, ushering a short, stocky bald man into the dressing room. The man's eyes light on me and Kick.

"Kick Raines and Mari Gold, I presume?"

"That's us." We both stand up to shake his hand.

"I'm Phil Brody from 30 Street Records."

"Oh, hi! Thank you so much for coming. This is our manager, Cass Zimmerman."

"Pleasure," Cass says.

"And our bass player, Miguel Diaz and our drummer, Mateo Diaz."

Handshakes and hellos are exchanged all around.

Phil crosses his arms over his broad chest. "I've been hearing a lot about you two since the tour started so when I got your invite, I knew I had to be here. Really interested to see your set."

"We hope you like what you hear," Kick says.

Phil's eyes find mine. "I'm especially interested in why you're choosing not to go by your real name?" He waits for my reply, like he just asked what I'm going to order for dinner.

"Sorry, what?"

"You're Penny Lovejoy, right?" He lifts one shoulder and drops it back down in a no-big-deal gesture. "Lots of people choose to use stage names but I'm surprised you chose not to go by Lovejoy. It's a well-respected name in the industry. I knew your father, John, back in the day. Great songwriter."

A loud whooshing sound fills my ears and my knees nearly give out on me. "I...sorry, I'm just a little stunned. How did you know I'm Penny Lovejoy?"

Kick gives Miguel and Mateo a reassuring look as Phil fishes his phone out of his pocket. "Your sister posted it on Instagram." He pulls up the post and hands me his phone.

Cass and Kick look over my shoulders and we all stare, mute. There I am, laughing, right after Kick's slung me over his shoulder in the T.O. photoshoot. This one and the one where Kick's looking back over his shoulder are both fan favorites.

Polly's caption reads: *So excited for my sister Penny to be out doing the damn thing! I guess talent really does run in the family. Although she's being sneaky and going by stage name Mari Gold. Go check her out on the Sparrow tour!*

She posted it three minutes ago and it has over five million likes.

Wordlessly, I hand the phone back to Phil.

"I take it you didn't know about the post," he says with a good-natured chuckle.

I do my best to recover, to act natural when my brain is screaming at full volume.

"I knew it was inevitable," I joke. "Was just trying to forge my own way outside of the LOVEJOY circus, if you know what I mean."

"Admirable," Phil says. "And from what I've seen, you're doing just that."

We chat for a few minutes about the tour and about 30 Street Records. Kick and Cass asks lots of great questions while I remain semi-catatonic. Once Phil leaves to go say hi to a few other people, I collapse into a heap.

"Are you okay?' Kick asks.

"We can handle this," Cass says.

"You're LOVEJOY's sister?" Mateo exclaims. "How did I not know this?"

Mateo and Miguel read comments from Polly's post.

I knew Mari Gold was LOVEJOY's sister the whole time. Anyone who didn't know isn't a true LOVEJOY fan.

Wish I was LOVEJOY's sister.

As long as she keeps singing with Kick Raines, I don't care who Mari Gold is.

Anyone think LOVEJOY will show up at a Sparrow show? Would die to see her.

"Someone posted a side-by-side of you and Polly that says, *These two are sisters? I don't see it.*"

Cass looks up at me with fierce determination. "I can call your mother. Or call Polly. Or like, hire a lawyer or something."

Everyone goes quiet, waiting to see what I'll say.

"It doesn't matter," I say, my voice quiet, my heart beating double-time. "Everyone knows. Or, they will soon enough."

Emily and Cheddar storm back in like their asses are on fire.

"What is this?" Cheddar says, shoving his phone into my face.

I don't have to look. I know what it is. "Aren't you thrilled? She just told her forty million followers to come to the tour."

"You told us we couldn't capitalize on this and now we've been scooped," Emily says, voice flat. "Anything we say now will have lost its fire, so, thanks for that." She gives Kick an accusatory look.

"Who cares anyway," Mateo says. His bulging arms are bowed at his sides like he's gunning for a fight. "Mari doesn't need to shout about being a Lovejoy. She's a kickass singer and guitar player."

I have seriously not given the Vampire Twins enough credit.

Emily seethes. She's lost the reigns and she knows it. "You two would be nothing without us. The only reason you even have a set for label people to come and see is because of me and Cheddar."

"Thanks for the vote of confidence," I say.

She breaths out hard, nostrils flaring. "We'll need to put out a response. About the Lovejoy connection. The media will expect details."

Jackson pops his head in, unaware of the tension in the room. "More label people here to see you."

"Give us a minute," Emily barks.

"We've got time," Kick says. "We'll come out."

The five of us file past Emily and Cheddar like rival middle school teams at the end of an intense basketball game. They don't follow, no doubt staying behind to strategize how to make this about them.

Two of the label people we invited are in the hall with Jackson. They don't mention Polly's post and I don't either. I know I'll have to deal with her announcement sooner than I'd like to, but I'm still hoping tonight can be about the music, about what Kick and I have together. We spend the next few minutes talking with the label people about the show, about the four of us, about our songs. Despite the hammering in my head, the conversation feels good, like we're sliding into the space we're meant to be in. The four of us plus Cass are a unit. A great one. Doing this together feels right.

When it's five minutes to show, Cass takes the label people side stage to watch our set. Miguel and Mateo leave for the stage. Kick and I head back to the dressing room to get our guitars. Inside, he pulls me into his arms with a soft smile.

"This is all because of you, you know. These label people wouldn't be here if it weren't for you. You were meant for this."

"Because I'm a Lovejoy? Because it's in my blood?"

That's always been the why. I've only ever meant something to someone because of who I happen to be related to.

He shakes his head. "Because you're a glowing ember on stage that can hold the attention of thousands of people at once. It's Mari Gold doing that, not your sister or your father, whoever he is. It's you. You were meant for this."

"You think we can we really do this? After everything? Polly's post…"

Kick reaches over to the couch where his guitar is propped and picks it up before handing me mine. "Let's go find out."

FORTY-THREE
COULD'VE BEEN

MOMENTS away from the start of the show, Deacon and Don stroll up next to us. Seeing Don up close and not acknowledging what I know is like trying to keep the air in a popped balloon. The most basic part of me wants to scream *Dad* and see what happens.

"Y'all ready for your first big Nashville show?" Don says, all smiles and distant friendliness.

"More than ready," Kick says, standing close to me, ready to scoop me up if I happen to fall.

All I can do is stare at Don. My maybe-father. The man who potentially knows exactly who I am but pretends I'm just a new artist on the tour. He's standing here, smiling at me, believing I'm oblivious.

He and Deacon head up on the stage and we follow them, just like we've done every other night on the tour.

"You okay?" Kick asks.

I nod and plug in my guitar.

As soon as Deacon and Don exit the stage, I exit them from my mind. Tonight's about me and Kick and making our dreams come true.

The crowd's buzzing as soon as Mateo starts us off with a

four count on the kick drum. This is our moment, the thing we do best.

Bum, bum, bum, bum.

"Hey there, Kick."

Bum, bum, bum, bum.

"Hey there, Mari."

Bum, bum, bum, bum.

The crowd's energy is swirling around us, lifting us off the stage.

"Gorgeous night in Nashville, isn't it?"

Bum, bum, bum, bum.

"I remember the last time we were in Nashville together," he says, his voice smoky and sexy and God, I love this man.

Bum, bum, bum, bum.

"Oh yeah? Remind me what happened?"

Bum, bum, bum, bum.

"You pulled me into an alcove and kissed me stupid."

Bum, bum, bum, bum.

"How dare you. I would never."

I can see my smile on the screen over Kick's head. It's wide and bright and alive.

Bum, bum, bum, bum.

"Never?"

Bum, bum, bum, bum.

"Well...maybe if you ask nicely."

We launch into "I Kissed Her In An Alcove." I know tonight isn't our only chance, but it feels like a big one, an important one, and we're leaving it all on the stage.

I shut everything and everyone else out and focus on Kick as he sings the words that started it all, the moment we first met, the first time we kissed, the first touch. I let myself feel all of it, the excitement and the pain and the confusion and the euphoria. It's all here, right now. We're letting everyone see the way we see each other. I'm not holding anything back, watching the way his body moves, drinking in the way he looks at me, the way his hands grip his guitar, the way he stomps the stage like he has too much energy to hold inside. As I'm playing, I move closer to him so that when it's my turn to sing, we're sharing the same mic, the same space, the same air.

I never want to stop sharing it all with him.

We sail through "Hot like Ice" and "Heaven" and "She's A Ten." There's a bigger than usual group of people standing side stage watching us—the label people we invited, several people from Sparrow's label, Emily and Cheddar, Cass, Jackson, Nic, Jasmine, Deacon and Don. One last person catches my eye right as we finish "She's A Ten."

My mother.

She's mingling with the label people, seemingly not paying attention to our performance, but I know she's catching every note.

She's here. Why is she here?

I look at over Kick and he nods, urging me to say what we practiced. I pull my shoulders back and blow out a breath. I'm not going to let anyone, not even my mother, ruin this moment.

"Nashville, you're such an amazing crowd. I wonder if you'd let us play a brand new song." The crowd cheers, eager, ready. "It's a song my father wrote a long time ago, but never got to finish." I glance over to make sure Don's watching. He is. So is my mother. "This one's for you, Dad."

Kick strums the first few notes, just like we practiced. Miguel and Mateo join in. I pick up on the fifth measure and start to sing.

Met too early
Fell in love too late
Should've found a way
To keep you
Dusty dry land
Filled with could've beens
Should've seen this flood coming

Should've recognized him
Now the water's rising
Carrying us away
The water keeps on rising
But it's too late
It's too late

As I sing, I sneak glances side stage but it's too dark to read anyone's expression or see any recognition. I don't know if this song is about my mother or about Sparrow, but I'm sure it's one of the two. Maybe now, since I'm singing their secrets to the entire Bridgestone Arena, someone will finally be honest with me.

FORTY-FOUR
A LOVEJOY BY ANY OTHER NAME

AS WE END THE SONG, I look side stage once more and Don's disappeared. My mother's still there, looking tortured. I've definitely stirred something up.

We've barely hit the last note on "Don't You Want Me" and are making our way off stage when I'm pulled through the black curtain that separates backstage from the lower concourse behind the stage. My mother's manicured nails are biting into my arm as she hustles me to the side. I look behind me and reach for Kick who's hot on my heels. Deacon and Don are right behind him.

"Candy," someone says, coming up and air kissing my mother's cheeks, "so good to run into you here. Is this your new artist? I just caught the show and it was phenomenal." She turns to me and Kick and holds out her hand. "Harper Deegan from Deegan Records. Thanks so much for inviting me out. Loved your set. Deacon, Don, great to see you both."

"Nice to see you, Harper, it's been a long time," Deacon says.

"Cass Zimmerman," Cass says, popping up behind me and reaching around to shake Harper's hand. "Kick and Mari's manager. Thank you so much for coming out tonight."

My mother's eyes bug out of her head at Cass's introduction but she quickly puts her pro face back on.

Kick and I shake hands and exchange hellos with Harper while my mother mentally scowls at me, her celebrity manager face perfectly engaged with Harper like this is a big, happy family reunion.

"This is my daughter, Penny Lovejoy," she offers. Her tone is light but commanding, leaving no room for a follow-up. Deacon glares at Don while Don stares blank-faced.

Harper startles. "Oh? So..."

"Mari Gold's my stage name," I offer.

"Don't want to be mistaken for your sister, I take it?" Harper says with a sparkling laugh, like this is all so easy and explainable.

"Daughter?" Deacon asks my mother, his eyes wide and a little scared.

"Harper," my mother says, voice dripping, "would you mind terribly if we have a little family catch-up and find you in a few?"

"Of course, yes. I'll be here."

"Thanks, Harper," I manage to say. "We'll definitely catch up with you."

I hold on tight to Kick's hand, letting him know I want him to stay, no matter what's about to happen. Cass is glued to my side, both she and Kick holding me up in case this all goes to hell, which at this moment, feels imminent.

"Candy," Deacon says. "What's going on?"

We're standing in a six-person circle, the intensity criss-crossing between us blocking out the backstage pandemonium happening all around us.

"It's good to see you guys," my mother says. "What's it been? Twenty years?"

She glances at me, her mask slipping, nerves breaking through.

"Almost twenty-five," Don says.

Deacon's shaking his head in confusion. "You said Mari's your daughter?"

"And you," Don says, turning to me, "where did you get that song?"

"Two minutes guys," Rod says, busting into the circle and calling the Sparrow brothers away.

They both look at my mother, conflicted and dumbstruck, but in different ways. "Will you stay?" Don asks.

She nods. "I'll be here. There's more to say."

I want to scream at her, want the band-aid ripped off, want answers to questions I've never known how to ask, but we're surrounded by more label people saying hi. Shawn Ware from Firelight. Harry Ortega from Anthill. Jeff Otto from Last Stop. Emily keeps walking by and glaring at us before donning her best schmooze voice, like she thinks by inserting herself she'll be able to change their minds about us. I can't care. We performed our asses off tonight. The label people will either like it or they won't.

I do my best to smile and be gracious. Kick and Cass easily charm everyone we meet even with my mother hovering over every conversation. I couldn't be prouder of Cass. Even though we semi-forced her into this role, she's handling it like she's been doing it for years. We get a short minute where we're not talking to any label people and I immediately pull my mother aside.

"Why did you lie to me about who my father is?" I know it's not the best opener, but I have to get it out before I talk myself out of it.

"Penny. Don't do this. Please."

I pull out my phone and show her the photo. "Who is this? You told me it was my father, but it's Don Sparrow isn't it? All this time, Don Sparrow was my father, my father was *alive*, and you decided, what, that I shouldn't know about that?"

"It's not that simple."

"It's actually pretty damn simple. Is John Lovejoy my father or isn't he?"

"Penny, this isn't the time or the place for a conversation this important."

"That's just it, Mother. You've never had a time or place. I had to change my name and get on a national tour to find out for myself."

She shakes her head. "I can't do this right now."

"Mom," I call as she hurries away through the crowd of people milling around the concourse. "Mom!"

FORTY-FIVE
THE TRUTH

KICK AND CASS are leaning against the cinderblock wall backstage watching me pace the floor. When Sparrow started playing the last song in their set, my skin pulled tight and my heart tried to abandon ship. I can't stop pacing, each step leading to another question, another worry, another twist I know is coming but can't see.

Nic finds us and asks us to follow him right as my mother shows back up.

"We have the meet-and-greet," Emily says, chasing after us.

"It'll have to wait," Cass says.

"You can't just abandon—"

Nic cuts her off with a wide sweep of his hand right in front of her face. "Not now."

We walk half-way around the backstage concourse, on the opposite side of the dressing rooms and catering, to a furnished, windowless room full of brown leather couches and low lighting.

"Deacon and Don asked y'all to wait here," Nic says.

The three couches are arranged in a u-shape. Kick and I sit next to each other on one, my mother and Cass across from us. My mother's eyes stay focused on the floor, which gives me a moment to really look at her. She looks older, tired, small lines have popped up around her eyes and her mouth is drawn down into a frown.

Cass raises her eyebrows at me, asking if I'm okay as Kick takes my hand in his. We're all bracing for whatever shitstorm is about to hit.

"I know I've made a lot of mistakes, Penny." My mother's voice has lost all its power. She's threading her fingers together in and out, in and out. "But I do love you."

"You love me, you just don't believe in my music and have been lying to me about who my father is my entire life. All this time you made me believe he was dead when I could have had a relationship with him. How could you do that to me?"

Deacon and Don come into the room before she can respond. They sit next to each other on the third couch in the middle.

Deacon raises his hands in the air and lets them fall. "Can someone tell me what the hell is going on?"

My mother starts talking, pain etched in every part of her face. "Penny is my daughter. She was born after John left the band. When he found out about…us…that's why he left, "she waves a hand in my direction, "because I was pregnant. I never told you because after everything that happened, it was too painful."

The room spins. Deacon's my father? Not Don? Deacon?

Deacon stares at the ceiling, a million emotions passing over his face. When he looks back at my mother, there's a hardness in his eyes I've never seen on him. "Why didn't you tell me?"

"You said you wanted to focus on your music, that there wasn't room in your life for 'all of that.' For me."

"But how did…" Deacon's voice trails off but we all know what he's trying to say. How did I get on this tour. How did the daughter he's never known about end up the opener of his show. "Did you send her here to ambush me? Is that it?"

"I had no idea she was on the tour until T.O. called and told me he'd just shot my daughter for the Sparrow tour. I was just as surprised as you."

"I've kept up with her," Don says, quietly. "With them."

"Wait." Deacon's hand closes into a fist in his lap. "You knew?"

"Look at her, Deacon. You really think she's John Lovejoy's kid?"

Everyone in the room stares at me, looking for Deacon in the lines of my face, the set of my shoulders, how I'm so much taller than my mother or Polly.

"I invited her to audition for the tour," Don says. "And I asked Cheddar and Emily to make sure she won."

"Why?" I ask.

It's the question that's been nagging at me more than anything else. If he knew who I was, if he made sure I got on the tour, why stay so distant? Why not say something? Get to know me?

"I knew Candy had never told you the truth about your father," Don says. "And I thought…" Don looks at Deacon, desperate. "I thought you'd see something of yourself in her. I thought you'd want to be in her life."

"That wasn't your decision to make," Deacon bites back. "I don't want this." He looks at me, heartless. "She's not my responsibility."

My heart plummets.

In all the time I've spent thinking about this moment, I never considered my real father wouldn't want to know me.

I look at my mother and there are tears streaming down her face. It's clear now why she never told me. She saw this coming. She knew Deacon would do this. She was trying to protect me.

"So, you're an asshole," I say to Deacon.

He jerks his head in my direction. "Watch your tone, honey. This is still my tour."

"She's your daughter, Deacon," my mother says, pleading.

"Look, Candy, we had some fun a long time ago. That was it.

How can you even be sure she's mine. If I remember right, there are more people you should consider than just me."

"You son of a bitch," she says.

"What? You want me to play daddy now? Want us to be a happy family? You had that with John and threw it away." He throws a hand out in my direction. "Besides, she's an adult. She doesn't need a father."

"Not one like you anyway," Cass says.

Deacon glares at her but Cass doesn't back down.

All Deacon's charm vanishes like smoke in the wind. I used to think he was this huge persona, someone to idolize, someone to aspire to. Now I can see him for who he really is—a narcissist who can't see past himself.

"I idolized you my whole life as the frontman of Sparrow," I say, "this mythical band I'd heard so much about but never got to know. And…I idolized John Lovejoy, the man I believed was my father. I thought if I could just meet him, the man who inspired me to become a songwriter, my life would make more sense, that things would fall into place. It's the whole reason I came to Nashville, chasing John Lovejoy's ghost."

"John was a good man," Don says which earns an eyeroll from Deacon.

"I have his old songwriting journal," I say to Don. "That's where I found that song you and John started."

"I love what you did with it," Don says.

"Can we get back to the conversation at hand," Deacon says. "I have places to be."

"I'm sorry," I say, "are we interrupting your plans to meet the next young woman you plan to use and throw away like you did my mother?"

"Don't you see the gift you've been given?" Kick says. "This woman, your daughter, is unmatched. I wouldn't be here, *couldn't* be here, without her encouragement and strength. She's so talented and inspiring and—"

"Not my responsibility," Deacon interrupts.

"It's not about responsibility," Kick argues. "It's about knowing this beautiful person who is a part of you."

"A sperm deposit during a meaningless fuck doesn't make anyone part of *my* life."

My mother gasps. We all do.

The room falls silent. Deacon is a man caught. He's avoiding everyone's eyes knowing there's nothing he can say or do. The veil has been lifted for all of us.

"I'm glad I came on this tour," I say. "I'm glad I learned who you really are. A small, selfish man who used my mother and destroyed my family without a hint of remorse. And thank you, honestly. Your gross behavior in this room has shown me who and what truly matters in my life." I look at Kick, his hand still holding mine so tight. "It's shown me how to recognize the people who truly love me." I stand up, ready for this conversation to be over. Kick stands with me. "I hope all your success was worth the people you trampled on to get it."

"You can't talk to me like that."

"Why not? Because you're my father? Because you're 'Deacon Sparrow?'"

He goes silent, furious. His whole career's built around everyone believing he's the charmer, the good-time guy, the artist with the enviable life, the rockstar everyone desires. He doesn't like being exposed as anything other than the man every other man wants to be.

"Penny, I'm sorry," my mother says. It's a loaded statement.

Don clears his throat. "I'm sorry too."

"Can we go?" I say, looking between Kick and Cass. "I'm done here."

Kick and Cass follow me out into the hallway.

He grabs me by the shoulders as soon as we're out the door. "If I wasn't already in love with you that would have sealed the deal."

"You just handed Deacon Sparrow his ass on a platter," Cass says.

I stare at them both, my breath catching in my throat. My heart's beating too fast. "I can't...I can't breathe. I think I'm in shock. Is this shock? Am I in shock?"

Kick pulls me into his arms. "It's a lot to take in, but you stood up for yourself and told the truth. You were incredible." When I don't say anything he pulls away to look at me. "Are you okay?"

"Yes. Or, I will be. I think? I'm...I'm proud of myself."

"I know that's right," Cass declares.

We all three smash into a group hug when someone tugs on my arm.

"Oh, thank God. I've been looking everywhere for you." It's Harper from Deegan Records. "Just wanted to say again how much I enjoyed your show. I know you're being pulled in a million directions right now, but I'd love to set up a meeting soon. I'd be happy to come out to a show."

The whiplash of the conversation with Deacon and Don and what Harper's saying has me spinning. I can't focus on one for worrying about the other.

"Absolutely," Cass says, pulling out her phone. "Let me give you my number and we'll get something set up."

Harper and Cass exchange numbers, Harper noticing my hand linked with Kick's.

"I'll be in touch," she says before waving good-bye and heading down the concourse.

We make our way down the hall and run into Jasmine, who halts to a stop when she sees me.

"I didn't know Candy was coming," she says, apologizing. "I would have given you a heads up."

"Did you know Deacon's my real father?"

Her shoulders shoot up as she inhales. She hisses out a breath as she lowers them in one long, fluid movement. "I suspected, but I didn't know for sure. Your father, John I mean, he took the affair really hard. Left the band. He loved your mom so much." She puts her hands on my shoulders. "I'm sorry I didn't tell you.

I didn't think it was my place to do so." I nod, letting her know I get it. And I do. "I'm here if you need to talk," she says. "About anything. Any time."

"Thanks, Jasmine."

She hugs me and squeezes Kick's hand. "You take care of this one. She's special."

He puts his arm around me, holding tight. "We take care of each other."

"Yes, I can see that," she says. "And listen, I know this might not be the moment, but there's a line of people waiting to meet you up on the main concourse. I can turn them away if you're not up for it tonight."

I probably shouldn't be up for it, should probably take some time to process everything that's happened tonight. But, the fans are waiting.

"Of course we're up for it," I say, waving my arms through the air. "We're Kick Raines and Mari Gold, the biggest new artist of the summer. We played our hearts out tonight and now we have fans to meet. Let's do it."

"I am so hot for you right now," Kick says.

"Honestly," Cass says, "me too."

FOR IMMEDIATE RELEASE

SURPRISE REVEAL WOWS FANS ON SPARROW GRAND TOTAL TOUR

LOVEJOY Social Post Spills The Beans, Revealing Opener Mari Gold As Stage Name For Penny Lovejoy

Nashville, TN (July 10th, 2025) In a revealing Instagram post that shook the music industry, Polly Lovejoy, known as LOVEJOY to her millions of fans worldwide, congratulated her sister, Penny Lovejoy, on her opening slot on Sparrow's sold out Grand Total Tour. Flying under the radar using stage name Mari Gold, Penny Lovejoy developed an enthusiastic following all too happy to learn of her family ties.

"People have been really supportive to learn I'm a Lovejoy," says Gold. "Kick and I really do have the best fans."

Performing as a duo with rocker Kick Raines, Penny Lovejoy plans to continue touring under stage name Mari Gold saying she likes the separation from her sister's pop star persona.

The sold out Grand Total Tour continues its run through August 21, 2025.

About Sparrow: Top-selling American folk rock band Sparrow are five-time PHONO® Award-nominated, two-time PHONO® Award-winning, Streamers Billionaires Club recipients with five *Charts* Music Awards. Their debut album, *Sparrow*, is RIAA-certified Double-Platinum with follow-up *Closer* RIAA-certified Platinum. The band's single "In A Dark Wood" remains one of the most-streamed folk rock songs of all time with over one billion streams. Sparrow are Deacon Sparrow (lead vocals, guitar), Don

Sparrow, (lead guitar, vocals), Randy Moore (bass, vocals) and Joe Collins (drums, vocals).

Press contact:
Emily Wu
emily@sparrowband.com

FORTY-SIX
CONTRACT HIGH

HARPER FROM DEEGAN RECORDS is coming out to our Louisville show to meet with us. It feels surreal, having a label person pursue us so pointedly. A couple of the other labels we invited to the Nashville show reached out to Cass saying to let them know when we have demos ready, but Harper's gone all in. Kick and I are a bundle of nerves for her and Cass to arrive.

"She's coming here," he says, dazed. "Harper Deegan is coming here to talk to us."

"Because she wants to sign us," I say. "To her label."

Mateo plays air guitar and jumps around the room. "We're gonna be rockstars."

"We still need a band name," Miguel says. "I'm voting for Genre Explosion."

I push him off the couch. "Let it go, man. Genre Explosion is never going to happen."

Miguel laughs. "I'll wear you down eventually."

Cass and Harper drive up from Nashville together, the two of them instant friends. Cass has been texting me the whole morning.

Cass: She loves y'all

Cass: She wants y'all

Cass: They will promote the shit out of you

Cass: This is going to be amazing

Harper and Cass show up by lunchtime and ask us to meet them at a bar and grill in downtown Louisville. When we get there, Harper and Cass are sitting at a big booth by the window and wave to us from the front door.

"Right on time. How's the tour going?"

Kick and I exchange a knowing look. "Chilly."

Since the Nashville show, things with Emily and Cheddar have been prickly. Polly's Instagram post predictably blew up but fans have been mostly supportive. Cass has fielded a million interview requests for me, most of them forwarded from Emily with a terse "for you," but the social chatter died down after a few days. Emily's been more than vocal about her irritation. I can't tell if she's mad about Kick not wanting to sign with them or that Polly's Instagram attack didn't crash and burn me.

"Thank you for coming all this way to see us," Kick says as we slide into the booth for six. Miguel and Mateo each take an end.

"If we work together," Harper says, "when we work together, I'll be traveling the world for you."

"As long as you don't force us to go on tour with LOVEJOY," I joke.

Everyone laughs and it's nice, being able to talk about my sister and know the people at this table are still here with me. No one's plotting to leave, angling to get to Polly, using me as a stepping stone. We're a bonded group, here for each other. It makes my heart ache with happiness.

"I know this might sound like a line coming from a label person trying to woo you," Harper says, "but we'd never force you to do anything you didn't want to do. We're partners with our artists. We like to make decisions together."

Lunch goes on like that, Harper saying the exact right things, things that feel like my life just got made. Judging by the way

Kick's squeezing my thigh under the table and the way Miguel and Mateo keep smiling at me, they all agree.

"One thing we haven't talked about yet," Cass says, "I'm sure you've worked out that Kick and Mari are together. Is that something...is that an issue at all?"

Cass warned me she was going to talk to Harper about this on the drive up, but I'm glad she's bringing it up with the group.

Harper folds her hands together on the table. "I'll be honest with you, we did discuss it internally. It's a risk, but to put it plainly, we want you bad enough to accept the risk. I'm not supposed to say that. I'm supposed to play a little hard to get, but we're all friends here, right?"

"Right," Mateo says and raises his hand for a high five. Harper laughs and slaps his hand with hers.

"The hard truth is," she says, "once you sign the contract, you are committed to the terms of that contract. If something happens between you two, you can't just walk away. We can negotiate terms once we get to that stage, but personally, I don't think it's something to be afraid of. Do you?"

"I'm not worried about it," Kick says, cool and not at all terrified. "We're ready for this."

"We're," I pause, trying to find the right words, "what Kick and I have is more than a flirty summer thing. I know you can't ever know the future, but I believe in us."

"I'm not worried," Miguel says. "These two burn hotter than any couple I know. They keep the whole bus up half the night trying to get it on in Mari's bunk."

Harper laughs and I feign shock. "That was one time, Miguel."

"So far," he says.

"We'll add a clause in the contract," Harper says, writing a pretend note on a napkin, "no nefarious activities on the bus if those activities keep other band members awake against their will."

Miguel and Mateo are laughing as Kick asks, "But what if we're quiet?"

"I sleep above Mari," Miguel says. "There's no way you two could ever be quiet."

After lunch, Harper excuses herself to make some calls and Cass leaves to find Mo. We have some time before soundcheck and I have an idea. As incredible as the night at Kick's was, and the next morning and the next afternoon, I need more of him. The more I get, the more I want.

"I wonder," I say, "if we could find somewhere we could be alone? We could practice being quiet."

Kick's eyes light up. "Come with me."

We practically run out to the bus and the thankfully empty back lounge. As soon as he closes the door I press into him, my hands on his neck, his thigh between my legs.

"You're so gorgeous when you're negotiating a record deal," he whispers, his lips against mine, his hands quickly unbuttoning my jeans. He kisses me hot and urgent and says, "I love watching you take charge."

"When you tell people you're not afraid of what comes next," I say, unzipping his pants, "it makes me want to do bad things to you."

He flips us around so my back is against the door. I let out a quiet cry of pleasure as he works me over, his mouth on my neck, his fingers taking me apart.

"What kind of bad things?" he asks.

I reach into his pants and show him what I mean.

He chuckles against my neck. "That's a very, very good thing, Goldie."

After, when we're collapsed on the couch, I consider suggesting round two. I can't get enough of the way he touches me, the way he kisses me, like I'm the only woman in the world. I can't get enough of his fearless love for me, his unwavering belief in us.

"I meant what I said at lunch, you know," he says, reading my mind. "I'm not afraid of what comes next."

"Once we sign that contract, it's official. Now's your only chance to run."

"I'm not running," he says. "I want to do this with you forever."

"You mean get each other off in the back lounge of the bus?"

He laughs loud and bright. "Yes. And the front lounge. And in my bunk. And in my dressing room." I shut him up with a kiss. "But everything else, too. I want all of it—the hard parts and the sad parts and the highs and the lows and everything in the boring middle. I want all of it with you."

FORTY-SEVEN
APPEARING IN STUDIO

THE TOUR'S in Arizona with two days off. Deegan Records flew us back to Nashville to record our first EP, *The Alcove Songs*. Don's producing. He and I have talked a few times and come to an understanding. I understand why he did what he did and he understands it will take me some time to warm up to him being my uncle. Despite the drama, I'm glad to have an uncle in my life, one who wants to know me and support me. One who is kind. It's a bonus he's a great songwriting mentor too.

Cass picks us up from the airport to take us to Don's studio. He took a red eye last night so he's already there getting everything set up. The four of us pile into Cass's SUV and head down to Franklin, happy for some time off from the tour and thrilled to be recording our songs.

When we get there, Harper's waiting at the door to greet us. We hug her hello and make our way into the studio. Don leans out from under the recording console where he's plugging in some cables.

"Hey, y'all. Glad you made it. Excited to get started?"

"You know it," Miguel says, rushing over to give Don a high five.

"I think we're still trying to wrap our heads around the fact that this is happening at all," I say.

"You wrote great songs," Don says. "Let's bring them to life."

Don shows us around the studio, a barn-like structure behind his main house. Inside it's dark and cozy, the floors covered in woven rugs with low-lit lamps scattered around. He has a huge recording console in the main room, the walls lined with a gorgeous collection of guitars. There's also a recording room and a vocal booth as well as a small hangout area and a kitchen.

"This is really nice," Kick says. "Thank you for letting us be the first to record here."

"We brought the contract." I pull it out of my bag with a flourish. "Signed and everything."

"Perfect." Harper already has her phone out, messaging someone. "We can get the team engaged right away, especially on socials."

"That would be helpful," I say. "Cheddar's been very hands-off since the Nashville show."

"It was quite a night, wasn't it?"

We turn to see my mother standing in the doorway. She's backlit by the sun, dressed down in simple black pants and a white button down with subtle make-up. Her hair is pulled back. She's in flat shoes.

"Candy," Harper says, surprised, "great to see you."

"Mind if I steal my daughter for a few minutes?"

"Oh, sure," Don says. "We're still getting things set up. Take your time."

Kick squeezes my hand and kisses my forehead. "I'm here if you need me."

I follow my mother outside the studio. We haven't talked since the big reveal. She took off as soon as the conversation with Deacon and Don was over and I haven't had it in me to be the first one to reach out.

Outside, I start walking down the long gravel driveway. This is just like my mother, showing up when I'm about to do something really exciting for me. I'm walking too fast, like my body is trying to keep up with my racing thoughts. Why did she think *now* was the right moment to talk about things? Today is supposed to be about the band and our music, not my family drama.

"I thought we should discuss what happened," she says, keeping pace with me. Her voice is measured, like she's scared I'll run if she says the wrong thing, which, I might.

"How did you even know I was here?"

She smooths her hands down her shirt. "It's a small industry."

Our footsteps crunch against the gravel. "So you've been talking to Don."

"Penny, I wanted to...all of this is...really difficult for me."

"Difficult for you?"

I glance at her out of the corner of my eye. Her expression is sad, defeated.

"For both of us," she says.

"Did you tell Polly to post that photo?"

She throws her hands up. "I still don't understand why you're performing under this other name. What's so wrong with being a Lovejoy?"

I stop walking and turn to her, arms crossed.

"But I'm not a Lovejoy, am I."

"The thing with Deacon was a mistake, a mistake I've regretted for twenty-five years. You're a Lovejoy." She clasps her hands in front of her, her fingers squeezing so tight her knuckles turn white. "That's what you've always been,

"But you never told me. There's been this huge truth out there about me, about who I am, and you kept it from me. All the years I didn't fit in, felt like my life didn't make sense, that there was something missing." I start walking again. "The whole reason I came to Nashville? I was looking for a connection to my father. Imagine what it was like for me to learn John Lovejoy wasn't my father at all."

She's a few steps behind me when she says, "But I'm still your mother."

I turn around. "Don't do that."

"Do what?"

"Make this about you. You and Polly have been doing that to me my entire life."

She shakes her head. "You've never been supportive of Polly's career. Or mine."

"You *left me*. I grew up alone in Polly's mansion. The housekeeper was more of a mother to me than—"

"Penny!"

She's hurt. She's angry. But I am too.

We both take a beat. There's so much unsaid between us I don't know how we'll ever dig it all out.

"Did you go on the Sparrow tour to punish me? Because of this...fantasy that I left you as a child?"

"I went on the Sparrow tour to have something that wasn't tainted by Polly's inescapable persona."

Her hands go to her hips. "We worked hard for that persona."

"Great. Good for you. But it's not what *I* want."

Mom steps off the driveway and sags against a tree. I can see her thoughts written across her furrowed brow. She'll never understand why I'm not head over heels to have a famous sister who never gave me the time of day.

"Does Polly know? About Deacon?"

Mom stares at the sky, her lips twitching. "She's known for a long time."

It'd be easier if she slapped me across the face. My relationship with my sister has always been strained. She's never liked me. Maybe now I finally understand why.

"Let me guess. She blames me for John Lovejoy's death?"

"This conversation is about you and me, not Polly."

We're interrupted by Kick jogging down the driveway, a hesitant look on his face. "Don says we're ready." He looks at me intently. "Do you want me to ask for more time?"

Even if I did, it wouldn't be enough to fix what's broken.

"I'll be right in."

He gives me a close-lipped smile and heads back inside.

"You're good together, you and Kick," Mom says. "I wish you'd let me manage you. I could make great things happen."

A humorless laugh escapes me. "You still don't get it, do you?"

"I just want to be a part of your life, Penny. I want you to let me in."

I steel myself and remember Cass's advice to focus on what I want, what I need. Challenging my mother isn't easy, but I've proven I'm able to stand on my own.

"If you want to be a part of my life, then be my mother, not my manager. Just be my mom. Support what I'm doing because it's what I love, not because it might make you money or help your profile. Be there for me, just because."

She nods, like all of this should be easy.

"I never meant to hurt you," she says, her voice thick with emotion. "I thought...I loved you the best way I knew how."

Despite the years of heartache, despite the deceit, I believe her. I'm not ready to forgive her, but I believe she never intended for things to end up the way they did. She's not evil, just... broken.

"I'm still really, really angry," I say, "about a lot of things. But I'm willing to acknowledge you're attempting to make an effort. So, let's try starting over. Be my mom. That's all I've ever wanted."

She walks over to me and takes my hands in hers. "I haven't been perfect, I know that, but I want to be in your life. Please believe me when I tell you that I promise to make things better between us."

It doesn't feel like nearly enough, but it's a start. Hopefully, it's a new beginning.

FORTY-EIGHT
MARICK, EVERYBODY

DEEGAN RECORDS SENT "I Kissed Her In An Alcove" out as the first single from Marick, our new band name. It debuted on the Hot 100 right as the Sparrow tour was ending, which was fun for Emily and Cheddar. Miguel's still bummed we're not called Genre Explosion.

Tonight's our first show on a new tour. We're co-openers with Shades of Grey, Deegan Records' other new act, opening for their biggest artist, The Research. Shades of Grey are such great guys and we're beyond excited to be able to tour with them. Don told me when Emily and Cheddar found out we're on the same label and on tour together, Emily threw Cheddar's iPad across the room and shattered the screen. Don also said Emily and Cheddar lost their investor and haven't been able to get their label off the ground. We chuckled about it over the phone and I found out Don is no fan of Emily Wu.

Don, ever the supportive uncle I never had, talks about Marick in interviews and on socials more than he talks about Sparrow, always hyping us up as the hottest new act he's seen in a long time.

For this tour, Kick and I are alternating with Shades of Grey for who plays first each night. Tonight, we're up first at the

Orpheum in Memphis, playing to a sold-out crowd. It's a much smaller venue than what we played on the Sparrow tour, but I couldn't be happier.

We're in the wings on the right side of the stage while Miguel and Mateo wait on the left side, all four of us brimming with excitement. I feel a tug on my arm and follow Kick as he pulls me into a tiny alcove carved into the wall, a look of utter glee on his face.

"Can you believe this is here?"

I look up and around. "What is this thing?"

He grins my favorite grin, eyes sparkling. Even after all this time, those palm branch eyelashes still make my toes curl.

"I think they call it an alcove." He brushes my hair behind my shoulder and wraps a warm hand softly around my neck. "It'll take a Costco-sized can of WD-40 to get us out of here."

He leans in and captures my lips in a hungry kiss, so familiar and still so new.

When he pulls away, we're both breathless, wide-eyed, just like the first time. I run my hands up his chest. "Can you believe this is happening?"

"Yes." He kisses my temple. "And no. It still doesn't feel real."

I lean around the corner of the alcove and peek out into the packed audience. My mother's sitting on the second row like a regular concertgoer, her way of showing me she's here for me as a mom, not a manager. We've both been working hard to fix what's broken between us, to build something we should have built a long time ago. I wouldn't say we're all the way there yet, but we're a lot closer than we were. I'm happy she's here tonight.

"Are you two serious right now?" Cass says, finding our hiding spot. She's flourished since becoming our official manager, running the Marick machine like a CEO in a power suit while still being as Cass as ever.

"Look," I say, "It's an alcove."

"It's show time," she replies, so done with us. "But first,

news. Kelly Clarkson is going to cover "I Kissed Her In An Alcove" on her show. And she wants you to come on as guests."

"Wait, wait, wait, wait, wait," I say, pushing out of the alcove. "Kelly Clarkson is going to cover our song? Kelly Clarkson. Like, *Kelly Clarkson*."

"Would you both think less of me if I fainted right now?" Kick says.

Cass laughs. "You can faint after the show. Now get out there and entertain the people."

I pull Kick toward the stage as he continues mumbling "Kelly Clarkson" under his breath.

Kick Raines, my love. The man who'd never written a song and is now being covered by one of the greatest singers of all time. Being with him is a daily surprise, my life taken over by his big, giant heart and unending capacity for love. I am the luckiest.

The DJ from the radio station sponsoring tonight's show appears on stage to introduce us. Kick and I run onto the dark stage and get into position. The DJ announces upcoming shows and throws station t-shirts into the crowd before booming into the mic, "Anybody here excited to see Marick tonight?" Loud cheers fill the theater. Fill my heart. "You're in luck, 'cause here they are. Marick, everybody!"

The spotlights hit us and Kick and I launch into a high speed drum duet. It's only two minutes long, something we cooked up a few days ago as we were rehearsing for the tour. We're totally showboating, playing into Emily's paparazzi-style creeper videos of us that have been gaining momentum online since the Sparrow tour. But it's also incredibly fun.

On the last beat, we jump up and jog to our microphones to thunderous applause. Our guitars are waiting for us, already plugged in. Kick gives Mateo a head nod and Mateo hits four beats on the kick drum.

Bum, bum, bum, bum

"Hey there, Mari," Kick says, smiling into the mic.

Bum, bum, bum, bum

"Hey there, Kick."

Bum, bum, bum, bum

"Beautiful night tonight in Memphis, isn't it?'

Bum, bum, bum, bum

"Love Memphis. Great barbeque."

The crowd cheers through four drum beats so we wait for four more.

Bum, bum, bum, bum.

"And the people are so nice. Very inviting."

Bum, bum, bum, bum.

"Reminds me of that night back in Nashville," I grin at him. "When you tried to kiss me in an alcove."

The crowd is eating it up, laughing and cheering, in on our little game.

"I think you've got that backwards. The way I remember, it was you who kissed me."

Bum, bum, bum, bum

"No, no," I say, smiling, "I'm pretty sure it was you doing the kissing."

Bum, bum, bum, bum

"Sure, okay, just as long as I get to kiss you again."

We hit the downbeat and launch into our songs, the songs that made us, the songs that survived us, the songs that are carrying us forward as we live out our wildest dreams. Together.

ACKNOWLEDGMENTS

None of my books would exist without the enormous time and effort put in by incredible people whose belief in me keeps the lights on. Thank you to Elise Stawarz for your unwavering support and enthusiasm for the stories I tell. You're the best pretend manager there is or ever will be. Thank you to Kristin Maher, Beth Lee, Kellie Harris, Drew Harris, Stacie Vining, Chuck Hargett, Brandi Manes, Sarah Jane Pounds and Sarah Van Goethem for reading and encouraging and being generally rad. Thank you to Brittany Kelley and Tiffany White for being great friends and cheerleaders, holding my hand, and giving me expert advice. Thank you to Tim Parker for designing another book cover that makes me scream with delight every time I look at it. Thank you to the NNF - Elise Stawarz, Beth Lee, Jill Tomalty, Kristin Byrne, Jordyn Harris and Nina Woodard - for keeping it real. Thank you to Ryan and Harry and Franklin for being my favorite musicians and the best part of every day. And a huge thank you to you, dear reader, for taking a chance on me. I am forever grateful.

Also by

JoAnna Illingworth

The Black Umbrella

Amelia Goes West